WHAT YOU CAN SEE FROM HERE

WHAT YOU CAN SEE FROM HERE

MARIANA LEKY

Translated from the German by Tess Lewis

Farrar, Straus and Giroux   New York

Farrar, Straus and Giroux
120 Broadway, New York 10271

Printed in the United States of America
Originally published in German in 2017 by DuMont Buchverlag, Germany,
as *Was man von hier aus sehen kann.*
English translation published in the United States by Farrar, Straus and Giroux
First American edition, 2021

Interior illustrations by EvaKate Gabrielsen.

Library of Congress Cataloging-in-Publication Data
Names: Leky, Mariana, 1973– author. | Lewis, Tess, translator.
Title: What you can see from here / Mariana Leky ; translated from the
     German by Tess Lewis.
Other titles: Was man von hier aus sehen kann. English
Description: First American edition. | New York : Farrar, Straus and Giroux,
     2021. | "Originally published in German in 2017 by DuMont Buchverlag,
     Cologne, Germany, as Was man von hier aus sehen kann"
Identifiers: LCCN 2020057983 | ISBN 9780374288822 (hardcover)
Classification: LCC PT2672.E38243 W3713 2021 | DDC 833/.92—dc23
LC record available at https://lccn.loc.gov/2020057983

Designed by Abby Kagan

Our books may be purchased in bulk for promotional, educational, or business
use. Please contact your local bookseller or the Macmillan Corporate and
Premium Sales Department at 1-800-221-7945, extension 5442, or by email at
MacmillanSpecialMarkets@macmillan.com.

www.fsgbooks.com
www.twitter.com/fsgbooks • www.facebook.com/fsgbooks

10 9 8 7 6 5 4 3 2 1

The translation of this work was supported by a grant from the Goethe-Institut.

For Martina

It's not the size of the stone I lift—it's the reason I lift it.

—HUGO GIRARD (World Muscle Power champion, 2004)

WHAT YOU CAN SEE FROM HERE

When you stare at something that is brightly lit for a long time and then close your eyes, your inner eye sees the same thing again as a static afterimage: what had actually been light is now dark and what had been dark appears light. If, for example, you watch a man walking down the street who repeatedly turns back to wave one last, one very last, one very, very last time, and then you close your eyes, on the inside of your eyelids you'll see the frozen movement of his very, very last wave, his frozen smile, and the man's dark hair will be light and his light-colored eyes will be very dark.

If what you were staring at was important, Selma says, something that upended the entire expanse of your life in a single movement, then its afterimage will resurface again and again. Even decades later, it will suddenly reappear, no matter what you were looking at just before you closed your eyes. The afterimage of the man waving for the very, very last time suddenly appears when, say, a mosquito flies into your eye as you're cleaning out the gutter. It appears when you briefly rest your eyes after staring for a long time at a surcharge on a bill that you don't understand. When you're sitting at the side of a child's bed to tell her a story and can't remember the princess's name or the story's happy ending because you're so very tired yourself. When you close your eyes because you're kissing someone. When you're stretched out on the forest floor, on a doctor's examination table, in a strange bed, in your own. When you close your eyes because you're lifting something very heavy. When you've been running around all day and stop just to retie your loose shoelaces and, with your head lowered, notice only then that you haven't stopped once the entire day. It appears when someone says, "Close your eyes," because they have a surprise for you. When you lean against the changing room wall because not even the very last pair of the pants you've been trying on fits. When you close your eyes just before you finally let something important slip out, such as: "I love you," or "But I don't love you." When you're frying potatoes at night. When you close your eyes because there is someone at the door you absolutely don't want to let in. When you close your eyes because some great worry has suddenly lifted—you've just found someone or something you'd lost: a letter, some hope, an earring, a runaway dog, your voice, or a child who found a perfect hiding place. Again and again, this afterimage suddenly reappears, this one particular image—it resurfaces like your life's screen saver, and often when you're not expecting it at all.

PART ONE

MEADOW, MEADOW

When Selma told us she had dreamed of an okapi the night before, we all knew that one of us was going to die in the next twenty-four hours. We were almost right. It took twenty-nine. Death arrived a bit late and very literally: he came in through the door. Maybe he was delayed because he had put it off for a long time, even past the last possible moment.

Selma had dreamed of an okapi three times in her life, and each time someone had then died. That's why we were convinced her dreams of an okapi were directly connected to death. That's how the mind works. It can draw connections between completely unrelated things in an instant. Coffeepots and shoelaces, for example, or deposit bottles and fir trees.

The optician had a mind especially adept in this. You could name two things that had absolutely nothing to do with each other, and right off the bat he would explain how they were closely related. And yet it was the optician of all people assuring us this latest okapi dream most certainly would not cause anyone's death, that death and Selma's dream were completely and absolutely not connected. But we knew that the optician, like us, believed they were. The optician more than anyone.

My father claimed it was complete and utter nonsense and that our delusion came from the fact that we allowed too little of the world into our lives. He was always saying: "You've got to let more of the world in."

Previously he would say this decisively and primarily to Selma. Afterward he said it only rarely.

The okapi is an incongruous animal, much more incongruous than death. It looks utterly disjointed, with its zebra shanks, its tapir haunches, its giraffe-like rust-red torso, its doe eyes and mouse ears. An okapi is completely implausible, every bit as implausible, in fact, as the sinister dreams of a woman from the Westerwald.

The okapi was officially discovered in Africa only eighty-two years ago. It's the last large mammal to be discovered by man, at least that is the consensus. In any case, no mammal could top it. No doubt someone unofficially discovered the okapi much earlier, but at the sight of it may have thought he was dreaming or had lost his mind, because an okapi, especially a sudden and unexpected one, looks completely invented.

An okapi does not look remotely sinister. It couldn't possibly, even if it tried very hard to, which, as far as anyone knows, it rarely does. Even if crows and screech owls had been fluttering around its head in Selma's dream—to a fully sinister effect—the okapi still would have made a very mild impression.

In Selma's dream the okapi stood in a meadow near the edge of the forest, in a group of fields and meadows that together are called the Uhlheck—the owl forest. People from the Westerwald often call things by a different or shorter name because they like to get any talking over with quickly. The okapi in the dream looked exactly as okapis do in real life, and Selma, too, looked exactly as she did in real life, namely like Rudi Carrell.

Surprisingly, we had never noticed Selma's perfect resemblance to the Dutch television host Rudi Carrell; it took someone from outside to come and point it out to us years later. But then the resemblance hit us with full force. Selma's long, slender body, her posture, her eyes, her nose, her mouth and hair: from head to toe, Selma resembled Rudi Carrell so perfectly that, from then on, in our eyes, he was nothing more than a poor copy of Selma.

In the dream, Selma and the okapi stood in the Uhlheck without moving. The okapi turned its head to the right, toward the forest. Selma stood a few steps away. As in each of these dreams, she was wearing the very same nightgown she was sleeping in; sometimes her nightgown was green, sometimes blue or white, but always ankle-length and always flowered. Her head lowered, she looked at her toes in the grass, long and old and crooked just like in real life. She glanced at the okapi now and then from the corner of her eye, looking up at it from below, the way you look at someone you love far more than you're prepared to admit.

Neither moved, neither made a sound, even the wind that always blows across the Uhlheck was still. Then Selma raised her head and the okapi turned toward her so that they were looking directly at each other. The okapi gazed at her with eyes that were very gentle, very black, very wet, and very large. It gave Selma a friendly look as if it wanted to ask her something, as if it were sorry that okapis can't ask any questions—even in dreams. This scene lasted a long time with the image of Selma and the okapi looking into each other's eyes.

Then the image disappeared, Selma woke up, and the dream was over, just as some life nearby would soon be over.

The following morning—it was April 18, 1983—Selma wanted to play down her dream of the okapi, so she put on an emphatically cheery front. She was about as slick in feigning cheerfulness as an okapi and believed the best way to show high spirits was to sashay around. And so, the morning after her dream, Selma sashayed into the kitchen wearing a crooked smile and I didn't notice that she looked just like Rudi Carrell when, in the opening of *Rudi's Daily Show*, he stepped out of a very large globe, a globe with light blue oceans, golden landmasses, and sliding doors.

My mother was still asleep in our apartment above Selma's. My father was already at his medical office. I was tired. I'd had trouble falling asleep the night before and Selma had stayed at my bedside for a long time. Maybe something in me had sensed what Selma would dream about and so wanted to keep her up.

Whenever I slept downstairs at Selma's she would tell me bedtime stories with happy endings. When I was little, after each story I would take hold of her wrist, lay my thumb on her pulse, and imagine that the whole world followed the rhythm of Selma's heartbeat. I pictured the optician grinding lenses, Martin lifting a heavy weight, Elsbeth trimming her hedges, the shopkeeper stacking cartons of juice, my mother layering fir branches, my father writing out prescriptions, all exactly to the beat of Selma's heart. This had always reliably put me to sleep, but now that I was ten years old, Selma felt I was too old for it.

As Selma sashayed into the kitchen, I was sitting at the table copying my completed geography assignment into Martin's notebook. I was surprised that instead of scolding me for doing Martin's homework for him yet again, she said, "Well, hello there," and poked me merrily in the ribs. Not once before in her life had Selma said, "Well, hello there," nor had she ever poked anyone merrily in the ribs.

"What's the matter?" I asked.

"Nothing," Selma warbled, and opened the refrigerator. She took out a package of sliced cheese and some liverwurst and waved them both in the air. "What will it be for your snack at school today?" she warbled. "My little mouse," she added, and now the warbling and the *little mouse* were truly alarming.

"Cheese, please," I said. "What's going on with you?"

"Like I said: nothing," she warbled. She spread butter on a piece of bread, and because she was still sashaying around, her wrist knocked the cheese off the counter.

Selma stopped moving and looked down at the package of cheese as if it were something valuable that had smashed into a thousand pieces.

I went over to her and picked up the cheese. I looked into her eyes from far below. Selma was even taller than most other grown-ups and was around sixty at the time: as high as a tower and as old as the hills, from my perspective. To me she seemed so tall that you could see far beyond the next village from her head, and so old that she had helped invent the world.

Even from down there, a meter from her eyes, I could see that something sinister had played out behind Selma's eyelids the night before.

Selma cleared her throat. "Don't tell anyone," she said softly, "but I'm afraid I dreamed of an okapi."

I was instantly wide awake. "Are you absolutely sure it was really an okapi?"

"What else would it have been?" Selma asked, adding that you can hardly mistake an okapi for another animal.

"Yes, you can," I said, and suggested that it might have been a misshapen cow, a badly assembled giraffe, a freak of nature, and besides, the stripes and reddish color are hard to see at night.

"Nonsense," Selma said, and rubbed her forehead, "I'm afraid that's just nonsense, Luisa."

She placed a slice of cheese on the bread, put the other piece of bread on top, and slipped it in my lunch box.

"Do you know exactly when you had the dream?"

"Around three," Selma said. She had woken with a start after the image of the okapi slipped away. She'd sat bolt upright in bed and had gasped at her nightgown, the same one she had been wearing just now standing in the Uhlheck in her dream, then at her alarm clock. Three o'clock.

"We probably shouldn't take it too seriously," Selma said, but like a TV detective who is not taking an anonymous letter too seriously.

Selma packed the lunch box into my schoolbag. I considered asking if I could stay home under the circumstances.

"Obviously you're still going to school today," said Selma, who always knew what I was thinking as if my thoughts hung in garlands of letters over my head, "You're not going to let a random dream stop you from doing anything."

"Can I tell Martin?" I asked.

Selma thought it over. "Fine," she decided. "But absolutely no one other than Martin."

Our village was too small to have a train station. It was also too small to have a school. Every morning, Martin and I took the bus to the small station in the next village and then caught the local train to the county seat, where we went to school.

While we waited for the train, Martin practiced lifting me. Martin had been training to be a weight lifter since kindergarten, and I was the only weight that was always at hand and never objected to being lifted. The twins from the upper village only let him lift them if he paid twenty pfennig each, grown-ups and calves were still too heavy for him, and everything else that might have been an adequate challenge— saplings, half-grown pigs—was either firmly rooted to the spot or would run away.

Martin and I were the same height. He would crouch down, grab me by the hips, and lift. He was at the point where he could hold me in the air for almost a minute. I only touched the ground if I stretched my toes down as far as I could. When Martin lifted me a second time, I said, "Last night my grandmother dreamed about an okapi."

I looked at Martin's part. His father had combed his blond hair with a wet comb and a few strands were still dark.

Martin's mouth was at the level of my belly button. "So is somebody going to die?" he asked into my sweater.

Maybe your father will be the one, I thought, but naturally didn't say it out loud, because fathers aren't supposed to die, no matter how bad they are. Martin put me down and exhaled.

"Do you believe in it?" he asked.

"No," I said.

The red-and-white crossing signal dropped with a clatter.

"Downright windy today," Martin said, even though it wasn't remotely true.

While Martin and I were on the train, Selma told her sister-in-law Elsbeth over the phone that she had dreamed of an okapi. She made Elsbeth promise to keep her lips sealed. Elsbeth then called the mayor's wife, actually just to talk over plans for the coming May Festival, but when the mayor's wife asked, "So, anything new?" the seal on Elsbeth's lips broke very quickly and in the blink of an eye the entire village knew about Selma's dream. Word spread so fast that Martin and I were still on the train to school when everyone in the village had heard.

The train ride lasted fifteen minutes, there were no intermediate stops. From our very first train ride, we always played the same game. We stood with our backs to the windows in facing doors; Martin closed his eyes and I looked out the window in the door behind him. In first grade, I had listed for Martin everything I saw during the ride and he tried to learn it all by heart. It worked so well that by second grade I no longer had to list anything, and Martin, with his back to the window and his eyes closed, could recite almost everything I was seeing through the foggy window: "Wire factory," he would say at the very moment we passed the wire factory. "Now field. Meadow. Crazy Hassel's farmhouse. Pasture. Forest. Forest. Hunting blind one. Field. Forest.

Pasture. Meadow, meadow. Tire factory. Village. Meadow. Field. Hunting blind two. Woodland. Farm. Field. Forest. Hunting blind three. Village."

In the beginning, Martin made careless mistakes. He would say "meadow" when we were actually passing a field or didn't call out the landscape fast enough when the train accelerated in the middle of the stretch. But before long he got everything exactly right. He said "field" when I saw a field, he said "farm" when the farm rushed past.

Now, in fourth grade, Martin could recite it all flawlessly, with precisely the right intervals, forward and backward. In winter, when the snow made the fields and pastures indistinguishable, Martin recited what the uneven white surface I saw rushing past actually was: field, forest, pasture, meadow, meadow.

Except for Selma's sister-in-law Elsbeth, people in the village were for the most part not superstitious. They blithely broke all of superstition's rules: They sat calmly under wall clocks even though the superstitious can die from it. They slept with their heads toward the door, though superstition claimed they'd soon be carried out that very door feetfirst. They hung laundry to dry between Christmas and New Year's, which, according to superstition, Elsbeth would remind them, amounts to suicide or accessory to murder. They were not frightened when owls hooted, when a horse in the stall broke into a heavy sweat, when a dog howled in the night with its head lowered.

Yet Selma's dreams did have an effect. When an okapi appeared to her in a dream, Death made an appearance in life. And everyone acted as if Death had appeared by surprise, as if he'd sashayed in unexpectedly and hadn't always been in the general vicinity, like a godmother sending you gifts small and large your entire life long.

The villagers were unsettled, you could tell, even though most of them tried not to let anything show. That morning, a few hours after Selma's dream, everyone moved through the village as if black ice had formed beneath their feet, not only outside, but inside their homes as well, black ice in their kitchens and living rooms. They moved as if their own bodies suddenly felt foreign to them, as if all their joints were inflamed and all the objects they handled were highly flammable. All day long, they eyed their lives suspiciously and, as far as possible, the lives of others as well. They kept looking around to check if someone filled with bloodlust were about to pounce—someone who had lost his reason and had nothing much to lose—and then they quickly looked straight ahead again because anyone who was out of his mind could very well attack from the front. They looked up to rule out falling roof tiles, branches, or heavy light fixtures. They avoided all animals because they believed animals were even more likely to lose it than their fellow humans. They kept clear of the good-natured cows who, they believed, might go berserk that day. They avoided all dogs, even the very old ones who could barely stand. On such days anything was possible, a senile dachshund could bite clean through one's throat, something which, in the end, was no more incongruous than an okapi.

Everyone was worried, but apart from Friedhelm, the shopkeeper's brother, no one was terrified, because being terrified usually requires some level of certainty. Friedhelm was as terrified as if the okapi in Selma's dream had whispered his name. He ran off stumbling through the forest, screaming and trembling, until the optician caught him and brought him to my father. My father was a doctor and gave Friedhelm a shot that made him so happy that he spent the rest of the day waltzing through the village singing, *Oh, you lovely Westerwald*, and getting on everyone's nerves.

The villagers also kept a suspicious eye on their hearts, which, unused to getting so much attention, raced at a disturbing pace. They remembered that the onset of a heart attack is accompanied by a tingling in the arm, but couldn't remember which one, so the villagers felt tingling in both arms. They kept a watchful eye on their state of mind, and these minds, also unused to so much attention, were set racing at a disturbing pace as well. They wondered, as they stepped into their cars, picked up a pitchfork, or took a pot of boiling water off the stove, if they might not lose their minds just then—be overcome by a bottomless despair and with it an urge to drive full speed into a tree, fall onto the pitchfork, or pour the boiling water over their heads. Or, if not to harm themselves, they might feel the urge to douse with boiling water, to stab with a pitchfork, or to run over someone close to them: their neighbor, their brother-in-law, their wife.

Some of the villagers avoided all activity the entire day; some even longer. Elsbeth once told Martin and me that years earlier, on the day after one of Selma's dreams, the retired mailman had stopped moving altogether. He was convinced that any movement could mean death; he remained convinced for days, even months after Selma's dream, long after someone had in fact died in accordance with the dream's dictate, the shoemaker's mother. The mailman simply stayed in his chair. His immobile joints became inflamed, his blood became clotted and finally came to a standstill halfway through his body at the very moment that his mistrusted heart stopped beating. The retired mailman lost his life from fear of losing it.

A few people felt it was high time to air hidden truths. They wrote unusually wordy letters with talk of *always* and *never*. They felt one should bring truthfulness to life—at least at the very last minute. And hidden truths, these people believed, are the most truthful of all. Left untouched, they harden over the years and, being kept secret and confined to immobility, these truths grow bulkier with time. Even truth itself wants out in extremis. Anyone holding a secret truth risks an especially agonizing end, a lengthy tug-of-war with Death pulling on one side and the bloated, hidden truth on the other. A secret truth does not want to perish in hiding. Having spent its life buried, it wants to be released, even if only for a short time, either to spread its fetid stink and appall everyone, or to show that, exposed to the light of day, it isn't so terrible or fearsome after all. Just before the supposed end, a hidden truth urgently wants a second opinion.

The only one who was happy about Selma's dream was old Farmer Häubel, a man who had lived so long he was almost transparent. When his great-grandson told him about Selma's dream, Farmer Häubel stood up from the breakfast table, nodded at his great-grandson, and climbed the stairs to his room in the attic. He lay down on his bed and watched the door like a birthday boy awoken early with excitement waiting impatiently for his parents to finally bring in the cake.

Farmer Häubel was sure that Death would be polite, just as he had been himself for his entire life. He was sure that Death would not wrench life away from him but would remove it gently. He pictured Death knocking softly, opening the door just a crack, and asking, "May I?" to which Farmer Häubel would naturally answer in the affirmative. "Of course," Farmer Häubel would say, "please come in," and Death would enter. He would stand next to Farmer Häubel's bed and ask: "Is this a good time? If not, I can always come back later." Farmer Häubel would sit up and say, "No, no, this is a very good time. Let's not put it off, who knows when you'll be able to arrange it again." And Death would sit on the chair placed and ready for him at the head of the bed. He would apologize in advance for his cold hands, which Farmer Häubel knew would not bother him at all, and then Death would lay a hand on Farmer Häubel's eyes.

That's how Farmer Häubel imagined it. He stood up one more time because he'd forgotten to open the roof hatch so his soul could fly right out.

THE OPTICIAN'S LOVE

There was nothing objectively terrible about the optician's truth that was trying to slip out on the morning after Selma's dream. The optician wasn't having an affair (nor was there anyone he wanted to have one with); he'd never stolen anything; and he had never lied for any length of time to anyone other than himself.

The optician's secret truth was that he was in love with Selma and had been for decades. He tried to hide this not only from others but also from himself. Nevertheless, his love for Selma always reappeared before long.

The optician was close by almost every day and always had been. From my perspective he was as ancient as Selma; therefore he had also helped to invent the world.

When Martin and I started kindergarten, Selma and the optician taught us how to tie our shoes. The four of us sat on the doorstep of Selma's house as she and the optician strained their backs teaching us, bending over our little shoes, tying and retying our laces in slow motion—Selma busy with my shoelaces, the optician with Martin's.

Selma and the optician also taught us to swim, both of them standing in the shallow pool, water up to their navels. Selma wore a large, frilled purple cap that looked like a hydrangea, which she had borrowed from Elsbeth to protect her Rudi Carrell hairdo. I lay facedown, held up by Selma's hands, Martin by the optician's. "We won't let go," they kept saying, and then at some point they said: "We're letting go." And Martin and I swam, awkwardly at first—our eyes wide with panic and pride—then ever more confidently. Selma hugged the optician joyfully and the optician's eyes welled with tears.

"It's just an allergic reaction," he said.

"To what?" asked Selma.

"To a particular material in that bathing cap's frills," the optician claimed.

Selma and the optician taught us to ride bicycles, the optician holding the rack on Martin's bike, Selma holding mine. "We won't let go," they kept saying, and then at some point they said: "We're letting go." And Martin and I rode, wobbling at first, then ever more confidently. Selma hugged the optician joyfully and the optician's eyes welled with tears.

"It's just an allergic reaction," he said.

"To what?" Selma asked.

"To a particular material in the bicycle seat," the optician claimed.

In front of the train station in the county seat, the optician and Selma taught us how to tell time. We four sat together looking up at the large round clockface, Selma and the optician pointing out the numbers and hands as if they were constellations. Once we understood how to tell time, the optician immediately explained how time zones work.

He insisted on explaining it, as if he knew, even then, how much and how often time would shift in my life.

The optician taught me how to read as we sat with Selma and Martin—who could already read—in the ice-cream parlor in the county seat. Alberto, the new owner of the parlor, had given his sundaes torrid names and maybe he had so few customers because people in the Westerwald would rather order "three assorted scoops" than Flaming Temptation or Hot Desire. "Secret Love sundae" was the first thing I learned to read. Soon after, I tried to decipher the horoscope on the sugar packet that came with Selma's coffee, hesitantly at first, then ever more confidently. "Leo," I read, "courageous, proud, open, vain, controlling." The optician's index finger moved under the words in pace with my reading and slowed at "controlling." When I read my first sugar packet fluently, a small Secret Love with whipped cream was my reward.

The optician always ordered a medium Secret Love without whipped cream. "A large Secret Love would be too much for me," he'd say, and glance at Selma out of the corner of his eye. But Selma had no feel for metaphors even when they were right in front of her, topped with a paper umbrella, on a table in an ice-cream parlor.

The optician was with us when Martin and I discovered a pop music show, which became the only thing we wanted to listen to from then on. We asked the optician to translate the lyrics for us even though we didn't understand them any better in our own language. We were ten years old and didn't know what burning desire or hot pain meant, whether in the ice-cream parlor or on the airwaves.

We huddled around the radio. The optician was concentrating hard. The radio was old and full of static and the singers sang very fast.

"Billie Jean is not my mistress," the optician translated for us.

"But Billie Jean sounds like a man's name," Selma said.

"Billie Jean isn't his *lover*, either," the optician said indignantly.

"Quiet!" Martin and I ordered.

"What a feeling," the optician translated, "take your ardor and make it happen."

"Maybe it should be 'your passion'?" Selma asked.

"Right," the optician said. Since he couldn't sit for long due to a herniated disk, we stretched out on a blanket on the floor next to the radio.

". . . lifts us up where we belong," he translated, "on a mountain high, where the eagles weep."

"Maybe it should be 'where the eagles cry'?" Selma asked.

"Six of one, half dozen of the other," the optician said.

"Quiet!" we shouted, then my father walked in and said it was time to go to bed. "Just one more song. Please," I begged. My father leaned against the doorframe.

"Words don't come easy to me," the optician translated, "how can I find a way to make you see I love you?"

"Seems to me he doesn't have any trouble finding words," Selma objected.

My father sighed and said, "You really need to let a bit more of the world in."

The optician took off his glasses, looked at my father, and said, "That's exactly what we're doing."

After he'd heard about Selma's dream and told anyone who would listen that he didn't believe in it at all, the optician put on his best suit, which was getting bigger with each passing year, picked up a stack of unfinished letters, which was also getting bigger with each passing year, and stuffed them into his large leather bag.

He set out for Selma's house. He could have walked there backward with his eyes closed: he had gone to her house every day for decades (though not wearing his best suit or carrying the stack of unfinished letters, but always carrying deep inside the secret love that now wanted to slip out of him at what could well be the very last minute).

As he strode toward Selma's house, his heart drummed loudly in his rib cage, beating in time with the secret truth as the leather bag bumped his hip at every step. The leather bag full of

Dear Selma, There's something I've wanted to say for years

Dear Selma, After so many years of friendship, it's surely ~~a mistake odd strange remarkable unexpected surprising~~ *a mistake*

Dear Selma, On the occasion of Inge and Dieter's wedding I'd like to finally

Dear Selma, You're going to laugh, but

Dear Selma, Once again your apple cake was exquisite. Speaking of exquisite, you

Dear Selma, We were just sharing a glass of wine and you rightly observed that the moon was especially

full and beautiful tonight. Speaking of ~~full and~~
beautiful

Dear Selma, Karl's illness hit me very hard even though
I couldn't put it into words earlier. It reminded me how
limited ~~life on earth our existence~~ everything is and
that's why I urgently want to tell

Dear Selma, Earlier you asked why I was so quiet. The
truth is

Dear Selma, Today it's Christmas, without a trace
of snow, which is not the way you like it. Speaking of
liking

Dear Selma, On the occasion of Inge and Dieter's divorce

Dear Selma, Since Christmas is the celebration of love

Dear Selma, On the occasion of Karl's funeral

Dear Selma, On the occasion of nothing at all

Dearest

Dear Selma, Unlike you, I'm convinced that we will
win the "Let's Beautify Our Village" competition. Your
beauty alone will guarantee us first place

Dear Selma, It's clear that we can't possibly win the
"Let's Beautify Our Village" competition. It's already
perfectly beautiful because you

Dear Selma, It's Christmas again already. I'm sitting here, looking out at the snow and wondering when it will melt. Speaking of melting

Dear Selma, Christmas is a time for gifts. Speaking of gifts, something I've long wanted to lay at your feet

Dear Selma, On a completely new topic

Dear Selma, By the way, I've always wanted to tell

Dear Selma, Christmas again.

Dear Selma, ~~BLAST~~

Dear Selma, When we were in the swimming pool with Luisa and Martin earlier, the blue of the water shone in the sun ~~like the blue of your ey~~

Dear Selma, Thanks for the tip on getting rid of molehills. Speaking of molehills, or rather mountains, even a mountain can't hide my

Dear Selma, Speaking of love

The optician hurried down the street to Selma's house without a glance to the left or right at the few houses along the way in which everyone was busy examining their hearts and their sanity and the people closest to them, ready to reveal or receive the secret truths about to emerge, truths that probably weren't so terrible after all in the light of day, but if one of the truths was, in fact, as awful as feared, the recipient of it might have a stroke and Selma's dream would have done its work.

The optician briefly mulled over truths capable of causing a stroke. They all seemed to him to be straight out of the American afternoon television show Selma always watched. Unlike Selma, the optician did not get a thrill from watching the show. What did give him a thrill was Selma's profile, and the show gave him the opportunity to gaze in rapture at Selma's profile from the corner of his eye for forty minutes while she gazed in rapture at the show. It seemed to him that truths capable of causing a stroke must sound like the sentences delivered at the end of each episode just before the theme music began playing, leaving Selma to wait an entire week for the aftermath—sentences like "I never loved you," or "Matthew is not your son," or "We're bankrupt."

It would have been better for the optician not to think of this because he couldn't get the theme music out of his head, a melody completely unsuited to declarations of love, and his inner voices immediately began to push him around.

There was an entire commune of voices living inside the optician. They were the worst lodgers imaginable. They were always too loud, especially after ten o'clock in the evening. They trashed the optician's interior. They were many of them, they never paid their rent, and they couldn't be evicted.

For years, his inner voices had been pleading in favor of keeping his love for Selma secret. So on the way to Selma's that day, the voices were naturally in favor of holding back the truth about his love. After all, he was skilled in the art of holding things back, which he'd done very successfully for decades. The voices conceded that without a declaration of love, nothing particularly wonderful had happened, but nothing particularly terrible had occurred, either, and that, after all, was the important thing.

The optician, who always expressed himself judiciously, stopped short, raised his head, and said, "Shut up!" in a loud voice. He knew it was impossible to have a reasonable conversation with the voices. He knew that the voices would grow extremely talkative if he didn't bark at them immediately.

And if the truth was out, the voices continued unfazed, something terrible very well could happen. Maybe, they hissed, Selma would find this truth—the optician's bloated, long-cloistered love—particularly threatening or unsightly. And if the optician were to die today, if he were the one intended by Selma's dream, then the last thing Selma should receive from him was something as unappetizing as his love, unaired for so many years.

The optician staggered a step to the right, as he did now and again. For a moment, he looked inebriated. Last year, Selma had talked him into getting a medical exam because of his sudden staggering. The optician had driven to the county seat with Selma. A neurologist had examined him but had not found anything. Inner voices, of course, cannot be detected by medical instruments. The optician had only gone to the neurologist so that Selma would leave him in peace. He knew in advance that nothing would be found; he knew he staggered because his inner voices jostled him.

"Shut up," the optician repeated even louder as he picked up his pace. "Selma rarely finds anything threatening or unsightly."

He was entirely correct but had unfortunately revealed more to the voices than he should have.

"That doesn't mean she won't think your love unsightly,"

the voices hissed. "After all, there are reasons you've kept the truth hidden so long," they continued.

"Cowardice," the optician said, and shifted the leather bag to his other hip because the bumping of the bag and the jostling of the voices had started to hurt.

"It was prudence," the voices retorted. "Fear sometimes gives good advice," they said, and hummed the show's theme music.

The optician's steps slowed. The walk to Selma's house, which only took ten minutes, suddenly seemed like a day's journey, a long day's journey with piles and piles of luggage.

He passed more houses, all full of secret truths, and as he walked he dredged up all the sayings about courage he had ever read. There were a lot of them. Whenever he drove Selma to the county seat so she could do her weekend shopping, he waited for her in front of an out-of-the-way gift shop. It was the ideal place to wait for her because she would never catch him smoking there. Nowhere were you safer from Selma than in front of a gift shop.

Waiting for Selma to do her errands had given the optician time to read through the gift shop's entire ninety-six-card display while bathing it in cigarette smoke. Each postcard showed a landscape that had nothing whatsoever to do with the county seat—in other words, an ocean or desert landscape or one with a waterfall—along with an inspirational quote that had nothing whatsoever to do with the optician. Now, having nearly reached Selma's doorstep, the voices still growing ever stronger and he ever weaker, he began to run through the quotes out loud.

"Courage stiffens the spine," the optician said.

"We already knew that," the voices answered.

"Fortune favors the brave," the optician said.

"Brave, schmave," the voices answered.

"Better to stumble on new paths than to get stuck on old ones," the optician said.

"Better to get stuck on old paths than to stumble on new ones, fall badly, and fracture a few vertebrae," the voices answered.

"Today is the first day of the rest of your life," the optician said.

"Not much left to the rest of your life, is there?" the voices asked. "Hardly worth the trouble, is it?"

"You have to climb the tree to pick the best fruit," the optician said, and the voices answered: "And the tree falls the minute the rotten optician reaches its crown."

The optician's pace was now very slow. The leather bag no longer bumped against his hip. His heart no longer drummed in his rib cage. The voices hummed the theme music and whispered, "We're bankrupt," and "Matthew is not your son."

"Shut up," the optician said. "Please."

Selma was sitting in front of her house and she saw the optician climbing the hill. She stood up and walked toward him. The dog sitting at her feet walked with her. It was just a puppy, but you could already see it would be huge one day, so huge that the optician wondered if it really was a dog and not some enormous, as-yet-undiscovered kind of land mammal.

"What are you mumbling?" Selma asked.

"I was just singing," the optician said.

"You look pale, but don't worry, you're definitely not the one," Selma said, even though she had no idea whom the dream intended, of course. "Nice suit, but it's not getting any younger. What was it you were singing?"

The optician shifted his bag to the other hip and said, "We're bankrupt."

Selma cocked her head, squinted, and peered at the optician's face like a dermatologist examining a particularly unusual mole.

Silence had fallen inside the optician. His inner voices had gone quiet, silent in the certainty that nothing would go wrong now.

It was silent inside the optician except for one sentence. It was a sentence that spread throughout his insides like spilled paint, a sentence that radiated weakness so powerfully it seemed to the optician as if all his muscles were melting, as if all the hair on his head that hadn't yet turned gray would do so immediately, as if the leaves on the trees around him and Selma would immediately wilt and the trees themselves collapse, exhausted by the sentence spreading through him; it seemed to him as if birds would fall from the sky, their wings paralyzed by the sentence, as if the legs of cows in the pasture would suddenly buckle and the three words inside the optician would lull to sleep the dog standing next to Selma—and it was a dog, what else could it be? Everything is wilting, the optician thought to himself, everything is shriveling, collapsing, falling down, and crumbling because of the sentence: "No, better not."

AN AS-YET-UNDISCOVERED LAND MAMMAL

The dog had appeared last year on Selma's birthday. My father had given Selma a book of photographs of Alaska and said with a wink: "There's another surprise coming."

Selma had never been to Alaska and didn't want to go. "Thank you," she said, and put the book on the shelf in the living room with the other photography books. Every year, my father gave her a new book of photographs showing the world he felt she urgently needed to let into her life.

Elsbeth gave Selma a pound of coffee and a jar of snail balm, which, according to Elsbeth, could turn gray hair blond. Sad Marlies gave her two cans of bargain mushrooms, and the optician gave her, on her request, ten boxes of Mon Chéri. What Selma liked best about Mon Chéri was the filling. "The filling is so calming," she would say. She usually bit off the front of the Mon Chéri, sucked out the cherry and the liqueur, and gave the chocolate shell to me.

We sang "Happy Birthday" and Martin took the opportunity to try to lift Selma but without success. We ate cake and my father told us about his psychoanalysis, something he loved to talk about. "Speaking of psychoanalysis," my father would say, even when no one in the room had said anything on the topic.

My father's psychoanalyst was Dr. Maschke, whose practice was in the county seat. Soon after my father announced that he was going into analysis—he announced it the way others announce they're getting married—there was a *Tatort* episode on television, in which the main suspect was also named Maschke. I wasn't allowed to see it, not being nearly old enough for a crime show, but I watched in secret through the crack of the living room door.

The *Tatort* police detective sensed that Maschke was a criminal from the very beginning. He'd received an anonymous letter that said, "Maschke is planning something." Since then, whenever my father said, "I'm off to Dr. Maschke's, see you later," I pictured the anonymous letter claiming Maschke was planning something, something serious enough to warrant an anonymous letter.

Knowing that my father talked about her to Dr. Maschke made Selma uncomfortable. Of course, he had to talk about her, since mothers are the main suspects in psychoanalysis. I didn't like the idea that my father was telling him absolutely everything about Selma either, because I worried that Maschke was planning something against her. I hadn't been able to see the whole *Tatort* episode because Selma caught me watching and sent me back to bed. So I only found out many years later that Maschke, the apparent prime suspect, was in fact completely innocent of all the terrible things that had occurred; Maschke had not tried to take anyone's life. Maschke hadn't been planning anything at all. In the end, it turned out that Maschke was one of the good guys.

On that day, too, over Selma's birthday cake, when the conversation was actually about Mon Chéri candy and the Piedmont cherry filling and Elsbeth declared that the liqueur-soaked cherries didn't come from Piedmont at all, it was just something she claimed when tipsy, my father responded, "Speaking of psychoanalysis . . ." He then told us that Dr. Maschke was a luminary in his field, something that had been proven yet again just the day before. Previously, the patient whose session was just before my father's had always come out of Dr. Maschke's office with a look of profound despair in his eyes.

"I'd never seen a look of such abysmal despair in anyone's eyes," he said. And now, a mere two sessions later, the very same patient practically skipped out of the office as if liberated. "So here's to psychoanalysis," my father said, and raised his glass. "And to the birthday girl, too, of course."

Sad Marlies asked, "Do you see despair in my eyes, too?"

My father turned to her, took her chin in his hand, and gazed into her eyes for a moment.

"No," he replied, "just an incipient eyelid inflammation."

The sound of my mother's steps echoed in the landing.

"Here's Astrid," my father said, "with the surprise."

My mother opened the kitchen door and walked in with the dog. My father jumped up, bounded over to my mother, and let the dog off the leash.

The dog looked around and ran to Martin and me. He greeted us exuberantly, as if we were old friends he had missed for a long time and unexpectedly met again at a lively surprise party in his honor. Martin put his arms around the dog and lifted him. Martin beamed with delight as I'd never seen him beam before.

Selma stood up abruptly, as if an invisible person had just said, "Please rise."

"It wasn't my idea," my mother said. "Happy birthday, Selma."

"What is it?" asked Elsbeth, who had started to wash the dessert plates and raised her rubber-gloved hands high, as if that would stop the dog from jumping up on her. He jumped up anyway.

"A mutt," my father said. "Part Irish wolfhound." Irish wolfhounds are the largest dogs in the world, as everyone in Selma's kitchen knew. My father had told us. "A shoulder height of thirty-six inches," he'd said.

My father liked to comment on the heights of humans and animals. As far as people were concerned, his estimates were often wrong, but he wouldn't let anyone correct him. He found Martin and me small for our age, even though we were both of average height. Even as a child he would say to Selma, who was taller than everyone around, "You're so small, Mama," when she bent down to him.

"I think he's also part poodle, so he shouldn't get *too* big," my father said in a conciliatory tone. He looked at the dog with satisfaction. "Maybe he's even got some cocker spaniel in him. They're not very intelligent, but they are friendly." My father smiled placatingly, as if that description fit each of us, too. "My guess is that he'll be medium-sized. Like a standard poodle."

Whenever a new person or animal joined us, we all started talking at once about what or whom he, she, or it resembled. Martin saw him as a young brown bear that had gotten its color and habitat wrong; Elsbeth saw a mini–Shetland pony who was missing hooves due to a caprice of nature; the optician suspected he was an as-yet-undiscovered land mammal;

and sad Marlies, who had taken out her compact and was examining her eyelids, glanced up and said, "I have no idea what it is, but somehow it looks like a bad winter."

It was true. The dog was the color of slush. It was watery gray and shaggy as only purebred Irish wolfhounds can be. Its body was still small, but its paws were as big as a bear's, and we all knew what that meant.

Selma was still standing in front of the kitchen bench. She looked at the dog for a long time. Then she looked at my father as if he were a gift shop.

"But I didn't ask for a dog," she said.

"You didn't ask for a coffee table book about Alaska, but you'll enjoy it for a long time," Elsbeth observed.

"You'll enjoy the dog, too, he seems very lively," the optician said, and Selma looked at the optician and Elsbeth as if they were purebred cocker spaniels.

"He's not for you. He's mine," my father said. "I bought him this morning."

Selma sighed with relief and sat down, but quickly stood up again when my father said, "I can only keep him if you'll look after him now and then."

"How often?" Selma asked.

"I've got to go," said my mother, who had remained standing in the doorway. "Unfortunately, I can't stay." My mother could never stay long.

"Well, relatively often," my father said, and everyone knew that "relatively often" meant during office hours.

"Bye, then," my mother said.

No one said anything for a long time, especially not Selma. Since the birthday girl wasn't talking anymore, everyone decided it was time to go. Besides, my father wasn't talking anymore either. Selma's and my father's combined

silence was at least as big as an Irish wolfhound with a shoulder height of eighty inches. So the optician kissed Selma on
the cheek and left. Elsbeth patted the dog, pulled off the rubber gloves, and left. Marlies stopped examining her supposedly visible incipient eyelid inflammation and her supposedly
invisible despair and left. Martin lifted the dog once more
and left. Selma and my father pushed their vigorous silence
outside onto the front doorsteps.

I sat down on the steps next to Selma and ate the empty
chocolate shell of a Mon Chéri. The dog lay down on my
feet. I could feel its heartbeat on my toes. The dog was tired.
It had been exhausting to encounter so many old, long-lost
friends he'd never met before.

On the far side of the meadow at the edge of the forest, a
deer appeared. Selma got up, walked to the garage, opened
the garage door, and slammed it shut with all her strength.
It was Tuesday, and on Tuesdays in season Martin's father,
Palm, went hunting, and Selma deliberately frightened the
deer so that it would disappear into the underbrush, safe
from Palm's shotgun.

The deer startled and disappeared. The dog startled, too,
but did not disappear. Selma returned to the house from the
garage, and it is incomprehensible that we still hadn't noticed
her resemblance to Rudi Carrell. "Here comes Rudi Carrell,"
would have been a perfectly justifiable reaction, "Rudi
Carrell is walking from the garage straight toward us."

Selma sat down on the doorsteps again, cleared her throat,
and looked at my father. "Can't Astrid watch him?"

"That's not possible with the flower shop," my father
said, and Selma looked like she suddenly wished she had a
shop, too.

"I bought him for therapeutic reasons," my father explained.

"So the dog is part of Dr. Maschke's nonsense," Selma said.

"Don't be so dismissive, it's because of my pain," my father said.

"What pain is that?"

"Mine," my father answered. "My encapsulated pain."

"But from what?" Selma asked, and my father replied, "That's just it. I don't know—it's encapsulated." And I thought that even with encapsulated things you know what's in them, but maybe that's only the case when there's no pain in the capsule, just medicine or astronauts.

My father explained that Dr. Maschke had figured out how his pain could be accessed.

"I have to externalize my pain, hence the dog," my father whispered excitedly.

"I beg your pardon?" Selma said. She wasn't indignant but instead seemed moved and a little incredulous. My father started to explain how important it was for him to external- ize his pain as Dr. Maschke recommended.

"Hang on a minute," Selma said. "So the dog is the pain. Have I got that right?"

"Exactly," my father said, relieved. "The dog is a meta- phor, so to speak, a metaphor for the pain."

"A standard poodle-sized pain," Selma said.

The dog raised his head and looked at me. His eyes were very gentle, very black, very wet, and very big. Suddenly I knew we'd all been waiting for him, especially Martin.

"You can leave him with Palm during your consulting hours," Selma suggested.

"Are you insane?" my father asked.

I looked at the dog. It was very clear that he'd be useless as a hunting dog. Palm only had hunting dogs. He kept them on chains in the yard; the chains stretched taut and held the dogs back as they lunged at me, barking, whenever I came to get Martin.

"He'd be a useless hunting dog," I said.

And Selma said, "That's exactly the point," because she believed she wouldn't have to worry about the deer as much if Palm had a gentle and therefore completely useless dog at his side.

I said, "Palm has no time for dogs that aren't aggressive."

There were many things Palm had no time for; actually, he had no time for anything besides high-proof hunting dogs and high-proof alcohol, certainly not for his own son, because Martin wasn't high-proof enough for him. Selma knew that. Everyone did.

Because Selma was so old, she knew Palm from another life, from life before Martin and me. Selma had told me that before he'd started drinking, Palm was exceptionally well informed about the world and its sources of light. He knew everything about the moon's elliptical orbit and its relation to the sun. A hunter, he believed, should know how the world is illuminated.

"Can we keep him, please?" I asked.

The deer reappeared in the meadow. This was unusual. Normally it was enough for Selma to slam the garage door once. She stood up and walked over to the garage. This time she slammed the door twice in a row and the deer disappeared.

Selma sat back down next to us.

"What should we call him?" she asked. "Did Dr. Maschke offer an opinion?"

"Pain," my father suggested. "Pain is a possibility."

"Not enough syllables," Selma said. "Imagine calling out 'Pain, come here, Pain!'" I desperately wanted to keep the dog, so I thought quickly and feverishly how you could best call "Pain." When I finally came up with something, I said it out loud, and the dog jumped up and ran off. Selma said that you couldn't blame him, she would have run away at that suggestion, too. We set off into the dusky forest and soon found the dog in the underbrush, where he had hidden from my suggestion like the deer from Palm's shotgun: I'd suggested, "Ouchy, we can call him Ouchy."

The dog (whom we finally named Alaska—it was Martin's idea; my father agreed because Alaska is big and cold and that's true of pain as well, at least of an encapsulated one) grew quickly. He surprised us every morning, because like everyone else he grew mostly at night. Some nights, I interrupted my own sleep and growth to watch Alaska as he slept and grew. In our house at night, the only thing you could hear was the creaking and rustling of the trees in the wind outside. In my ears, however, it didn't sound like the creaking and rustling of trees in the wind but like the creaking and rustling of bones, the sound of Alaska's bones growing in all directions as he slept.

MON CHÉRI

I f Selma hadn't dreamed of the okapi the previous night, Martin and I would have gone to the Uhlheck after school like we always did. We would have rebuilt our hut in the forest, which Palm often knocked down when he drank. It didn't take much. Our hut was already shaky, and the fact that it collapsed so easily provoked Palm to such a degree that he always trampled the remains after it fell.

We would have played weight lifting in the field like we always did. Martin was the weight lifter and I was the audience. Martin would find a branch that didn't actually weigh very much and would lift it above his head as if it weighed a ton. "And now you must be wondering how the super-heavyweight Vasily Alekseyev was able to lift a hundred and eighty kilos in the snatch. You have to picture it more or less this way," he would say, holding the branch over his head, letting his narrow shoulders and thin arms tremble and holding his breath until his face turned as bright red as weight lifters' faces turn in competitions. "He was also called 'the Crane of Shakhty,'" Martin would say proudly as he took a bow. I would clap. "I'm sure you want to know how Blagoy Blagoev was able to lift a full hundred and eighty-five kilos," Martin would say with another demonstration of trembling and shaking, and I would clap.

"You have to clap with more enthusiasm," Martin would say after about the fourth demonstration. I'd try to clap more enthusiastically and would add: "Amazing."

But that day, after Selma's dream, we avoided the Uhlheck. Despite the clear blue sky, we were afraid lightning might strike us on the field, a bolt of lightning that couldn't care less about being meteorologically impossible. We were afraid we might meet something in the forest even more dangerous than Palm, maybe a hellhound that couldn't care less that it didn't exist.

From the train station, we went straight to Selma's. We felt safer there on the day after her dream. We were ten years old and afraid of deaths that could not possibly occur instead of the real one that came in through the door.

The optician was sitting at Selma's kitchen table. He held a large leather bag on his lap and was unusually quiet. Selma bustled about, doing housework, wiping away dirt that didn't exist.

Martin and I sat on the floor and talked the optician into playing the similarity game with us. In the similarity game we would name two things that had nothing to do with each other and the optician had to find a connection.

"Mathematics and calf's liver," I said.

"You have to absorb them both and neither is to your taste," the optician said.

"What does *absorb* mean?" Martin asked.

"To make something a part of you," Selma replied.

She stepped onto the kitchen bench next to the optician and brushed would-be dust from the photograph of my grandfather. Selma's shoelace had come untied.

"A coffeepot and a shoelace," I said. The optician thought for a moment and Selma stepped down from the bench and tied her shoe.

"Both are used first thing in the morning," the optician explained, "and when used, they both get your heart rate going."

"That's a bit of a stretch," Selma remarked.

"Doesn't matter, it's still true," the optician said.

"A glass soda bottle and a Christmas tree," Martin said, and the optician answered: "That one's easy. Both are most often dark green, both whistle when people or the wind blow in them."

Selma took a stack of leaflets and television guides from a chair to fluff up the cushion. One of the covers showed the actress who played Maggie in Selma's series. Last week Maggie's husband, who was severely injured from an accident, had been unplugged from the machines in the hospital. "Love and death," I said.

"That one's easy, too," the optician said. "You can't practice for either one and you can't escape them—both will befall you."

"What's befall?" I asked.

"When something bowls you over," Selma explained.

"And now, outside with both of you," she said, because she didn't want us to hide. She wanted us to do what we always did, despite her dream, and it was clear that she would not be contradicted.

"And take Alaska with you," she said. Alaska stood up.

It always takes a while for something big to get up fully, even when still young.

We crossed the apple orchard to Elsbeth's house. It was four o'clock in the afternoon. On my fingers, I counted how many hours were left until we could be sure everyone survived Selma's dream. There were eleven.

Alaska stopped under an apple tree and found a bird that had fallen from its nest. It was still alive and already had feathers but couldn't fly yet. I wanted to take the bird straight to Selma, convinced she could raise it so that, although it was born a titmouse, it would later trace artistic circles in the air over the Uhlheck.

"Let's take it with us," I said.

"No, let's leave it in peace," Martin objected.

"Then it will die."

"Yes. Then it will die."

I tried to give Martin a look from Selma's television show and said, "We can't let that happen."

"Yes, we can," Martin said. "It's the way of the world," he added, which had also been said in Selma's show. "Let's just hope a fox comes soon."

Then the twins from the upper village ran up. They'd apparently discovered the bird before we did.

"We went to get sticks to kill it," they said.

"Not a chance," I said.

"We're just putting an end to its suffering," the twins said, the same way Palm would say, "I'm just doing my part to protect the environment," before going off to shoot animals in the forest.

"Can't we just wait for a fox?" I asked, but the twins were

already beating with their sticks. The first blow missed. The second slipped and wasn't decisive enough. It just grazed the bird's head. I saw its little eyes turn red before Martin took my head and pressed my face into his neck. "Don't watch," he said. I could still hear the blows of the sticks and I heard Martin yell: "You idiots, just get it over with."

I decided I would marry Martin one day because I believed that someone who would spare you from having to watch the world take its course had to be the right person.

"Oh, it's just you. That's a nice change," Elsbeth said when we stood at her door, because half the village had already rung her doorbell that day.

Half the village had slipped through Elsbeth's garden gate with their coat collars turned up. They'd looked around several times, the way men in the county seat turned up their collars and looked around when they opened the door to Gaby's Erotic Boutique.

After Selma's dream, those in the village who were not truly superstitious naturally wanted to do everything they could to ward off possible death and reasoned that maybe it could be deflected with a little trinket. After all, you can never be sure. They rang the bell, flitted into Elsbeth's front hall, and said contritely, "I just wanted to ask if there's anything that can be done to protect against death." Elsbeth looked at them the way a priest looks at congregants who only come to church on Christmas.

Elsbeth had something to guard against gout, against unhappy love, against childlessness, against inopportune hemorrhoids and calves born breech. She had several things to ward off the dead; she knew how to cajole their restless souls out of this world and keep them from coming back. She even had something to erase memory and, of course, had a whole bunch of cures for warts, but she had nothing to protect against death itself. Elsbeth was reluctant to admit it, though, especially if people were finally coming to her for help, so that morning she had told the mayor's wife that leaning your forehead against that of a horse would keep death away, even though it really only helped ease headaches. But then Elsbeth's conscience wouldn't let her rest, so she went looking for the mayor's wife. She found her in the stall, her forehead pressed against a horse's. Elsbeth had rarely seen the mayor's wife so relaxed. The mayor's wife and the horse were standing very still, just like Selma and the okapi in the dream. Elsbeth gently put her hand on the mayor's wife's shoulder and said, "I lied to you. It only helps with headaches. I don't have anything to protect against death."

The mayor's wife answered without looking up, "But this is very nice, and I think it's working."

Elsbeth's doorbell rang every few minutes. The three of us sat together on the sofa. Alaska curled up next to Elsbeth's beige-tiled coffee table on which she'd placed two champagne glasses filled with lemonade, and the doorbell kept ringing. And each time she'd just finished asking how school was or what Martin had lifted that day or if we'd rebuilt our hut in the woods, she'd have to jump up and run to the door. Then we'd hear someone ask if she possibly had something to guard against death, we'd hear the someone leave, and Elsbeth calling after: "I do have remedies for toothache or unrequited love, if you ever need them."

Through the living room window we saw people wave goodbye politely and fold their coat collars back down outside her garden gate.

Martin, Alaska, and I watched Elsbeth as she kept jumping up and running back and forth. She always wore the same style of slippers—she had since the beginning of the world. When the outside edges of the soles wore down because of her bow legs, she switched the right slipper to her left foot and the left slipper to her right, and this lasted for a while until someone took pity on her and gave her a new pair.

Elsbeth was small and round, so round that when she drove, she put a piece of carpet on her stomach so the steering wheel wouldn't chafe her. Elsbeth's body was not made for so much back-and-forth. Dark spots formed under her arms and down the back of her dress, which had flowers as big as the ones on the living room wallpaper. Finally she said, "Children, you see how busy it is here. Go and see sad Marlies."

"Do we have to?" we asked.

"Be nice," Elsbeth said, and jumped up when the doorbell rang again. "Someone has to check on her."

Strictly speaking, Marlies wasn't sad, she was bad-tempered. The grown-ups always spoke of Marlies's sadness to Martin and me to make us feel bad for her. They knew if they told us Marlies was sad, we'd have to visit her out of decency and then they wouldn't have to go themselves. Visiting Marlies was not exactly fun, so they always sent us.

She lived at the end of the village. Martin said this was convenient because if robbers tried to attack the village from the back, Marlies's foul mood would scare them away.

We went through her garden gate and made a wide arc around her mailbox, where a bee nest hung, which Marlies simply would not allow to be removed. The mailman refused to put letters in Marlies's mailbox because of the bees, so he stuck them in the garden gate, where they always ended up soaked in the rain.

"Can we come in?" we asked when Marlies opened the door a crack, and Marlies said, "I don't want the dog in here."

"Sit, Alaska," I said. Alaska stretched out in front of the steps to Marlies's little house because he suspected we could be a while.

We followed her into the kitchen. Marlies had not chosen a single thing in the house herself. The house and every last piece of furniture had belonged to her aunt: the bed upstairs, the night table, the wardrobe, the dark three-piece suite, the wrought-iron shelves in the living room, the carpet, the moldy cupboards, the stove and refrigerator, the kitchen table, the two chairs, even the heavy, sticky pans hanging above the stove.

Marlies's aunt had hanged herself in the kitchen at the age of ninety-two, which Marlies could not understand. In her opinion, committing suicide at ninety-two was hardly worth the trouble. Marlies often talked about her aunt, an intolerably prickly person, utterly unreasonable and always in a foul mood.

"And that's where she was hanging," Marlies said every time we came into her kitchen. She said it this time, too, and pointed to the hook next to the ceiling light. Martin and I did not look up.

The only thing in the house that came from Marlies was the smell. The house smelled of cigarettes, of cheap deodorant's feeble efforts against acrid sweat, of food left out for days, of cheerfulness that had expired decades ago, of smoldering fires extinguished in ashtrays, of garbage, of tree-shaped air fresheners and damp laundry left too long in the basket. Marlies walked with a stoop even though she was in her twenties. Her perm was half grown out, and her hair was as brittle as straw. Whenever I saw Marlies's hair, I thought of the shampoo in the local shop, "Schauma for assaulted hair." Martin and I found the wording odd because we thought you could only be assaulted by hellhounds, lightning, Palm, or criminals, and even then they didn't usually attack your hair. Through Marlies we learned that chronic bad temper, too, could be belligerent and attack hair as well.

Marlies dropped onto a kitchen chair. As usual, she wore only a baggy Norwegian sweater and underwear. Her panties were the kind sold in the local shop in packages of three colors. Selma wore the same kind. However, you never knew if Marlies was wearing the yellow, apricot, or light blue pair because they were all as faded as the look she gave us when she asked, "So, what's up?"

"We just wanted to see how you're doing," Martin said.

"Don't worry about me, I'm definitely not the one," Marlies said regretfully, as if she were playing a lottery with extremely low odds of winning.

"Do you want something to eat?" Marlies asked, a question we'd been dreading.

"Yes," we said. We desperately wanted to say no, but Elsbeth had drummed into us that if we didn't eat sad Marlies's food, she would be even sadder.

Marlies went to the stove, poured peas from an open can onto two dessert plates, slapped a lump of cold mashed potatoes next to them, and topped each plate with a slice of boiled ham. She set the plates on the table and dropped back onto her chair.

There was only one other chair in the kitchen. "Do you have anything else to sit on?" I asked.

"No," Marlies said, and turned on the small television on top of the refrigerator. Selma's show was on.

Martin sat down and patted his thigh. I sat on his lap.

The mashed potatoes were the same indeterminate color as Marlies's underwear. The peas lay in a snot-colored puddle. The ham was shiny and covered with spots that looked like badly healed vaccination marks.

Martin and I simultaneously stuffed a forkful into our mouths and looked at each other. Martin chewed. "Get it over with as fast as you can," he said, and shoveled it all quickly into his mouth.

The peas in my mouth didn't get smaller, they swelled. I glanced at Marlies, who was watching Selma's show, and I spit the peas and mashed potatoes back onto my plate. "I an't eat it, Martin," I whispered.

Martin's plate was soon empty. He grabbed a bottle of water and washed down the peas and potatoes. Then he looked at my full plate. "I'm sorry," he said, "but there's no way I can get that down, too. It would make me throw up."

He burped and, looking panicky, he put his hand over his mouth. Marlies turned toward him.

"Taste good?"

"Yes, thanks," Martin said.

"You've hardly touched yours. Eat up before it gets cold," she said to me, as if the food had ever been warm, and then turned back to the television. On the screen were Matthew and Melissa, whose destinies Selma was following feverishly. They were standing in the middle of a field, and Matthew said, "I love you, Melissa, but you know our love doesn't stand a chance."

"Stand up for a second," Martin whispered. I got up

quietly so that Marlies wouldn't look around, but she was watching Melissa say, "I love you, too."

Martin scooped my peas and mashed potatoes onto one slice of ham and covered it with the other. Then he slipped the badly packed mush into the front pocket of his shorts. Martin wore light red Bermuda shorts with deep pockets.

On the television, Melissa said, "But, Matthew, we belong together," and the theme music started playing. Marlies turned off the television and faced us.

"Seconds?"

"Thanks, but no," Martin said.

"Why are you standing there?" Marlies asked. I was standing because I didn't want to smoosh the pea-and-potato mush into Martin's shorts.

"Because there's no chair," I said.

"Sit back down on your friend's lap," Marlies said, "you're making me nervous standing there."

I thought of the optician, who often couldn't sit because of his back trouble. "I've got a problem with my disks because of my primarily sedentary occupation."

"So young, and already falling apart." Marlies sighed.

She lit another cigarette, a long Peer 100. She smoked and tapped her ashes onto my empty plate. Marlies started muttering. She could just as well have been talking to Matthew and Melissa. I stood next to the kitchen table and watched from the corner of my eye as an enormous dark patch spread rapidly over Martin's light red shorts. Martin scooted his chair close to the table so Marlies wouldn't notice anything if she stood up. But she stayed in her chair and told us that she didn't like the television show and hadn't liked the last May Festival and she definitely wouldn't like the next episode or the next May Festival, either. "Why didn't you like the last May Festival?" Martin asked, pulling in his stomach because the mush had reached his waistband.

"Because I've never liked it," Marlies said.

"Come on, Martin, let's go," I whispered.

"Why do you watch the show if you don't even like it?" Martin asked.

I bent down as if I had to tie my shoes. I looked under the table. The ham-and-pea goo kept spreading. Martin's calf was covered with goose bumps, and a trickle of greenish canned pea liquid ran down his leg.

"Because the other shows are even worse garbage," Marlies said.

"Unfortunately, we really have to go now," I said.

We stood up, and Martin slipped close behind me. "Bye, Marlies," we said, and Martin followed me out right on my heels.

"Thanks," I said outside. "For that you can lift me a thousand times."

Martin laughed. "But not right now," he said.

Behind Marlies's house he took off his shorts and shook out the pocket. The ham and mush fell on the grass. We pulled the pocket inside out and scraped off the peas and clumps of mashed potatoes.

"I need new shorts," Martin said.

Our hands were sticky. We held them out to Alaska, but he refused to lick them clean. Martin pulled his shorts back on and we ran to his house.

We stopped abruptly when we saw Palm standing at their

garden gate. We hadn't expected to see Palm. We thought he'd be out in the field.

"Let's go to my house," I whispered. "I'll lend you some shorts." But his father had seen us.

"Come here, right now," he shouted, and we approached the fence behind which the dogs were barking. Alaska tried to hide behind Martin's legs.

Palm stared at Martin's shorts. "Did you piss yourself or what?" he yelled. He stank of schnapps and shook Martin by the shoulder. Martin's head swung back and forth. Martin didn't say a word and shut his eyes.

"It's not his fault," I said. "He scooped up my peas. It's not his fault, Palm."

"Are you a goddamn baby or what?" Palm roared, and Martin kept his eyes closed. He seemed strangely relaxed, as if he were standing in front of the local train door reciting what I was looking at: field, forest, pasture, meadow, meadow.

"He only wanted to help me," I said.

Palm bent down toward me and stared. His complexion was mottled, as if he had once had feathers and someone had yanked them out. Whenever Palm looked at me, I wondered how someone so filled with darkness could ever have known anything about luminous bodies.

"You think you can make a fool of me," he hissed, and his hiss was even worse than his yelling.

I thought of the little bird, of its eye that turned red with the first blow, and I didn't want the world to take its course, the world in the form of Palm.

I stood in front of Martin. "Leave him alone," I shouted.

Palm pushed me away. Light as I was, I fell down even

faster than the hut in the forest. Palm grabbed Martin, whose eyes were still closed, and dragged him into the house. Alaska growled for the first and only time in his life. The door slammed so hard it seemed it would never open again.

I felt nauseated. Death between four walls instead of outdoors suddenly no longer seemed so unlikely. The dogs in the yard barked. I stood there, staring at the door behind which Martin had disappeared, and then at everything around it. Pasture, field. Forest.

WITH DEEPEST SYMPATHIES

After Palm had pulled Martin inside, I ran to my mother's flower shop, the closest refuge. Her store was called Fresh as a Daisy. My mother was proud of the name, but my father thought it was fatuous. It smelled of lilies and pine trees because my mother kept a lot of wreaths in stock. She supplied flowers and funeral wreaths not just to our village, but to the surrounding villages as well. She was always very busy. Whenever I rushed to see her, I had to brake and wait until she finished something or other: a phone call about the phrasing for the bow on a wreath or about the color of the flower arrangements for a wedding banquet, or a conversation with the mayor's wife, who needed a bouquet for the wife of the mayor in the neighboring village.

Eventually my mother would finish what she was doing and turn to me. But there was always something else that needed to be done. She was always occupied with something, even when she turned to me, and this something was a question—one that had lived inside her for more than five years.

My mother had been wondering if she should leave my father. This question filled her from head to toe. She only ever asked herself, but she asked it so often and with such intensity that she never had time to find an answer. The constant questioning even caused her to hallucinate. Looking at the funeral wreath ribbons, she did not read "Sincere Condolences," "With Deepest Sympathies," or "In Eternal Memory," but "Should I Leave Him?" in a bold and suitably decorative font.

"Should I Leave Him?" didn't just appear on the funeral wreath ribbons. It was everywhere. When my mother opened her eyes in the morning, the question was already wide awake and dancing under her nose. It swirled in her cup when she poured milk into her first coffee of the day and formed in the smoke of her first cigarette. It dusted the coat collars of the customers in the flower shop or stuck in their hats. It was imprinted on the wrapping paper for the flowers and it steamed from the pot when she cooked dinner.

The question could also get violent. It rooted around inside my mother the way you rummage in a bag for your keys. It fished everything out of my mother that it didn't need, and that was a lot.

"Are you actually listening to me?" I sometimes asked when telling her I'd learned something new—how to tell time, say, or how to tie a bow. And my mother would reply, "Of course I'm listening, sweetheart," and she would try to listen, but her question was always louder than anything I was saying. Much later I wondered if the question would have given up and made room for me if Selma and the optician hadn't always been there, if I hadn't always had them to turn to, if they hadn't invented the world together.

"So, what's the matter, Luisy?" my mother asked.

"I'm afraid something will happen to Martin because of Selma's dream and because of Palm."

My mother stroked my hair. "I'm sorry," she said.

"Are you even listening to me?" I asked.

"Of course I am. Why don't you just go over to Martin's and cheer him up," she said, and a customer from the next village came in, so I ran to Selma's.

The baying dogs in Palm's yard were on long chains. Alaska stopped at the fence. Selma and I pressed up against the side of the house. The dogs lunged at us, but the chains yanked them back mid-leap. They fell backward, but immediately scrambled onto their feet again.

I grabbed Selma's hand. "Do you think the chains will hold?" I asked.

"They won't break. Palm has good chains," Selma said.

She grabbed a broom leaning against the house next to the door and tried to sweep the dogs away. "Get lost, you hellhounds," she yelled, which didn't impress the dogs. She hammered on the door with her fist.

A window on the second floor opened and Palm looked out.

"Call off your dogs and let your son be. And if you touch Luisa one more time I'm going to poison your goddamn mutts, I swear."

Palm grinned and shouted, "I can't hear you, the dogs are too loud."

Selma slung the broom at the dogs. It hit one on the leg. The dog tripped, yelped, and scrambled back up. "Leave my dogs alone," Palm roared. I closed my eyes tight and buried my face in Selma's shirt. Her chest rose as she took a deep breath.

"Listen to me, Palm," she said more calmly. "Luisa's afraid you'll do something to Martin."

"*Do something*," Palm mimicked her. He reached to the right and pulled Martin to the window. "Did I do anything to you?" Palm asked.

As usual, one strand was standing up on Martin's always well-combed head. You could flatten it as often as you'd like, it would be standing on end again after a few minutes, as if it wanted to point out something overhead.

Martin cleared his throat. "No," he said.

The dogs bayed. "Listen to me, Martin. I've got my eye on your father. We've all got our eyes on your father."

Friedhelm came waltzing down the street, his arms spread as if he were dancing with someone we couldn't see, singing, *Oh, you lovely Westerwald.*

The shutters came rattling down on the house across the street. Palm laughed.

"If I were you, I'd get lost, Selma," he shouted. "Those chains have seen better days." Then he closed the window.

We turned to face the dogs. Selma pulled off a shoe, threw it into the pack, and hit one of the dogs on the head. It fell, yelped, and scrambled back up. Selma's shoe was lost. The dogs crowded around it as if it were a slain rabbit. "I'm watching you, Palm," Selma shouted, and threw her other shoe at the dogs. We went home, Selma barefoot.

It was five o'clock in the evening. Ten more hours, I thought, and wanted to count them off just to make sure, but Selma took my hand, with its fingers spread for counting, closed it into a fist, and held it in her own until we got home.

At that time, at five o'clock, when half the village had already been to see Elsbeth and it was quieter at her place than she liked, an imp jumped onto the nape of her neck. It was one of those invisible hobgoblins that usually leap onto the shoulders of people out wandering at night. But since Elsbeth was constantly roaming through her house with the silence roaring in her ears like a forest at night, she wasn't at all surprised that the imp had perched on her by mistake.

The imp repeated what half the village had said. It chattered about Selma's dream and said that possibly, but probably not, no, certainly not, but then again just maybe, yes, definitely, someone was going to die.

With the imp perched on her neck, Elsbeth went to the telephone. She had a few truths of her own that wanted out at the very last minute, and the imp was whispering that the very last minute might well come soon.

Elsbeth called Selma, because Selma was the best person to call when you were afraid. No one answered. Selma had her hands full with other hellhounds at that very moment. Elsbeth stood in front of the little telephone side table for a long time, an endless ringing in her ear.

She knew what Selma would say, namely: "Do exactly what you would do on any other day."

Elsbeth hung up.

"What would I do right now on any other day?" she asked, and the imp said, "Unfortunately, today is not any other day."

Elsbeth tried not to listen. "What would I do now?" she asked again, louder.

"You should be afraid," the imp replied.

"No," Elsbeth said. "I should go buy some cornstarch."

The line in the general store was short. While she waited, Elsbeth tried to free herself from the imp's grip, but it wasn't easy, unfortunately, because with the cornstarch she only had one hand free. She paid and hurried out. The sound of ringing echoed in her head, the telephone ringing endlessly at Selma's. Elsbeth didn't know how to make it stop, the ringing or the imp's intrusions, and then suddenly the optician was standing in front of her.

"Hello," he said. The ringing stopped and the imp, too, was silenced.

"Hello," Elsbeth said. "Did you do your shopping?"

"Yes, heat patches for my back," the optician said.

"Cornstarch for me," Elsbeth said.

The shopkeeper's supplier was pushing a cart as tall as he was, filled with groceries and covered with a gray tarp, into the store. He stopped halfway through the doorway to tie his shoelaces. The cart looks like a monstrous gray wall of regret, before which we will all eventually kneel, Elsbeth thought.

"How poetic," the imp remarked, and Elsbeth, embarrassed, was suddenly unsure if she had said it out loud.

"Would you like one?" the optician asked.

"One what?"

"A heat patch. I mean, just because you keep grabbing at the back of your neck. It's great for aching muscles," the optician said.

"Yes, please," Elsbeth said.

The optician's shop was right next to the general store. "Come in. I'll put one on you right now."

He unlocked the door and took off his jacket. On his sweater vest was a small badge that said *Employee of the Month*.

"But you're the only one here," Elsbeth said.

"I know, it's supposed to be a joke."

"I see." Elsbeth was never good at getting jokes. Suddenly she could hear her dead husband's exasperated voice in her ear, "For God's sake, Elsbeth, it was a joke," but maybe it was the imp.

"Martin and Luisa think it's funny," the optician said.

"So do I," Elsbeth reassured him. "Very funny, even."

And the optician said, "Go on, have a seat."

Elsbeth sat down on the stool in front of the phoropter, the instrument the optician used to test vision. When we were younger, the optician told Martin and me that you could see the future with it. Given the way a phoropter looks, we believed it immediately, and secretly did for a long time.

"You'll have to uncover your shoulder area," the optician said.

Elsbeth raised both hands to the nape of her neck and undid the zipper on the back of her tight dress. This alone provided some relief. She pulled the neckline down over her round shoulders to completely uncover the back of her neck—as uncovered as something can be with an imp sitting on it, an imp with very tired little arms who had luckily become very taciturn.

The optician opened the package of heat patches and peeled away the protective paper. "This isn't the right size for your neck, but it will stay," he said.

Elsbeth thought of the very last minute and asked herself if the optician was made for secret truths.

The optician carefully placed the heat patch on the nape of her neck and pressed it with his hands so it would stick. The warmth slowly crept under Elsbeth's skin. The imp jumped off.

"Can I tell you a secret?" Elsbeth asked.

SEX WITH RENATA BLOWS MY MIND

Selma and I went home. Her two-story house was built on a slope with the forest at its back. It was a ramshackle building, and the optician was convinced that Selma's love was all that held it upright. My father had suggested several times that she should have it torn down and a new one built in its place, but Selma didn't want to hear it. She knew my father saw the house as a metaphor for nothing less than life, an off-kilter life in danger of collapse.

My dead grandfather, Selma's husband, had built the house, so how could she let it be torn down?

My grandfather had shown Selma an okapi for the first time, in a black-and-white photograph he had found in a newspaper. He'd shown it to her with as much joy as if he had been the first to discover the okapi in real life and hadn't merely found it in a newspaper.

"What kind of creature is that?" Selma had asked.

"It's an okapi, my dearest, and if such a thing exists,

then anything is possible—even that you might marry me and that I might build us a house," my grandfather had said. "Yes, me," he'd added when Selma looked at him skeptically. My grandfather had distinguished himself as her great love, but not so much as a carpenter.

His name was Heinrich, like Iron Henry in the fairy tale of the Frog King, but he must not have been particularly ironclad, since he died long before I was born. But whenever anyone said "Heinrich," Martin and I still shouted the line from the fairy tale in chorus, "The coach is breaking!"— which Selma didn't find the least bit funny.

No one had explicitly told me that my grandfather had died; it was something I had concluded on my own. Selma claimed that Heinrich had fallen in the war, which sounded to me like he had tripped. My father said he hadn't come home from the war, which sounded to me like the war was somewhere you stayed for a long time at some point in your life.

Martin and I admired my grandfather because he'd often behaved more mischievously, if not outrageously, than we would ever dare. Again and again we asked Elsbeth to tell us how as a child my grandfather had been suspended from school because he'd hoisted the principal's camel-hair coat up the flagpole, or how he'd shown up in school one day with a homemade bandage wrapped around his head and claimed that he hadn't been able to do his homework because of a basilar skull fracture. We'd shout, "The coach is breaking!" and sometimes my father would add, "Not the coach but the house," which also didn't amuse Selma.

In fact, the floor in the downstairs apartment was so thin

in places that Selma had broken through several times. Far from being rattled, she would almost wax nostalgic about it. Once she had broken through the kitchen floor while holding the roasted Christmas goose. From her hips down, Selma had dangled into the cellar and still managed to hold the roast goose steady. The optician had helped her out and repaired the hole in the floor with my father's help. Neither the optician nor my father was particularly skilled at home repair. Palm would have done a much better job, but no one wanted to ask him.

Because the floor was, accordingly, unreliably repaired, the optician marked the patched sections with red packing tape so we could avoid them. The optician also marked the spot in the living room floor where Selma's foot had broken through right after my father had said, "I've started psycho-analysis." We all automatically avoided the patched spots, and even Alaska, when he entered the kitchen for the first time on Selma's birthday, had instinctively stayed clear of the area marked in red.

Selma loved her house, and every time she left it, she patted the façade like the flank of an old horse.

"You should let more of the world in," my father would say, "instead of living in a house that is always on the verge of collapsing."

"As long as it's only on the verge," Selma would answer.

"That's exactly the problem," my father would continue, "that it's not worse." Then he would start in again on how the house should be torn down and a new one built, one with more room, since the upstairs apartment had always been too small, with or without extensions. Selma would become furious and tell my father that he should take his wasteful tendencies elsewhere, but please watch where he stepped on his way out.

When we got home, my father was sitting on the front steps. His consulting hours were over. "You're not wearing shoes," he said to Selma. "Are you going senile? Or did you have one Mon Chéri too many today?"

"I threw my shoes at some dogs," Selma said.

"That's not exactly a sign of mental health, either," my father remarked.

"Yes, it is," Selma said. She opened the door. "Come in."

The optician lifted his hands off the hot compress, took Elsbeth by the shoulders, and turned her to face him. "Of course," he said, "you can tell me anything."

"It's just that I'd like to confess something in case I . . . in case today something . . ." Elsbeth said.

"Because of the dream," the optician said.

"Exactly, even though I don't actually believe anything will happen," she lied.

"Neither do I," the optician lied right back. "I think it's extremely unlikely that the dream is foretelling anyone's death. It's nonsense, if you ask me."

It's very calming to tell a few small lies when you know a hidden truth is about to be revealed. The optician thought of Martin, who always hopped up and down a little before trying to lift something almost impossibly heavy.

"It's not easy," Elsbeth said.

"If you'd like, I'll tell you a secret in return," the optician offered.

Elsbeth looked at him long and hard. Everyone in the village knew the optician was in love with Selma—but he didn't know that everyone knew. He still thought his love for Selma was a truth that could remain hidden, while for years everyone had wondered when he would finally admit what had been obvious for ages.

Elsbeth, however, was not sure if Selma herself was aware of the optician's love. Elsbeth had been there the one time my mother tried to talk to Selma about her relationship with the optician. Elsbeth had not thought it was a particularly good idea, but she couldn't talk my mother out of it.

"What do you think, Selma, can you see it working with the optician?" my mother had asked.

"I don't need to work with him, he's self-sufficient," Selma had replied.

"I mean as a companion."

"He already is that," Selma had said.

"Say, Astrid, since you know a lot about flowers," Elsbeth interrupted in the hopes of steering the conversation in another direction, "did you know that buttercups are good for hemorrhoids?"

"No, Selma, I mean as a couple," my mother had insisted. "I mean have you thought of being a couple with the optician?"

Selma had looked at my mother as if she were a cocker spaniel and said, "But I already had my couple."

In Elsbeth's view, Selma had only enough love for one person—it was a very generous amount and it was all for Heinrich. Heinrich was Elsbeth's older brother. Elsbeth had known Heinrich and Selma as a couple and was quite certain that nothing would follow.

Seated on the optician's examination chair, Elsbeth could not believe that after so many years she would be the first to learn what everyone already knew.

"You first," the optician said.

He sat on his desk across from Elsbeth. The compress had become very warm. Elsbeth took a deep breath. "Rudolf cheated on me for a long time," she said. Rudolf was her dead husband. "And I know this because I read his diaries. All of them."

It was not clear which Elsbeth thought worse: that her husband had cheated on her or that she had read all his diaries.

"I've tried everything I could think of to forget. You lose your memory when you eat bread that you've found, did you know that? I tried it, but it didn't work. Probably because I had lost the bread on purpose beforehand."

"You can't decide to find something by accident," the optician agreed. "Did you ever talk about it with Rudolf?"

Elsbeth zipped up her dress. "Rudolf's diaries are yellow. Lined notebooks wrapped in a bright warm sunflower shade of yellow."

"Did you ever talk about it with Rudolf?" the optician asked again.

"No," Elsbeth said. She raised her hand to her neck and pressed the compress tighter. "I pretended I didn't know what I knew. And now it's too late."

The optician knew this feeling well. He felt it every time he'd tried to hide his love for Selma from himself.

"There were a lot of sunflower-yellow notebooks, and even though I only read them once, I still know exactly what is in them. Often, when I'm lying in bed, I hear my inner voice reading from them."

"What exactly does it read to you?" the optician asked.

"Things about the other woman."

"Give me an example, just a sentence, if you want," the optician proposed. "Then I'll have the sentence. That way it can move in with me instead."

Elsbeth closed her eyes and pressed the bridge of her nose between her thumb and forefinger as if she had a headache. Then she said: "Sex with Renata blows my mind." At exactly that moment the doorbell rang, and the shopkeeper's wife burst in. "Hi, there!" she called, and came up to them. "Oh, a vision test?"

"Of a kind," the optician said.

Elsbeth said nothing because she was feverishly wondering if the shopkeeper's wife had heard the last sentence and could be thinking that Elsbeth had had mind-blowing sex with some woman named Renata

The shopkeeper's wife needed a new eyeglass chain. Fortunately, she quickly decided on one with rhinestones. "I'm going to the city tomorrow. To get my hair done. Could you watch Trixie tomorrow?" she asked Elsbeth.

Trixie was her terrier, and now Elsbeth was sure the shopkeeper's wife hadn't heard the sentence, because not in a million years would she leave her terrier with Elsbeth if she thought Elsbeth was having mind-blowing sex with some Renata or other.

"I'd be very happy to," Elsbeth said.

"Assuming we're all still alive tomorrow," the shopkeeper's wife said cheerily.

"That would be helpful," the optician said, and opened the door for the shopkeeper's wife. Then he sat back down on the desk across from Elsbeth.

The optician looked at Elsbeth as if he had all the time in the world for her. Even if he were the one to die that day, he still had all the time in the world in that moment.

He crossed his legs. "If you ask me: The fact that sex with Renata blew your husband's mind doesn't necessarily reflect on the quality of their relationship. Bashing someone on the head with a skillet also blows their mind."

Elsbeth smiled. Her bound-up truth had been massive and very heavy. It still was, but it did her good to see that the optician could carry it so lightly.

"Earlier, a deliveryman pushed a cart covered with a gray tarp into the store and it looked like a wall, like the wall of regret we all kneel before. Wouldn't you agree?"

"Unfortunately, I didn't see it," the optician said, "but I can imagine that's exactly what it looked like."

"I didn't have aching muscles," Elsbeth said. "I had an imp."

"I know," the optician said. "But heat works wonders against imps, too."

Elsbeth cleared her throat. "You were going to tell me something." She sat up straight and folded her hands in her lap.

The optician ran his hand through his hair. He stood up and paced back and forth in front of the shelves with eyeglass frames and cases. Now and then he took a small, involuntary step to the right, as he always did when his inner voices accosted him.

Elsbeth considered what would be best for him. When he confessed his love for Selma, should she act surprised, and would she actually be able to say, after all these years, "Well, now, that *is* news"? She wondered whether she should advise the optician to tell Selma, and whether he might not have a stroke when he realized that he had spent decades trying to conceal a truth that was much too big to hide and so had been standing behind him for all to see.

"So," the optician said, "Palm has absolutely no time for Martin."

"I know," Elsbeth said, and gave him an encouraging look.

"He has made it clear to Martin from day one. And he also chased away Martin's mother."

"I know," Elsbeth said, and asked herself how the optician would segue to Selma. "And he probably beats Martin sometimes, too."

"Yes, I'm also afraid of that."

The optician was still pacing back and forth. "He shoots drunkenly at deer and doesn't hit them. Once, on a binge, he threatened Selma with a broken bottle."

"Yes," Elsbeth said, and remembered that the optician had a habit of connecting the most disparate things; he could surely find a connection between Palm and his love for Selma.

The optician stood still and looked at Elsbeth. "This is the secret: last night I took a saw to the posts of his hunting blind."

IT'S BEAUTIFUL HERE

Night was falling, and Selma repeated what she had been saying all day long: "Do exactly what you'd do on a normal day." So I went to give Alaska a bath. Since Alaska didn't fit into Selma's shower, I had to wash his front half first and then his back half while the rest of him stuck out of the shower stall. The door was open, and I heard Selma say to my father: "Everyone is afraid of my dream."

My father laughed. "Mama, please, it's nothing but nonsense."

Selma got a box of Mon Chéri. "It probably is, but that doesn't make things any better."

"Dr. Maschke will laugh himself silly when I tell him about it."

"How nice that you entertain Dr. Maschke so well."

My father sighed. "I wanted to talk with you about something completely different," he said, and added in a louder voice, "Come here, Luisy, I have something to tell you both."

I had toweled off Alaska all over, but he was still dripping. I thought of what the sentence "I have something to tell you" introduced in Selma's television series. We're bankrupt; I'm leaving you; Matthew is not your son; William is clinically dead; we're going to unplug the machines.

I went into the kitchen with the dog. My father was sitting on a stool. Selma was leaning on the kitchen table. "Alaska is still dripping," she said.

"Do you remember Otto?" my father asked.

"Of course," we said.

Otto was the retired mailman who died after Selma's dream because he had completely stopped moving.

"Here's the thing," my father said. "I think I'm going to give it all up. Probably. I'm going on a long trip."

"And when will you be back?" I asked.

"And where will you go?" Selma asked.

"Out into the world," he said. "To Africa or Asia or somewhere."

"Or somewhere," Selma echoed. "And when?"

"I don't know yet," my father said, "I'm still thinking it over. I'm just letting you know that I'm considering it."

"And why?" Selma asked. This was an unusual question. When someone says he's going on a trip around the world, usually no one asks why. No one needs to explain why he wants to get out into the world.

"Because I don't want to rot in this backwater," he said.

"Thanks very much," Selma said.

Alaska was still dripping. I suddenly felt very tired. As if I hadn't just returned from the bathroom but from a day's journey, a long day's journey with piles and piles of luggage.

I tried to think of how I could persuade my father to stay.

"But it's so beautiful here," I finally said, "we live in a glorious symphony of green, blue, and gold."

That's what the optician said sometimes. We lived in

a picturesque area, in a gorgeous, heavenly area, as was written in elegant script on the postcards displayed on the counter of the general store. Yet hardly anyone in the village noticed. We overlooked and ignored the beauty that surrounded us—we gave it the cold shoulder—but we'd be the first to complain vociferously if the beauty in our surroundings failed to show up one day. The only one who occasionally felt pangs of conscience over our daily neglect of beauty was the optician. He would stop short, up in the Uhlheck, for example, and put his arms around Martin's and my shoulders.

"Just look how unbelievably beautiful it is here, in this glorious symphony of green, blue, and gold," he'd say, with a grand gesture at the fir trees, the fields of wheat, and the immense sky above. We'd look at the familiar firs and the familiar sky and then would be ready to move on. "Just savor it for a moment," the optician would say, and we'd give him the same look we gave Elsbeth when she would tell us to go and see sad Marlies.

"That's true," my father said. "And I'll come back."

"When?" I asked.

Selma looked at me, sat down next to me on the kitchen bench, and took my hand in hers. I leaned against her shoulder and thought that we could just stay here, Selma and me, and rot here together.

"Could we have a few more details?" she asked. "Is this more of Dr. Maschke's nonsense?"

My father raised his head and murmured, "Don't be so dismissive." It was clear that he was not prepared for our questions and had hoped we would say, "Fine, go ahead, have fun, and stay in touch."

"And what does Astrid think about this?" Selma asked.

"And what about Alaska? He's hardly had a chance to prove himself as an encapsulated pain."

"For goodness' sake, I'm only telling you that I'm thinking about it."

This was not true. My father had decided long before, but here, at Selma's kitchen table, he was as unaware of that fact as Selma and I were, and we were also unaware that Alaska would become Selma's dog because my father couldn't take him out into the world, since Alaska, my father would claim, was not made for adventure.

Selma and I sat on the kitchen bench across from my father, thinking of the same thing, of Dr. Maschke's office in the county seat, which my father had described to us. The room was filled with posters of the same landscapes as those on the postcards outside the gift shop, that is, of the sea, mountains, and undulating prairies, just bigger and without inspirational quotes, since Dr. Maschke delivered these personally. There were also objects mounted on the walls of Dr. Maschke's office. While he was searching for encapsulated pain in what my father was saying, my father was looking at an African mask, a Buddha doweled into the wall, a sequined shawl, a leather canteen, a scimitar.

Dr. Maschke's hallmark, my father had told us, was a black leather jacket, which he never took off during their sessions. The leather jacket creaked whenever Dr. Maschke leaned forward or back in his chair.

At that moment, sitting at the kitchen table, Selma and I were sure that it was actually Dr. Maschke who wanted to give everything up—except for his leather jacket—and that he was actually the one who wanted to travel around the world but, for the sake of convenience, had planted the seed of this idea in my father's mind through some adage or other.

He was sending my father out into a creaking world and be-cause of him we would all be given up and left behind to rot. That's what Dr. Maschke had been scheming from the very beginning.

"And when will you be back?" I asked again.

Friedhelm waltzed by under Selma's window, singing loudly that even the smallest ray of sunshine can reach deep into the heart.

"That's enough," my father said, and stood up. He ran outside, grabbed Friedhelm, and drove him to his office. My father had medicine for and against every emotional state and he gave Friedhelm another shot that made him tired, so irresistibly tired that Friedhelm fell asleep on the examina-tion table and didn't wake up until noon the following day, completely confused, into a world in which, for a while, no one, aside from me, was able to sleep.

Selma and I stayed in the kitchen.

"I'll be all yours in just a moment," she said, and stroked my arm. I thought Selma would stand up and go into another room, but she kept sitting next to me on the bench, looking out the window. The silence that emanated from her grew much more quickly than the puddle spreading under Alaska. Just when I'd begun to wonder when I might be allowed to interrupt Selma's silence, the doorbell did it for me.

Martin stood on the doorstep. He was wearing a clean pair of shorts and his hair was freshly plastered down.

"He let you go out again," I said.

"Yes, he's asleep. Can I come in?"

I glanced into the kitchen. The silence had risen higher than the dog's shoulder.

"What's going on?" Martin asked.

"Nothing," I said.

The hand rake Selma had left in the gutter above the kitchen door fell to the ground.

"Some wind we've got today," Martin said, even though it wasn't true.

He was pale but smiling.

"Can I lift you?"

"Yes, please, lift me up," I said, and put my arm around Martin's neck.

EMPLOYEE OF THE MONTH

Martin and I went into the kitchen and looked at Selma, wide-eyed. We must have looked pretty helpless, because she cleared her throat, took a deep breath, and said, "Well, you two bewildered children. You may not believe it right now, but everything will work out. You both have strange fathers, but they'll come to their senses at some point. You can take my word for it."

We did. We believed everything Selma said. When a suspicious-looking mole was found on her back some years before, Selma had written a card to a worried acquaintance the night before she received the biopsy results. "Everything went well," Selma had written, and she had been right.

"But you dreamed about an okapi," Martin said. "Someone is going to die."

Selma sighed. She looked at the clock. It was almost six-thirty, and every evening at six-thirty Selma went for a walk in the Uhlheck, and had since she invented the world.

"Let's go," she said.

"Even today?" we asked, because we were still afraid of a nonexistent hellhound or an impossible lightning strike.

"Especially today," Selma said. "We're not going to let anything stop us."

It was dark in the Uhlheck. The wind blew through the trees. Martin and I held Selma's hands. We didn't talk. We especially didn't talk about the fact that according to my calculations, Death only had eight hours left in which to strike. I counted off the hours on the fingers of my free hand and Selma pretended not to notice.

"What do you two want to be when you grow up?" she suddenly asked.

"A doctor," I exclaimed.

"Oh Lord," Selma said. "Still, better than a psychiatrist. And you?"

"The optician saw in his phoropter that I'll be a weight lifter," Martin said. "And it's true."

"Of course it's true," Selma said.

Martin looked up at her. "And you?" he asked.

Selma caressed Martin's hair. "Maybe a veterinarian," she said.

Martin picked up a stick that lay across the path. "You surely want to see exactly how Igor Nikitin was able to lift a hundred and sixty-five kilos," he said.

Selma smiled. "Absolutely," she said.

Martin pretended the stick bore a tremendous weight, lifted it over his head, held it there, his arms trembling, and let it fall. We clapped for a long time. Martin beamed and took a bow.

"Let's go back," Selma said after thirty minutes had passed and rain had begun to fall. We turned around. The way back was shrouded in darkness.

"Let's play Hat, Stick, Umbrella; I'll be last," Selma said. We lined up in a row. "A hat, a stick, an umbrella," we sang. "Forward, backward, sideways, stop." We played the entire dark way home and arrived at Selma's door before we knew it.

Selma pan-fried us some potatoes. Then she called Palm and asked if Martin could spend the night, but he wasn't allowed, not even as an exception.

At two o'clock in the morning, Elsbeth climbed out of bed and dressed. She had been lying awake for hours and had made a decision.

She opened her front door and went out into the night, a tube of superglue and a roll of wire in one hand, the determination to save the optician in the other.

Palm's hunting blind was in a meadow that could only be reached by going through the forest. The forest was as black as the bow on a funeral wreath. Elsbeth peered into the darkness and longed for a bright, warm, sunflower shade of yellow.

At the forest's edge, she hesitated one last time. On the one hand, going into the forest at night alone after Selma's dream seemed like sending Death an invitation, like throwing herself into his arms. On the other hand, it would have been cheap of Death to take advantage of such an easy opportunity. On yet another hand, Death was now under enormous pressure, since he only had about an hour left to strike, and in such circumstances, people aren't as choosy and are more likely to be satisfied with easy solutions. On top of that, the more she thought about it, the more trouble Elsbeth had coming up with any suitably dramatic kind of death, but she came up with quite a few that would count as an easy way out.

Elsbeth went into the forest; she did not want to go back on her decision.

She remembered that singing helped when you were afraid. Elsbeth sang the lullaby "The Forest Is Dark and Silent." It was, in fact, pitch-black, but it was not at all silent. There was rustling and cracking on all sides: above, behind, in front of, and next to Elsbeth. Maybe it was the imps, who were afraid of the optician's heat patch, which she still had on. She stopped singing because her voice sounded so lost, and singing the praises of a marvelous rising fog that, in reality, was not the least bit marvelous, seemed rather desperate to her. Besides, she was afraid of attracting or not hearing something.

Unfortunately, Elsbeth knew all about creatures you could encounter in the forest at night. She thought of the shrub woman, who emerges from the underbrush every hundred years with a basket on her back and wants to be scratched and have her hair deloused. Those who scratch her back and delouse her hair are rewarded with leaves of gold. Those who don't are carried off.

Elsbeth had no interest in leaves of gold. She pictured the squinty-eyed shrub woman coming out from between the fir trees, grabbing Elsbeth with twisted fingers. She pictured the shrub woman pushing Elsbeth's hand into her matted hair so she could find the lice—but how on earth could the shrub woman expect her to see anything in the dark? Then Elsbeth pictured how, and above all, *where*, the shrub woman would want to be scratched, and then she thought about mind-blowing sex with Renata and how a skillet to the head and a shrub woman could both blow one's mind as well, *which doesn't necessarily reflect on the quality of their relationship, if you ask me*, and she remembered that she had decided to save the optician and that saving the optician meant saving Palm.

Elsbeth did not have appropriate footwear. She was wearing fake leather pumps with the toes split open and the heels worn down. Elsbeth never wore rubber boots because they weren't flattering, and whenever she went out, even if just to Selma's or the general store, Elsbeth tried to look chic because, she always said, you never know who you'll meet. The dampness of the fallen leaves crept up over the edges of her pumps and into her black nylons, making them even blacker.

The forest suddenly opened up. In our region, there are no transitions. There's no gradually clearing forest, no slightly lower trees as intermediaries between forest and meadow. In the middle of the abrupt meadow, Palm's hunting blind rose like an unfinished monument, like the crow's nest on a ghost ship. As she approached the blind, Elsbeth wondered if anyone had ever been here so late at night, anyone who was not a fox, a deer, or a wild boar, anyone the shrub woman could have asked to scratch and delouse her. The meadow was very still. Elsbeth longed for the cracking and creaking of the forest, because it's scary being the only one making noise. Her steps and her breathing were suddenly as loud as in a *Tatort* episode just before the victim is overcome and mangled with such barbarity that even the taciturn pathologist blanches and the police commissioners who had come running have to vomit.

Elsbeth stepped up to the stand's rear posts. On both posts, she felt for the spot the optician had sawed. The posts were almost completely severed. Severed, Elsbeth thought, and the throat of the young girl in the last episode flashed before her eyes. She unscrewed the tube of superglue and squeezed the contents first in one crack, then in the other. Don't think of the shrub woman, she thought, don't think of severed things. Most of all she was afraid of her own breathing, which was much too rapid and improbably loud.

The wire made a deafening sound when she unrolled it to wrap it around the first post. Her hands shook as if they weren't her hands at all but hands from a *Tatort* episode.

And then, above her, someone coughed.

Elsbeth closed her eyes. I'm the one, she thought. I'm the one who dies from Selma's dream.

"Get lost," someone hissed from above. Elsbeth looked up and in the hunting blind's paneless window she saw Palm.

Someone whose life is being saved does not murder his rescuer.

"Good evening, Palm," Elsbeth said. "I'm sorry, but you have to come down right now."

"Get lost," Palm said, "you're scaring away the pigs." It took Elsbeth a moment to realize that he was actually talking about the wild boar.

"Night hunting is forbidden," Elsbeth said bravely, but when he was drunk, Palm was no more worried about laws against hunting than he was about the shrub woman.

She started to wrap the wire around the first sawn post. Some of the glue had dripped down the post like resin and begun to harden.

"Are you out of your mind?" Palm hissed.

Elsbeth considered. "When you're afraid of dying, you should wrap a hunting blind in wire."

Palm said nothing.

"Seven times, and never in moonlight," Elsbeth continued.

"Besides, you shouldn't sit in a hunting blind when you're afraid of dying."

"But I'm not afraid of dying," Palm said, and he was serious. Palm didn't know that he was afraid of dying, deathly afraid even. He couldn't know, because he hadn't experienced real terror before Death came in through the door.

"But Selma dreamed of an okapi," Elsbeth said.

Palm took a gulp from his bottle. "You're all nuts. I can't believe you people," he said.

Elsbeth kept wrapping wire around the post.

It's true, I am nuts—this will never hold, Elsbeth thought.

Palm burped. "Here comes another idiot," he said.

Elsbeth spun around. Someone with a headlamp came running toward her over the meadow. He was tall and coming very quickly. It was the optician.

He had run the entire way from his door, across the village, through the forest, over the meadow, carrying a sack with nails, a hammer, and several pieces of wood. He didn't even notice that when he was running, his inner voices were silent. For the first time, the voices didn't constantly want to be scratched and deloused, because such voices step aside with unexpected politeness when you're running somewhere, determined to save a life.

Out of breath, the optician stood in front of Elsbeth. "What are you doing here?" he asked.

"I'm saving you," Elsbeth said.

The optician had run out without his jacket. He was still wearing his sweater vest with the *Employee of the Month* badge. He emptied his sack at Elsbeth's feet, stuck a few nails between his lips, and began hectically hammering the pieces of wood over the sawn cracks. The noise was deafening.

"What's going on now?" Palm asked overhead. "Would you piss off already?" he hissed. "You're scaring away the pigs."

The optician froze and looked up. "You have to come down right now," Elsbeth called.

"No!" the optician yelled, and the nails fell from his mouth. "For God's sake, Palm, stay up there. Don't move!"

He leaned toward Elsbeth. "If he climbs down now, the thing will collapse," he whispered, and hammered with all his strength. His heart hammered to the same beat, as if to help.

"Would you stop with this shit?" Palm hissed.

"I'm sorry, I was wrong," Elsbeth said. "Instead of wrapping wire around the post seven times, you're supposed to hammer it."

Palm started yelling.

"I've had it with both of you," he roared, then grabbed his rifle and stood up.

"Stay up there," Elsbeth shouted.

"Don't come down," the optician shouted. But Palm turned around and started to climb down the ladder, still yelling ferociously.

"If you're not afraid of dying, you have to stay up in a hunting blind no matter what," Elsbeth shouted.

"Stay up there!" the optician shouted, and hammered. Palm swayed on the ladder. The optician stopped hammering, leapt to the post that was most unstable, and wrapped his arms around it to stabilize it with his own body.

"You're the one scaring away the pigs," Elsbeth shouted, and when Palm reached the sixth rung from the top, he slipped and fell.

Palm fell far. The optician let go of the post and leapt to the ladder, believing he could catch Palm. Even though it seemed to Elsbeth that Palm was falling astonishingly slowly, as if he were falling in slow motion, the optician still wasn't fast enough.

He's the one, Elsbeth thought, Palm's the one who will die, and Palm hit the ground right in front of the optician.

Elsbeth and the optician knelt down next to him. Palm didn't move. His eyes were closed. He breathed heavily and stank of schnapps.

Elsbeth asked herself if anyone other than Martin and Martin's mother had ever dared get this close to him. She examined Palm as closely as she would a stuffed predator.

"Palm, say something!" the optician said.

Palm was silent.

"Can you move your legs?" Elsbeth asked.

Palm remained silent but rolled to his side.

Palm was not the one who would die.

The headlamp illuminated his profile, his nose's cratered landscape, the blond hair stuck to the nape of his neck. Elsbeth took hold of his wrist. His pulse thundered over the meadow.

Elsbeth was about to set down Palm's arm when her eye fell on his wristwatch. "Look," she yelled to the optician, even though he was kneeling right next to her, and she waved Palm's arm in front of his face. "It's three o'clock, it's three o'clock! It's over. It's three o'clock and we're not dead."

"Congratulations," the optician said softly. "You, too, Werner Palm."

Without raising his head, Palm shook off Elsbeth's hand and slipped his arm under his head. He seemed to be in a stable recovery position.

"I'm going to kill you, you jackasses," he murmured, "I'm going to blow you away."

Elsbeth patted his head as if he were the shopkeeper's wife's terrier. "Of course you will, Palm," she said, then laughed and slapped the optician on the thigh, because now that the twenty-four hours were up, she felt that everything was immortal again for the time being.

Far behind in the village, old Farmer Häubel looked at the clock and felt himself immortal for the time being, but, unlike Elsbeth, he wasn't in the least bit happy about it. He stood up laboriously and, nearly transparent as he was, he shuffled over to the roof hatch and shut it, since no souls would be flying through it anytime soon.

THE TWENTY-NINTH HOUR

When the new day began, twenty-six hours after Selma's dream, the villagers found themselves in their pajamas, their hearts still intact, their minds still intact, with their hastily burned and hastily written letters.

They were overjoyed and resolved to delight in and be grateful for everything in the future because they were still alive. They resolved, for example, to finally fully appreciate the morning sun playing in the branches of the apple trees. The villagers made such resolutions often, when a falling roof tile narrowly missed them, for example, or a feared diagnosis was ruled out. But inevitably, after a short time, a burst pipe or an unexpected surcharge quickly diluted their brief spell of joy and gratitude, and the sunlight in the apple trees could call it quits.

When the mailman came to empty the mailbox at the crack of dawn, a few people were already waiting to reclaim their hastily mailed letters because the letters now made them uncomfortable, the words having become unsuitably grandiose for a continuing life—*always* appeared far too often, as did *never*. The mailman patiently waited as they rummaged through his mailbag and recovered their escaped truths.

The truths people had said to each other at the supposedly very last minute could not be recovered. The cobbler left his wife at daybreak and moved to the neighboring village because she had told him that his son wasn't, strictly speaking, *his* son, and this long-confined truth spread an awful stink and a great commotion.

One liberated truth, which no one tried to recapture and could therefore romp about freely, belonged to Farmer Häubel's great-grandson. He had finally told the mayor's daughter that at the last May Festival he had danced only with the shopkeeper's daughter simply out of pique because he had thought she didn't want to dance with him. After Selma's dream, Häubel's great-grandson told the mayor's daughter that he actually loved no one but her and that he was convinced nothing could ever get in the way of his love. The mayor's daughter also loved Häubel's great-grandson, and everyone was happy that this truth was out. It had escaped at the very last minute not because death was near but because otherwise life would have taken a wrong turn. Häubel's great-grandson had almost moved to the county seat out of pique and the mayor's daughter had almost begun to talk herself into believing that Häubel's great-grandson was not the right one for her. Everyone was happy that this truth was free to romp about and they would all have liked to celebrate the marriage right away if not for what happened next, after which no one wanted to celebrate any wedding ever again, at least not for a while.

At six-fifteen, twenty-seven hours and fifteen minutes after her dream, when everyone assumed time had saved them, Selma packed my lunch box. I sat at the kitchen table. I was late and wouldn't have time to copy all my homework into Martin's notebook. I can still remember that my shoes were too tight, that I said to Selma, "I need new shoes," and she answered that we would drive to the county seat the next day and get new ones—Elsbeth also needed new shoes.

Naturally, I didn't know that there would be no tomorrow for buying new shoes in the county seat. I didn't know that a few days later, I'd be wearing my too-large Sunday shoes and holding Selma's hand in the cemetery and everyone close to me, including the optician, the "Employee of the Month," shaking with sobs, would form a circle around me so I wouldn't see the course the world had taken, so I wouldn't see too clearly how the coffin was lowered, a coffin, the priest said, of a size showing that here lay someone who had not been granted even half a life; but I saw it very clearly, not even all of them together were enough to hide it. And naturally I didn't know that as soon as the coffin was set down almost without a sound, I would turn and run, and that Selma, of course it was Selma, would find me exactly in the spot under her kitchen table where my feet in their too-small shoes now stood, that I would be huddled there, my face smeared with a sticky red paste and countless Mon Chéri wrappers at my feet; I didn't know that Selma would crouch down and I would see her tear-streaked face, that Selma would creep under the table with me and say, "Come here, you little praline," and everything would go dark because I would press my face against Selma's black shirt, black as the bow on a funeral wreath; naturally, I didn't know any of this because if we did know such things in advance, if we knew in advance that the entire expanse of life could be upended in less than an hour, we would lose our minds.

At seven-fifteen, Martin and I were standing in the train. Martin had not lifted me on the platform. I had dictated my homework to him as fast as possible.

"Go," Martin said when the train started, leaning his back with his backpack against the train door and closing his eyes. I stood against the facing door and looked outside.

"Wire factory," Martin said exactly at the moment we passed the wire factory.

"Right," I said.

"Field, meadow, crazy Hassel's farmhouse," he said.

"Right," I said.

"Pasture," Martin said. "Forest. Forest. Hunting blind two."

"Hunting blind one," I said.

"Sorry," Martin said, and smiled. "Hunting blind one. Now field again."

"Perfect," I said.

I looked outside over Martin's head. The strand on Martin's head was still stuck down but it would be standing up again before we got to school.

"Forest, pasture," Martin recited quickly, because we

were approaching the section where the train sped up, the section in which naming everything at exactly the right moment was especially challenging. "Meadow, meadow," he said.

Then suddenly the door sprang open.

PART TWO

SOMEONE OUTSIDE

Please close the door," Mr. Rödder said.

He knew this wasn't possible. The door did not close completely because the doorframe had warped and the brown carpet squares that looked like wire-haired dachshund fur were too thick. For the door to close even halfway, you had to lean your entire body weight against it as if you were trying at all costs to prevent someone outside from pushing in. And yet, no one ever wanted to come in here; no one except for Mr. Rödder and me ever wanted to come into the bookstore's tiny, windowless, musty back room.

Even without the two of us, the room was completely full. Along with a folding table holding a coffee maker, it held old fax machines, discarded cash registers, rolls of crumpled promotional posters, and display stands.

In the midst of all these things lay Alaska. Alaska was old, much older than dogs generally grow to be. It seemed as if he had been allotted several lives and was living them one after the other without dying in between.

Mr. Rödder hated Alaska. He hated it when I had to bring him with me to the bookstore. Alaska was clumsy and shaggy and enormous and gray. He smelled like an unaired truth. Every time I came in through the door with Alaska and countless excuses and apologies, Mr. Rödder reached for the aerosol can next to the cash register without a word and filled the room with Blue Ocean Breeze air freshener, but it wasn't much help. "It doesn't work with this wreck of a creature," Mr. Rödder always said after spraying Alaska and shooing him into the back room. "These living conditions are not at all suitable for the species," he would say when Alaska lay down between the many broken objects, and he would say it with as much indignation as if he were talking about his own life, not Alaska's.

Because of Alaska, the tiny back room was filled with the odors of dog and blue ocean breeze from a spray can. Mr. Rödder and I stood close to each other and, as with every time we were both in this room, it was unclear how we had found enough space among the clutter. It always seemed that we hadn't come in through the door that didn't close but had been deposited here by some giant hand that had raised the roof and carefully fit us in the room without having to remove anything.

"I have to speak with you about something," Mr. Rödder said. His breath smelled of the violet pastilles he was constantly sucking because he was afraid of having bad breath. He had even offered Alaska some, but I argued that they weren't suitable for the species, and Alaska had ignored them. Mr. Rödder's breath smelled of old funeral decorations and I didn't dare tell him that this, too, was a kind of bad breath.

"Marlies Klamp came in this morning," he said. "She complained yet again about your recommendation. She didn't like the book. It would be very nice if you could develop a better sense of our customers."

"But I do have a good sense of them," I objected. "Marlies never likes anything."

"Then get an even better sense of them," Mr. Rödder said.

He held his face close to mine. His eyebrows looked like wire-haired dachshund fur. They stuck out in all directions. Mr. Rödder's eyebrows were in a constant state of agitation.

"Otherwise you won't pass the trial period," Mr. Rödder said as if it were a matter of life and death, and I couldn't believe that it would depend on Marlies, of all people.

Marlies hardly left her house anymore, and when she did it was only to complain about something. She complained to the shopkeeper about a frozen dinner that didn't taste good. She complained to the optician that her glasses were always crooked. She complained in the gift shop that they didn't have any good ideas for presents, and she complained to Mr. Rödder about my recommendations.

I had gone to see her the previous week. "No one's home," Marlies had called through the closed door. I went around her house and looked in through the kitchen window. It was dark and I couldn't see anything. The window was ajar.

"I'll be quick, Marlies," I said. "Could you please stop complaining to Mr. Rödder about me? Otherwise I won't pass the trial period."

Marlies did not answer.

"What would you like me to recommend?" I asked through the window. I thought of the day Alaska came to us and I had feverishly tried to think of a name, only to come up with the wrong one. Martin knew the right name immediately.

"I'm going to keep complaining," Marlies had answered. "Deal with it. Now go away."

"Fine," I said to Mr. Rödder. "I'll get an even better sense of our customers."

"I very much hope you will," he said. He put his hands in his pockets and rocked back and forth on his toes. He did this often and his rocking made him seem like he wanted to gallop away that instant and knock someone over with his enormous belly. "That will be all."

"I've also got something on my mind," I said. "I wanted to ask if I could have a few days off next week. Can you believe it? Someone is coming to visit me from Japan."

"Good Lord," Mr. Rödder said, as if a visitor from Japan were an attack of rheumatism.

"Just two days," I said.

Alaska woke up. He raised his head and wagged his tail, knocking over a colony of promotional poster rolls. Mr. Rödder sighed. "That really is a lot to ask," he said.

"I know, and I'm very sorry."

The door chimes jingled.

"Customer," Mr. Rödder said.

"Maybe you could consider it," I said.

"Customer," Mr. Rödder repeated.

We struggled through all the broken objects and climbed over Alaska to the door that didn't shut completely or open fully.

———

The optician was standing next to the door, and when he saw us coming he grabbed a book from a stack of new titles and came up to us.

"Good evening," he said to Mr. Rödder. "I simply must tell you that your colleague always gives me excellent recommendations."

"I see," Mr. Rödder said.

"She knows exactly what I want before I do," the optician said. He was wearing the *Employee of the Month* badge on his sweater vest.

"It's okay," I whispered.

"Aren't you the optician from Luisa's village?" Mr. Rödder asked suspiciously. "You two know each other personally, don't you?"

"Vaguely," the optician said. "What I wanted to tell you is that your colleague reads me like an open book."

"We're closing now," I said, pushing the optician toward the door.

In the doorway, the optician turned to Mr. Rödder. "No one has ever given me as many exceptional recommendations as she has. And I've been given a lot of recommendations in my life," he said, and I pushed him out onto the sidewalk.

"Thanks," I said outside, "but that wasn't necessary."

The optician beamed at me. "Good idea, wasn't it? I'm sure it worked."

That evening I unlocked the door to my apartment, went into the kitchen with Alaska, and hid his evening pill in a ball of liverwurst. The answering machine light was blinking. Its display showed five new messages. The answering machine actually should have been in Mr. Rödder's back room with all the other broken things. It always showed many more new messages than there actually were. The answering machine regularly hung up on callers after a few seconds, said connections were maintained that weren't, and repeated three times that a message was done at the end.

"You have forty-seven new messages," the answering machine announced. The first was from my father. The connection was terrible.

"The connection is terrible," he said from somewhere far away. The farther away he was, the more his voice echoed, as if he were in an empty room that kept getting bigger.

I could not understand much of what he said and only caught "in touch" and "Alaska." I didn't know if he meant the place or the dog because the answering machine cut my father off and announced the next message.

"Werner Palm here," Palm said. Then he paused as if giving the answering machine a chance to greet him by name. "I just wanted to ask if you were coming this weekend. As always, I wanted to wish you—" Palm said, and the answering machine cut him off.

"God's merciful blessings," I said.

"Next message," the answering machine announced.

"God's merciful blessings," Palm said.

"Rödder here." Mr. Rödder spoke very quickly because he knew the answering machine well. "It's Monday evening, six fifty-seven. You left the store a few minutes ago. I'd like to let you know that I have decided to grant your request for time off this coming week as a rare exception—" and the answering machine cut him off. Then Frederik said, "It's me."

"Frederik," I said.

"Don't be alarmed, Luisa," Frederik said. "I wanted to

tell you—" The answering machine cut him off because it did not discriminate—everyone was equal in the eyes of this answering machine—and I was alarmed by Frederik's request that I not be alarmed. He's not coming, I thought. He's about to tell me that he isn't coming.

"Next message," the answering machine announced.

"As I was saying, I wanted to tell you there's been a change in plans." And the answering machine cut him off and said, "Your connection is maintained," then announced the next message. And I thought, Frederik's not coming; the connection has not been maintained. And Frederik said, "I'm coming today. In fact, I'm almost there."

Then he was silent. The answering machine was silent, too, and did not cut him off. Maybe the answering machine was also blindsided by this message, thrown off its egalitarian disinterest, maybe it had no idea, either, what to do after receiving such a message, and therefore unintentionally did exactly the right thing—in other words, it kept recording.

Alaska and I stared at the blinking light. We stared at Frederik's silence, and I tried to grasp that Frederik was almost here.

"I was expecting to be cut off," Frederik finally said. "I'm sorry I wasn't able to let you know sooner. I hope it's all right with you. See you soon, Luisa."

"End of message," the answering machine said quickly, "end of message, end of message." And then, exceptionally, to be absolutely certain, it repeated a fourth time, "end of message."

I dialed the number almost everyone I knew dialed in an emergency.

Selma answered after the third ring. It always took a while before the receiver reached her ear. On the other end of the line you heard nothing but a protracted rustling, as if the receiver were a detector that first had to scan Selma's entire body before it finally reached her ear.

"Hello?" Selma finally said.

"Frederik is coming," I said.

"I know that." Selma sighed. "Next week."

Alaska looked at me. My voice sounded shrill.

"Calm down," Selma said. "In fact, it's actually good news."

"What is?"

"That he's almost here."

"What?"

"It's exactly what you wanted."

"I don't remember that it's exactly what I wanted," I said, and I heard Selma smile and say, "But I do."

"What should I do now?" I asked. "And don't tell me to do exactly what I would do on any other day."

"But there's no okapi involved," Selma said.

"It feels like there is, though."

"You're getting mixed up there," she said. "I'd take a quick shower. You sound like you're in a sweat."

The doorbell rang. Alaska stood up.

"The doorbell," Selma said.

"It's him," I said.

"I suspect it is," Selma said. "Deodorant works, too."

The doorbell rang again.

"What should I do now?" I asked, and Selma answered, "Open the door, Luisa."

OPEN THE DOOR

After I had closed my eyes under Selma's kitchen table on the day Martin was buried and pressed my face against her shirt that was as black as the bow on a funeral wreath, I didn't open them again for a very long time.

At some point Selma had crawled out from under the table with me in her arms. I held tight to her neck with both arms and she sat down on a chair with me on her lap. I slept.

My parents came, knelt next to Selma and me, and tried to whisper me awake. My mother had the hiccups. She always got the hiccups from crying. Because she was responsible for all the funeral wreaths in the area, she also made the one for Martin's burial. "Not that one," she had said at first, "I refuse to make that wreath." She made it after all, the night before the burial, and until the next morning there was no other sound in the entire village and the surrounding forest aside from my mother's hiccuping and the rustling of the bow in her hands.

"Luisa," my mother whispered. "Luisa?"

"Let's lay her on the sofa," my father whispered. He carefully tried to loosen my arms from Selma's neck, but it didn't work. As soon as my father tried to lift me from Selma's lap, I just clung to her more tightly, and I was surprisingly powerful in my sleep.

"Let go," Selma said. "I'll just sit here. She'll wake up soon."

She was wrong. I slept for three days. Selma later claimed it was a hundred years.

Because I wouldn't let her put me down, Selma carried me for three days without interruption. A sleeping ten-year-old is much heavier than one who is awake, and Selma wondered if Martin could have held me up asleep for even a minute.

As long as I wouldn't let go, Selma did not trust she would remember to avoid the weak spots in the kitchen and living room floors and started reminding herself out loud. "Don't step there," she murmured when she came close to one of the sections marked with red tape, because falling through the floor alone was entirely different from falling through with someone in your arms.

Selma carried me in front of her chest, on her back, over her shoulder. When she had to go to the bathroom, she pulled her stockings and underwear down with one hand and balanced me on her lap. When she was hungry, she tore open a packet of dried soup with her teeth. She soon learned how to unwrap a Mon Chéri candy with one hand. When she went to bed, I lay against her chest or her back, my arms around her neck. For three days, Selma not only kept me on her, she also kept on her funeral-wreath-bow-black shirt; undressing and washing were impossible as long as I wouldn't let go.

On the second day, Selma walked through the village to the shop with me on her back. The shopkeeper was also still wearing black. He was sitting in front of his store, which was closed. DUE TO A BEREAVEMENT, read the sign on the door, as if everyone didn't know.

"Could you please open for a minute?" Selma asked. The shopkeeper stood up and didn't seem at all surprised to see me draped over Selma's shoulder, asleep.

"Do you have dry dog food?"

"Unfortunately not, only canned," the shopkeeper said.

Selma considered. "How much bologna do you have in stock?"

The shopkeeper went to check. "Nine packs," he answered.

"I'll take them all," Selma said, "and it would be a help if you could open all the packages right now. And then put them in here." She turned around and the shopkeeper took the bag that hung from Selma's fingers interlaced under my bottom. He opened the nine packages in silence and laid the stack of bologna slices in the bag.

"Could you take out my wallet?" Selma asked, gesturing with her chin at the pocket in her black skirt.

"It's on the house," the shopkeeper said.

Selma passed the optician's shop and was mirrored in his display window. I clung to Selma's back like an imp and the bag dangled below me. The optician didn't see Selma, or he would have come out right away and tried to carry everything for her. But Selma did see the optician, also in black, in his best suit, which got bigger with each passing year. He was sitting on his stool, his head hidden in the hemisphere of the arc perimeter he had purchased from an eye doctor in the county seat.

The optician was measuring his field of vision. In front of him he saw nothing other than light gray with a friendly red spot in the center of a limited area the shape of a half sphere. At the edge of his field of vision were smaller, flashing dots, which the optician indicated he had seen. Sticking his head in the hemisphere and confirming that the flashing dots were there reassured him.

Selma passed Elsbeth's house. Elsbeth, also still in black, stood in her garden with a leaf blower. She held the blower up to the apple tree. It was April and the leaves were accordingly young.

"What are you doing?" Selma shouted over the roar of the leaf blower.

Elsbeth did not turn to face her. "I want time to pass," she shouted. "I want it to be autumn already. The autumn after the autumn after this one."

It didn't occur to the leaves to let themselves be blown off their branches. They were young and strong. They didn't understand what Elsbeth had in mind and didn't feel in the least bit threatened; in fact, they felt like they were getting a blow-dry.

"Put it on turbo," Selma suggested. Elsbeth didn't hear her.

"And what are you doing?" she called loudly without turning around.

"I'm carrying Luisa," Selma shouted back, and Elsbeth answered, "That's good, too."

Selma nodded at Elsbeth's back and continued on to Palm's house.

Selma had briefly considered letting the dogs starve. Palm had not fed them for days. Since Martin's death he had not left his house, not even for the funeral. Selma had wanted to bring him to the funeral since she suspected he would not come. She went to his house. Famished, the dogs bayed even louder than usual. She had slipped past them, knocked, and rung the bell, but Palm had not answered the door.

"Palm, you have to come," she had finally yelled up from under his kitchen window. Then she had cleared her throat and added, "You have to carry his coffin." As she shouted this last sentence, she had squeezed her eyes shut. Such a sentence should never be shouted; even in a whisper it would be too loud. "There's no other way, Palm," Selma had shouted then, twice.

Palm had not opened the door and so there was another way.

Now, standing before Palm's house, Selma briefly thought of going back to Elsbeth, back to the optician, so they could help her with the bologna slices. She decided it was too much trouble.

Selma always found letting others help her to be too much trouble. The worst part, she thought, was thanking them afterward. She would rather fall from an unstable ladder, get an electric shock from a lamp cable or an unelectrified shock from an engine cover, suffer lower back pain from carrying a heavy bag, or break through the floor in her apartment than accept assistance and have to express gratitude afterward.

Bending forward, Selma stretched out her arms and poured the contents of her bag onto the ground. Then she crouched down, trying to keep me from slipping off her back. Selma's disks also tried to keep from slipping, and even then, her face bright red and her disks indignant with the strain, she still found it all less trouble than saying thank you. She threw the slices of bologna over Palm's fence and the dogs went crazy.

Selma held me tight and stood up. She sighed, and her disks sighed with her in chorus. She went to the back of the house. The basement door was unlocked.

She climbed up the basement stairs and crossed the kitchen, trying not to see the half-eaten toast with Nutella that still lay on a plate. She went through the living room, trying to overlook the Obelix pajamas still draped over the back of the sofa, and went into the bedroom.

Palm's bedroom had probably not been aired for years. There was an enormous dark wardrobe next to a dark double bed with two mattresses, one yellow and bare, the other covered with rumpled sheets and pillows on the foot of the bed. The room was dim. Selma turned on the light.

Palm lay on the floor, on his side. He was asleep, his head resting on Martin's schoolbag.

The schoolbag had been found a hundred meters down the tracks. The bag was almost intact, only the right shoulder strap torn.

Selma sat on the bed on the rumpled side. She shifted me from her back, over her shoulder, and onto her lap. My head was cradled in her elbow. Selma could feel her heart beating irregularly. These days, she often felt her heart take a step out of line, like the optician when his inner voices accosted him.

She looked at Palm asleep; she looked at me asleep. Two broken hearts and one faulty one, Selma thought. Then she thought of Iron Henry in the fairy tale and of his heart, and let herself fall backward onto Palm's blankets, which smelled acrid—of schnapps and rage.

The ceiling lamp hung right above Selma's head. In its bowl lay a dead moth with its dead moth heart. Selma closed her eyes.

A fixed afterimage appeared behind her eyelids in which what was actually dark appeared light and what was actually light appeared dark. She saw Heinrich walk down the street and turn back, as he always did, to wave one last, one very last time. Selma looked at the image on the inside of her eyelids, at the stopped motion of the very, very last wave, the frozen smile, and Heinrich's dark hair was light and his light eyes very dark.

Selma lay there for a long time. Then she lifted me back over her shoulder. She swayed briefly and her heart stepped to the right. As she stood, Selma pulled the blanket from the bed, dragged it behind her until it covered Palm's stomach and legs. She let go.

"You have to put her down for a bit," the optician said.

"I should examine her," my father said.

"She should eat something," my mother said.

"You're already all crooked," Marlies said.

"You should eat something, too," Elsbeth said.

Everyone said something, except for me, Palm, and Alaska.

"She won't let go," Selma said. And: "She'll wake soon." And: "She's not very heavy." That last one was a lie. I was as heavy as a boulder.

Selma decided to do exactly what she always did, because otherwise she'd run the risk of never doing anything again, and at some point, as with the dead retired mailman, her blood and mind would congeal, she'd die or go crazy, neither of which Selma could afford to do at the moment.

Because it was Thursday and that's what she did every Thursday, she turned on her television series. I slept on her lap. In the series, at the very beginning, a completely unknown man in a very good mood entered the gate of the Victorian manor house and was greeted by Melissa as Matthew, even though he was not Matthew. Selma scooted closer to the screen and opened her eyes wide, but it truly wasn't Matthew. He just vaguely resembled him. Apparently the actor who had played Matthew didn't want to anymore, or had been hired away to another series, or had died and so at the last minute they'd had to find someone similar to play Matthew.

Selma turned off the television and started writing a letter to the producer. She wrote that this was not acceptable. She wrote that if someone had died or been hired away, he couldn't simply be replaced by someone else who pretended to have always been Matthew. One shouldn't stoop to such cheap solutions, not even on American-Victorian landed estates. It's undignified.

Selma offered her explanation over three closely written pages. Then the optician came over and found Selma at the kitchen table, writing her letter with me across her lap like a blanket. Selma looked up at him and he handed her a handkerchief.

Because Selma wanted to get back to doing what she always did as soon as possible, she went for a walk in the Uhlheck at six-thirty. "Come, Alaska," she said, but Alaska didn't want to; in fact, in those days Alaska also wanted to do nothing but sleep.

The optician followed Selma to the Uhlheck in case I slipped or her disks did. The optician looked at the ground. His eyes stung from crying, from too many field-of-vision tests. Besides, he felt there was nothing left worth seeing. The symphonic beauty he had always tried to get Martin and me to appreciate had been retired to storage like an old theater backdrop.

On the third evening, it started to rain over the Uhlheck. As a precaution, the optician had brought along Selma's raincoat and rain hat, a transparent bonnet with white polka dots. He draped the raincoat over me on Selma's back, gently placed the rain hat on her head so nothing would happen to her hairdo, and tied the bands carefully under her chin. Then they started walking again, but after a short distance Selma stopped in her tracks and the optician, who hadn't expected this, ran into her from behind. Selma swayed and the optician held her tightly. He tried to stabilize her and me with his own body as he had the sawn post of the hunting blind.

"To be honest, she's becoming rather heavy," Selma said.

She turned around and started for home. For the first time since the invention of the world, she didn't want to walk for the full thirty minutes in the Uhlheck. The optician was surprised when Selma didn't climb the hill toward her house but continued downhill until she reached the general store. She stopped in front of the cigarette vending machine.

"Do you have any change?" she asked, and shifted me over her shoulder and farther down her back. My head hung just above her rear end.

Selma had smoked when Heinrich was still alive. In many of the gray photographs of her and Heinrich, they both had a cigarette in the corner of their mouths and if they didn't, Selma claimed, it was only because they laughed so hard the cigarettes had fallen out. Selma had stopped smoking when she was pregnant with my father and had become one of those people who wave their hands reproachfully and cough indignantly when anyone is smoking any distance away.

"Selma, now, this is no reason to start smoking again," the optician said, and as soon as the sentence was out of his mouth, he knew it was the most idiotic sentence said in a long while, and this at a time hardly lacking in idiotic sentences. It was more idiotic than the one about time healing all wounds, more idiotic than the one about God working in mysterious ways.

"Then give me a better reason," Selma said. "Give me just one reason in the entire world that is better than this one."

"I'm sorry," the optician said.

He took his change purse from his jacket pocket and handed her four marks. Selma inserted them into the vending machine and pulled the handle of the first silver-colored compartment. It didn't open. First Selma pulled, then she yanked the handle. Then she yanked all the other handles, my head bouncing side to side on her back. None of the compartments opened.

"Piece-of-shit vending machine," Selma said.

"Let it go," the optician said, "I have some."

"You do? But you don't even smoke."

"Apparently I do," the optician said.

He took a pack and his lighter from his trouser pocket, tapped out a cigarette, lit it, and handed it to Selma. Selma inhaled deeply, all the way to her belly button. She leaned her free shoulder against the vending machine and closed her eyes.

"Glorious," she said.

Selma smoked the entire cigarette leaning against the vending machine with her eyes closed and her see-through rain hat on her head, and the optician watched her. Selma's beauty was the only beauty that hadn't been packed up and taken away, and a dozen opening lines from the letters flashed through his mind during the span of the cigarette. He looked into the darkening sky. Above the optician spread a vast expanse in which bright points would soon appear, and there wasn't any way whatsoever to indicate that they had been seen.

Selma opened her eyes, threw the cigarette butt on the ground, and crushed it thoroughly. "I had no idea you smoked," she said.

The optician almost replied, "There are quite a few things you don't know, Selma, quite a few," but his inner voices accosted him and he swayed to the right for a half second. "Definitely not a good time," the voices said, and for once, they were right.

Selma and the optician returned to our house. Selma swung me from her shoulder to her stomach—by now she'd had quite a bit of practice—and stretched out with me on her bed.

The optician sat on the edge of the bed. He had never sat

there before. Selma's bed, the bed in which she occasionally dreamed of an okapi, was narrow. A flowery quilted coverlet lay over a puffy duvet.

Selma switched on the lamp on her night table. A folding traveling alarm clock in brown imitation leather sat next to it, ticking loudly. Over her bed hung a painting in a gold frame that showed a boy with a shawm sitting happily among his lambs.

If the optician had looked at the painting, he would have noticed that the boy looked like he had never been accosted by anything or anyone. If the optician had had eyes for anything other than Selma and me, he would have found the room to be very beautiful: the diarrhea-colored alarm clock that ticked too loudly, the large flower-patterned quilt, the fat lambs, the bronze bedside lamp with a frosted glass shade shaped like a gnome's hat; the optician's hidden love was so vast, he would have found all this to be sublime. But he only saw Selma and me, lying on her bed facing each other, my arm around her neck.

Selma looked at the optician. He nodded.

"Luisa," she whispered, "you have to let go. It's time."

She took hold of my hands and they relaxed their grip. I turned onto my back without opening my eyes.

"Is everyone still here?" I asked.

Selma and the optician exchanged glances, and Selma invented the world for the second time.

"No, not everyone is still here. But the world is. The whole world minus one person."

"Alaska isn't big enough," I said.

Selma and the optician exchanged glances again. The optician gave her a puzzled look and Selma formed a word silently with her lips, which the optician couldn't understand.

So she formed the word a second time, and because the optician still didn't get it, she finally grimaced, forming the word with her entire face: *pain*. She looked so comical, the optician almost burst out laughing.

"You're right," Selma said. "Alaska isn't nearly big enough."

"He's also not heavy enough," I said. "What's the heaviest animal in the world?"

"An elephant, I believe," Selma answered, "but that wouldn't be enough either."

"We need ten elephants," I said, and the optician cleared his throat.

"I beg your pardon, but that's not correct," he said. "The heaviest animal in the world is not the elephant, but the blue whale. A fully grown blue whale can weigh up to two hundred tons. There's nothing heavier in the world."

The optician leaned toward me. He was glad there was something he could explain at a moment when sound explanations were in short supply.

"A blue whale's tongue alone weighs as much as an elephant, and a blue whale weighs fifty times as much as its own tongue. Just imagine."

Selma looked at the optician. "How do you know that?" she whispered.

"No idea," he whispered back.

"It sounds made-up," whispered Selma, and the optician whispered, "But I believe it's true."

"If you only weigh fifty times as much as your tongue, then you're pretty light," I said.

"Not if you're a blue whale," Selma said.

"With a single breath, a blue whale could blow up two thousand balloons," the optician said.

Selma gave him a look. He shrugged. "It's true," he said.

"Two thousand balloons aren't very heavy either," I said. "Why would anyone do that?"

"Do what?" the optician asked.

"Blow up two thousand balloons with the single breath of a blue whale."

"I don't know," the optician said. "Maybe to have decorations. For a celebration."

"Why would anyone want to celebrate?" I asked.

Selma stroked my forehead again and again. Her small fingers occasionally brushed my closed eyelids.

"The heart of a blue whale only beats two to six times a minute, presumably because it's so heavy," the optician explained. "A blue whale's heart is also unimaginably heavy. It weighs more than a ton."

"Martin could lift it," I said.

"He could even lift ten fully grown blue whales," Selma said, "all at the same time. Ten fully grown blue whales piled one on top of the other. Heavy tongues and hearts included."

"Martin is not fully grown," I said.

"That would be almost two thousand tons," the optician calculated, and Selma said, "He could do it easily."

"I don't want to grow up," I said. For a while, the only sound was the ticking of the alarm clock.

"I know," Selma finally said. "But we'd be very happy if you decided to grow up anyway."

"That's true," the optician said. He cleared his throat several times, but whatever was stuck in his throat would not be cleared. The optician gingerly stroked my cheek, slowly and gingerly, as if he were sounding out a particularly difficult word in a sugar package horoscope. "You have no idea how happy we'd be, Luisa, if you decided to grow up after all. My dear child," he said quickly and softly, the way you rush to finish saying something before you start to cry and can't say any more.

I opened my eyes. Selma and the optician smiled at me in the dim light of the bedside lamp. Tears were streaming down the optician's face. They rolled out from under his glasses and down his cheeks.

I looked around. Selma's bedroom, the entire world, was as small as the stomach of a blue whale. Selma stroked my forehead, again and again.

And again.

IT'S LIKE THIS

Frederik had appeared six months earlier, the day Alaska disappeared. The previous evening Selma hadn't closed the door properly, and in the morning it stood wide open and Alaska was gone.

The optician supposed he had gone off in search of my father, who had been traveling almost constantly. Selma believed Alaska had run away because we were too caught up in ourselves and had noticed him as little as we noticed the landscape.

I was caught up in myself because I had to deal with Mr. Rödder. I had started an apprenticeship with him despite my father's recommendation that I move abroad for a time or at the very least to a big city, because, he explained, you only become someone when you've been away. Instead of moving far away, I stuck around. I moved to the county seat, into a one-room apartment, and into Mr. Rödder's bookstore.

"Oh well," my father said over the phone, "you're not made for adventure. Neither you nor Alaska."

Selma was caught up in herself because she had started

to suffer from rheumatism. Her joints were slowly becoming deformed, especially the knuckles on her left hand. After the diagnosis my father had called from some coastal city or other and said that rheumatism wouldn't be an issue if Selma would just let more of the world in. He'd called to ask Dr. Maschke about Selma, and Dr. Maschke, in his leather jacket, which you could even hear creak over the phone, said that you get rheumatism from trying to hold on to things that are impossible to hold. Selma had switched the receiver from her left hand, which was starting to become deformed, to her right, and asked my father to finally, finally stop pestering her about the world, and my father hung up on her.

We searched for Alaska the entire day. Marlies had joined in at first; Elsbeth had talked her into it for the fresh air, which would surely do her good.

Marlies turned around after ten minutes. "The dog's gone," she'd said, "deal with it."

We combed the forest, clambered over roots and rotten tree trunks. We bent back low-hanging branches, calling Alaska's name continuously. I followed Selma, Elsbeth, and the optician. Selma had linked arms with the optician, and Elsbeth walked at Selma's right in her worn-down pumps. All three were in their seventies. The week before we had celebrated my twenty-second birthday. The optician had passed his finger through the birthday candle flames. "How can anyone be so young?" he had asked.

"I have no idea," I'd answered, even though the optician had only asked rhetorically.

Alaska was already much older than a dog should be. Selma had recently seen a television documentary about criminals who stole dogs to turn them into what she called "animal experiments." Selma was very worried.

"I don't believe anyone would want to turn Alaska into an animal experiment," Elsbeth said. "What test could they run on such an old dog?"

"The secret of immortality," Selma said.

I didn't believe in Alaska's scientifically appealing immortality. On the contrary, I was afraid he had gone off somewhere to die. It wasn't Alaska's way to withdraw, but until now it hadn't been his way to die either. With every fallen tree I approached, every pile of leaves I saw, I worried Alaska might have decided it was a good place to die.

Early in the morning, as soon as we'd noticed that Alaska had disappeared, I'd called Palm because I was afraid he might have gone hunting and confused Alaska with a deer.

"I would never do that, Luisa," Palm had said. "Do you want me to help look for him?"

In the twelve years since Martin's death, Palm had not touched a drop of alcohol. With Selma's help, he had thrown out all the schnapps bottles, empty as well as full, from under his sink, under his bed, in his bedroom and bathroom closets. Selma and he had gone to the glass recycling drop-off five times.

Palm had also become religious. Bible quotes were plastered throughout his house, most of them about light. I AM THE LIGHT OF THE WORLD hung over Palm's refrigerator. I HAVE COME INTO THE WORLD AS LIGHT hung over the sideboard. I AM THE LIGHT THAT IS OVER ALL THINGS hung on the dark wardrobe in his bedroom.

Elsbeth could not understand it. "What's the point of becoming religious at the very moment God has shown His very worst side?" she kept asking. Selma told her it made more sense than wanting to blow the leaves off trees in April and, after all, Palm had always known a thing or two about illumination.

In the period following Martin's death, I was afraid of Palm, but it was a different kind of fear than before. After Martin's death, I was afraid of Palm's pain. I didn't know how to approach him, in the same way you don't know how or if you should approach a motionless animal you've never seen before. Pain had uprooted everything inside him it couldn't use, and with Palm this meant just about everything. Even his rage had drained away, and without rage he seemed even more ominous to me than he had been with it.

The look in Palm's eyes was no longer wild, nor was his hair. Every morning he combed his hair and smoothed it down, and soon after, as with Martin, a strand always stood up. If anyone mentioned it, Palm would say, "It's pointing at the Lord."

Since Martin's death, Palm would visit Elsbeth, the optician, or Selma to discuss passages in the Bible. They let Palm sit in their kitchens, living rooms, or examination chairs. Over the years, faith had anchored itself in Palm, but no one was sure if this faith was solid enough to withstand uninterrupted hours in Palm's silent house or strong enough to lift all that was no longer there.

Most of the time on his visits Palm discussed the Bible passages with himself, anticipating the rare questions about his explications. "You surely want to know why Jesus told the blind man that he should not return to the village," Palm would say. "Well, I can tell you." He would say, "Surely you've often wondered exactly how Jesus healed the paralyzed man. Well, I'll gladly explain," and then Palm would explain, and the optician, silently stirring his coffee, would let the explanation wash over him. Even Elsbeth, who struggled to follow him, would nod off sooner or later. She slept sitting upright on her sofa, her mouth hanging open, and Palm continued undeterred.

The only one who asked questions during Palm's biblical exegeses, the only one who at least said, "Yes, Palm, I have been wondering about that, please explain it again," was Selma. She asked about many things so he could extend his exegeses, so he could kill a few more hours, because that, Selma believed, was the point: killing time so he wouldn't have to spend yet more hours alone. Now and then during Palm's visits, Selma would go into the bathroom and gobble down five Mon Chéris at once. Because of the increasing deformation of her left hand, she would unwrap the candies single-handedly, as she had when carrying me for three days. After the Mon Chéris, she would take a deep breath, pop a eucalyptus lozenge in her mouth, and return to the kitchen, where Palm was waiting with further explanations.

None of us dared touch Palm. We'd shake his hand, that was all. We never hugged him or patted his shoulder. On no account did Palm want anyone to touch him, this we knew. As if he risked crumbling into dust.

"Thank you, but that's not necessary," I'd answered when Palm had offered to help search for Alaska, because I was afraid he would quote Bible verses the entire time, and the Bible, after all, is bristling with passages that are suitable for when you're searching for someone.

"May the Lord bless you in your search," Palm said.

"Seek and you shall find," I replied to make Palm happy, and it worked.

————

We searched until evening. "Alaska!" we called. "Alaska!" We passed through the two neighboring villages and asked everyone we met if they'd seen a dog that was much too big. For hours Elsbeth asked us over and over again if any of us happened to feel tingling in our right hands, which was as exhausting as Palm's biblical exegeses would have been. Elsbeth had explained that you find someone you've lost when your right hand tingles. "No, still no tingling," we'd answer each time.

"I can't go any farther," Selma finally announced.

"Let's stop for now," the optician suggested. "We can look for him again tomorrow. Maybe Alaska is sitting by the front door waiting for us."

I didn't want to stop. I feared that the person you're looking for is truly lost if you stop searching. I was afraid my father might call. He loved Alaska. My father saw him only rarely, which made love much simpler, because those who are absent can't misbehave. My father had called that morning and the connection had been terrible. Selma told him that Alaska had disappeared, even though we were all standing around her, waving our arms to signal that she shouldn't say anything about Alaska's disappearance, not yet. But Selma hadn't understood what we were trying to tell her and had only looked at us, astonished at the way we were all flailing our arms as if we'd all burned our hands at the same time.

"You absolutely have to find him," my father had said, at least as far as Selma could understand over the terrible connection, and he promised to call again that evening. I could picture Selma telling him that we'd looked everywhere for Alaska but hadn't found him. I could see my father, in a telephone booth somewhere far away with a bad connection, only able to understand "everywhere" and "not."

"Go home," I said. "I'm going to keep looking a bit longer."

I didn't return through the villages but instead followed the edge of the forest. Night was falling. When I reached the Uhl-heck, in the meadow where Selma had seen the okapi in her dream, three men emerged from between the tree trunks. They appeared so suddenly and so silently, it was as if they hadn't stepped out of the forest but out of the void.

I stood still. The men were bald and wore black cowls and sandals. Three monks had burst out of the underbrush. The sudden appearance of an okapi would not have been more incongruous.

The monks were staring at the ground with intense con-centration. A few steps from me, they finally raised their heads and stood still.

They stood before me in a row. It was like a lineup in *Tatort* when an eyewitness behind a one-way mirror has to identify the suspect among several people standing in a row. To make the identification more difficult, everyone in the lineup looks very similar. "The perpetrator wore a black cowl and a friendly smile," the witness would have said in this case.

"Good evening," said the monk in the middle. "We didn't mean to frighten you."

I hadn't been frightened, and only then, when the monk in the middle said that, did I feel alarmed, like an eyewit-ness who recognizes the main suspect beyond the shadow of a doubt. I felt dizzy and staggered a step to the right, not because anything accosted me from within or from with-out but because I had a presentiment when the monk in the middle said "Good evening" that he would upend the entire expanse of my life in a single movement.

I had always believed that you could never know something like this in advance, but there, in the Uhlheck, I realized you could.

"What are you doing here?" I asked, because it is an appropriate question to ask someone who is about to change your life.

"Walking meditation," the monk replied. "We're here for a retreat in the village back there, in that house with the pensive name." He pointed behind him, meaning on the other side of the forest.

"The House of Contemplation," I offered.

Years ago, a widow in the neighboring village had converted her farm into an inn, which she mostly rented out on weekends to therapy groups. When I was a child, primal scream therapy was in vogue. Sometimes, when Martin and I were passing through the neighboring village, piercing screams echoed from the House of Contemplation and the shutters of all the surrounding houses were closed tight. Amused, Martin and I screamed back as loud as we could until the owner of one of the houses came out and said despairingly, "Please, not you, too."

"And you?" the monk in the middle asked.

He was still just the monk in the middle, still nameless. The monk in the middle's name could still have been Jörn or Sigurd, which would have been unfortunate in light of the still-unestablished fact that I would eventually say his name around seventy-five thousand times and would think it around a hundred and eighty thousand times.

"I'm looking for Alaska," I said.

One of the monks giggled. He was at least as old as Farmer Häubel.

"Is that a metaphor?" the monk in the middle asked.

"No," I replied, then thought of my father and Dr. Maschke. "Well, yes, it's also a metaphor. But it's primarily a dog."

"How long has it been gone?"

"Since last night, I think," I said, because you lose track of time and no longer know the difference between last night and the coming night when you sense your life is in the process of being upended.

The monk in the middle looked at the ancient monk, who nodded. "We'll help you," he said.

"Look for the dog?" I asked, because you become slow on the uptake when you've lost track of time.

"That's right, to find the dog," the monk said.

"To look for."

"To find," he insisted.

"It's roughly the same thing," the ancient monk said.

"You're Buddhist monks," I said, and all three nodded as if I'd answered the grand-prize-winning question.

"What does the dog look like?" the ancient monk asked.

"Big, gray, and old," I said.

"All right, let's spread out," the ancient monk said.

He turned and walked straight back into the forest. The second monk turned to the right. The monk who had been the monk in the middle rested his hand on my shoulder and smiled at me. His eyes were very blue, almost turquoise. "As blue as the Masurian Lakeland," Selma would later say. "As blue as the Mediterranean Sea in the Mediterranean midday," Elsbeth would later say. "It's some shade of cyan blue, to be precise," the optician would later say, and "As blue as blue, that's all," Marlies would later say.

"Shall we look together?" he asked me. "My name is Frederik, by the way."

We walked next to each other, keeping a lookout, and Frederik kept looking at me out of the corner of his eye, the way Selma had looked at the okapi in her dream. Frederik was tall. He had pushed up the sleeves of his cowl. His arms were tanned as if they had just returned from summer vacation, and covered with fine hairs, blond ones; you could tell that the hair on his head would have been blond, too, if it hadn't been shaved.

For a long time, neither of us said anything. I frantically tried to come up with a question, but because too many questions arise when a Buddhist monk is suddenly walking beside you in the Uhlheck, especially when it's one who is about to upend your life, the questions all get wedged together and none can get free from the others.

Frederik didn't look as if he had a question. I figured Buddhist monks likely never have any questions, but that wasn't the case. At my side, Frederik was also trying to figure out how to separate questions that had gotten wedged together. "What do you think?" he wrote me much later. "That kind of thing doesn't happen to me every day either."

Frederik stuck his hand into his cowl pocket and pulled out a chocolate bar. It was a Mars bar. He unwrapped it and held it out to me.

"Want some?"

"No, thanks."

"What kind of dog is Alaska?"

"He belongs to my father," I said.

We crossed the Uhlheck. Frederik ate the Mars bar and kept glancing at me, then at the landscape that was now dressed to the nines, like Elsbeth when she had Sunday visitors. The ears of wheat were truly golden, the sky perfectly clear.

"It's beautiful here," Frederik said.

"It is, isn't it," I agreed, "a glorious symphony of green, blue, and gold."

Everything about Frederik was light: the hair missing from his head, his very present turquoise-colored eyes. How can anyone be so beautiful? I thought. My thought had the same intonation as the optician's when he had asked no one in particular how anyone could be so young.

Then I stopped and grabbed Frederik's sleeve.

"It's like this," I said. "I'm twenty-two years old. My best friend died because he leaned against a door on the local train that wasn't properly shut. That was twelve years ago. Whenever my grandmother dreams of an okapi, someone dies soon after. My father believes you can only become yourself somewhere far from home, so he's traveling. My mother has a flower shop and is having an affair with the owner of an ice-cream parlor whose name is Alberto. The optician took a saw to the posts of that hunting blind there"—I pointed at the adjacent meadow—"because he wanted to kill the hunter. The optician is in love with my grandmother but won't tell her. I'm doing a bookseller apprenticeship."

I had never told anyone all these things because some were already known by everyone I knew and some were things that no one should know. I told them all to Frederik so he could jump right in.

Frederik looked over the fields and listened to me like

someone listening closely to directions so he can remember them exactly.

"That pretty much sums it up," I said.

Frederik laid his hand on mine, which was still clutching his sleeve, and kept looking into the distance.

"Is that him?" he asked.

"Who?"

"Alaska."

From far, far away, something was running toward us, a small gray thing that got bigger and bigger and looked more and more like Alaska as it got closer. When it got very close, when it reached us, it truly was him. "You can become yourself somewhere nearby, too," Frederik said.

I knelt down and threw my arms around the breathless dog, who was covered with twigs and leaves. "I'm so happy, so happy," I cried, "but where have you been?" For once, I was surprised Alaska didn't answer.

I plucked the twigs and leaves from his fur and looked him over to see if he had any injuries. He was intact.

"That's a very handsome dog," Frederik said, lying to me for the first and only time. Alaska was friendly but by no means was he handsome.

I stood up. Frederik and I stood facing each other and I tried to think of something else I could lose, on the spot, so that he and I still had something to look for.

Frederik scratched his bald head. "I should start back," he said. "How do I get to the House of Contemplation from here?"

"We'll walk you there," I said, a little too loud and with the delight you feel when you've managed to make an imminent farewell somewhat less imminent. "We'll just take you all the way to the House of Contemplation."

We walked along the forest edge, Alaska between us, my hand resting on his back as if on a handrail. We kept walking straight ahead until the neighboring village appeared much too quickly.

"It's like this," Frederik announced abruptly when we had almost reached the House of Contemplation. "I'm actually from Hessen."

"I thought you came from the void."

"It's pretty much the same thing. Two years ago, I dropped out of university to—"

"How old are you?" I asked, because suddenly all the questions had become untangled and were ready for use.

"Twenty-five. I dropped out to go to Japan and live in a monastery, and—"

"Why?"

"Stop interrupting me," Frederik said. "I didn't interrupt you. I spent a few weeks in a Buddhist monastery. And I decided to follow this path. Actually, what time is it?"

We were standing on the doorstep of the House of Contemplation. A small wreath hung on the door. I recognized the model. The House of Contemplation must have bought it from my mother. The wreath was called Autumn Dream and was constructed out of cloth leaves in atmospheric fall colors. It's still summer, I thought, way too early for an autumn dream.

Frederik took his watch from his pocket. Way too early, I thought. "It's way too late," he said, "I have to go in now."

Alaska had sat down in front of Frederik as if he wanted to block his way.

"Thanks for your help," I said softly, because you can't constantly keep being snatched from the jaws of a farewell. Unless, I thought, the House of Contemplation were to

collapse all of a sudden because the walls had become unstable as a delayed side effect of too much primal scream
therapy.

Frederik looked at me. "Goodbye, Luisa," he said. "Meeting you was an adventure."

"You too," I said.

Frederik patted my shoulder. I closed my eyes. When I
opened them again, Frederik was halfway through the door.
The door started to close after him and I sensed that it was a
door that, unlike other doors, would close perfectly.

It's said that when someone dies, their life flashes before
their eyes. That must happen very quickly sometimes, when
you fall out of something, for example, or when you've got
the barrel of a gun under your chin. As the door was closing
behind Frederik, I thought at the speed of a life in free fall
that Alaska had gone in search of adventure even though my
father had denied that he had any capacity for it. I thought
that it may be impossible to judge anyone's level of adventurousness if you've known them for too long, that a person's
adventurousness can only reliably be assessed by someone
who happens to stumble out of the underbrush. I thought, as
I watched the door closing, that Frederik had said he had decided to follow this path, and I thought that I'd never decided
on anything in my life, that things just happened to me. I had
never really said yes to anything before, I'd only ever said no.
I thought that you shouldn't let yourself be intimidated by an
overstuffed farewell, that you can, in fact, escape its jaws,
because as long as no one dies, every farewell is negotiable.
Faulty doors on a local commuter train are not negotiable, but
the closing of a door decorated with an unseasonable autumn wreath certainly is. And at the very last second, before

the latch fell, before a life had time to pass before anyone's eyes, I leapt forward and stuck my foot in the doorway.

"Ouch," Frederik said, because the door had hit his forehead.

"I'm sorry," I said, "but I need your phone number."

I beamed at Frederik, because I had finally let the world in, and that alone was so extraordinary I simply didn't care if the world were to say, "Get lost!"

Frederik rubbed his forehead. "Phone calls are very complicated. In fact, we never get calls."

"Give me your number anyway."

He smiled. "You're very stubborn," he said, something no one had ever said to me before. He took a pen from his pocket. "Do you have a piece of paper?"

"No." I held my hand out. "Write it here."

"One hand isn't enough," he said.

I turned my arm over. Frederik took hold of my wrist and wrote his number on the inside of my forearm. The pen tickled. Frederik wrote and wrote. The number reached from my wrist almost to my elbow. Almost all the telephone numbers I knew only had four digits.

"Thank you," I said. "But you're already late, so you really should go."

"Goodbye, then," Frederik said. He turned around and closed the door.

"Come, Alaska," I said, and after we'd walked away, when we were some distance from the House of Contemplation, the door opened again.

"Luisa," Frederik called, "what's an okapi?"

I turned around.

"An okapi is an incongruous animal that lives in the rain

forest," I called back. "It was the last large mammal discovered by man. It looks like a mix of zebra, tapir, deer, mouse, and giraffe."

"I've never heard of it."

"See you later," I called. The door closed and I bowed to Alaska because there was no other audience around. I bowed the way Martin would after lifting a stick over his head. Anyhow, I did stick my foot in the door, and I did teach Frederik about an animal that nothing can top.

Alaska and I ran all the way back to our village. Selma and the optician, who had been sitting on the front steps of our house, jumped up and ran to meet us. "You're here," they cried, "thank goodness, where have you been?" Alaska didn't answer and I didn't answer, either, because I was out of breath.

When Selma and the optician were done welcoming Alaska home, they looked up at me. "What's the matter with you?" Selma asked, because I obviously looked as if I'd just barely managed to free Alaska from violent criminals who had been about to turn him into an animal experiment and me into something similar.

"He's a monk," I said, "a Buddhist monk. He lives in Japan."

"Who?" the optician asked.

"Hang on," Selma said, because it was Tuesday and the deer had appeared at the edge of the forest. Selma now gave Palm free rein with everything except the deer. For a long time, it had been a different deer than before. Another deer had taken over the original deer's role ages ago, but unlike changing actors in her television series, it made no difference to Selma. She went to the garage, opened the door, and slammed it shut with all her strength. The deer disappeared, Selma came back to the front steps and sat down next to the optician. They looked at me expectantly as if I had announced that I was about to recite a poem.

"Well, who?" the optician asked.

I told them about the monks who had burst out of the underbrush, about the monk in the middle who was Frederik, about Hessen and Japan and how I stuck my foot in the door of the House of Contemplation at the very last minute. I recounted it all breathlessly as if I were still running on the spot.

"But what is a Buddhist monk from Japan doing here, of all places?" the optician asked.

"Walking meditation," I said solemnly.

I held my forearm out to both of them the way my father's patients had held their arms out for blood samples to be taken. "We have to write it down before it gets smudged. Have you ever seen such a long number?"

"The longer the number, the farther away the person," Selma said.

We went back to the house and sat at the kitchen table. Because she was so happy to have him home, Selma held Alaska on her lap. He hadn't been held on anyone's lap since he was full-grown; Selma was completely hidden behind him.

Next to me, the optician took his fountain pen from the breast pocket of his shirt and put on his reading glasses. I placed my forearm on the table in front of him and he began copying down the numbers onto a piece of paper. It took a while.

"I'm sure this number has a lovely melody," he said. Selma

had recently had to replace her rotary telephone and now had a phone with buttons and with accompanying beeps.

"Yes, probably the wedding march," Selma said from behind Alaska.

The optician was done writing and he blew on the ink so it wouldn't smudge.

"Thanks," I said. I stood up and pinned the number on the bulletin board over Selma's refrigerator.

The optician and I stood before the telephone number the way we'd once stood in front of the train station where he had taught Martin and me how to tell time and had explained how time zones work.

"I don't know," Selma said, still completely hidden behind Alaska, so that it looked like Alaska was ventriloquizing. "Couldn't it have been somebody nearby? That nice boy from your vocational school, maybe?"

"Unfortunately not," I said.

The new telephone rang. I ran to it and picked up the receiver. I knew it was my father before he'd even had a chance to say, "Hello, the connection is terrible."

"I found him, Papa," I said, "and the dog, too."

I JUST WANTED TO ASK HOW ALASKA IS DOING

When you desperately want to call someone but dread it just as much, you suddenly notice how many telephones there are. There was the new touch-tone telephone in Selma's living room, and in the living room one floor above it was my mother's elegant, slender phone. There was the telephone in the optician's back room, the telephone covered in hunter-green velvet on Elsbeth's side table. There was the telephone in my apartment in the county seat, the one next to the cash register in Mr. Rödder's bookstore. There was a yellow phone booth on the way from my apartment to the bookstore. "We're ready," all these telephones said, "it's up to you."

The optician was also ready. The day after Frederik had burst from the underbrush, he had come into the bookstore with a list of books about Buddhism. We didn't have a single one in stock. When Mr. Rödder called the distributor to place the order, both he and the sales rep despaired over the Japanese names. Mr. Rödder shouted the letters into the receiver as if the distributor were out on the high seas.

When the books arrived, the optician sat down with them and a highlighter at Selma's kitchen table. He read with intense concentration and marked many passages, murmuring all the while, "Selma, I'm telling you, this is all absolutely wonderful."

Selma sat across from the optician. She had darned socks, filled out bank transfer forms, and was gluing stamps to envelopes, smoothing the stamps with the index finger on her crooked left hand. She always does everything as if for the first or last time, the optician thought. Then he said, "Did you know that there is no 'I'? The so-called I is nothing but a swinging door through which the breath passes in and out?"

"You're a swinging door with very red cheeks," Selma replied.

"Just breathe," the optician said.

"I've been breathing all my life."

"Yes, but now do it right," the optician said, and inhaled and exhaled deeply. "Here it says that every illumination begins and ends with cleaning the floor. Did you know that?"

"I didn't know that, but I should certainly hope it would," Selma said.

"And did you know that nothing is ever truly lost?"

Selma looked at the optician. Then she put the last stamped envelope on top of the others and stood up. "You know, I've got enough to do with Palm's explications. It would be nice if you didn't start explicating, too."

"Sorry," the optician said. He read further. "Just one more thing, Selma," he said a minute later. "It'll be very quick. Listen to this: *When we look at something, it can disappear from our sight, but if we do not try to see this something, it cannot disappear.* I don't understand. Do you?"

"No," Selma said, and added that it would be fine with her if the optician disappeared at this point, which couldn't be all that difficult since he has no "I." The optician, however, stayed where he was and kept underlining passages.

"When Luisa calls him, she absolutely must ask him what it means," he murmured, and just then I telephoned Selma.

"Well? Have you called him yet?" she asked.

"Of course not," I replied.

I hadn't called Frederik yet because I was afraid I'd get stuck. With anything important, I always suddenly got stuck. I almost failed my graduation exam. I failed my first driving test: my mind stalled, so the car did, too. Mr. Rödder hired me despite my mind going blank during my interview; no one else had applied.

"I decided I'd rather call you," I told Selma. "How are you?"

"I'm fine," Selma said, "but the optician isn't. He claims he's a swinging door."

"Tell her she should ask him about disappearing," the optician called out.

"And you're supposed to ask the monk how it is that you can't see something if you're not trying to see it. Or something like that," Selma said.

"So she hasn't called him yet?" the optician asked.

"No," Selma whispered.

"In Buddhism, there's often great emphasis on non-action," the optician said.

"I'll come over this evening," I said. When I arrived at Selma's, the optician was still reading at the kitchen table and

Selma was busy with a potato masher, mashing potatoes as if she wanted to prove that things very well could disappear.

"Do I seem unstuck right now?" I asked.

"Yes," said the optician, who was too engrossed in his reading to listen.

"Yes," said Selma, who was too engrossed in mashing potatoes to listen.

"Then I'll do it, I'll call him now," I said.

"Good," Selma and the optician said, the one not looking up from the potatoes mashed beyond recognition, the other not looking up from his thoroughly highlighted reading.

I went into the living room, picked up the receiver, and started dialing. When I was about halfway through the number, the optician stormed into the room and cut off the call.

"Don't do it," he said.

I stared at him.

"Different time zone," he said. "It's four in the morning there."

I spent the night in Selma's living room on the fold-out couch, a red corduroy monstrosity. I often spent the night either with Selma in the ground-floor apartment or with my mother on the floor above. Nights at Selma's in the village, unlike those in the county seat, were as uncompromisingly silent and dark as nights should be.

I woke at two in the morning. I turned on the small lamp on the side table, stood up, and went to the window, skirting the dangerously weak sections on the floor that the optician had marked with red. It was dark outside. I couldn't see anything except my own blurred image in the windowpane.

I was wearing one of Selma's nightgowns, blurry, ankle-length, and flowered.

I calculated eight hours ahead. If I don't call now, I thought, I never will, and time would shift forever and I'll never see him again. I took the rolled-up phone cord from the hook and carried the phone to the window. I dialed Frederik's number.

It rang for a very long time, as if the ring had to struggle laboriously all the way to Japan: from here to the county seat—which was difficult enough—then over the Carpathian Mountains, the Ukrainian plain, the Caspian Sea, across Russia, Kazakhstan, and China. Just when I was becoming convinced that it was impossible for a ring to make it from the Westerwald all the way to Japan, someone picked up on the other end of the line.

"Moshi moshi," said a cheerful voice. It sounded like the name of a children's game.

"Hello," I said in English, "I'm sorry. I don't speak Japanese. My name is Luisa and I'm calling from Germany."

"No problem," the cheerful voice said. "Hello."

"I would like to speak to Frederik," I said into the receiver in the darkness before the window, "to Monk Frederik." And it sounded like I wanted to speak to a mountain named after Frederik.

"No problem," the voice said again, and I liked the way there apparently seemed to be so few problems in Japan.

For a very long time I heard nothing but rustling. While the cheerful voice was looking for Frederik, I looked for a cheerful opening sentence. I should have thought of it earlier. I should have worked on a first-rate opening sentence with Selma and the optician, but now it was too late. Now there weren't even any second-rate opening sentences to be found in the thicket of darkness outside the window. "Hello, Frederik," I thought, "I have a technical question about Buddhism; Hello, Frederik, so, how was your flight?; Hello, Frederik, about Hessen . . ." Another monk who wasn't Frederik came on the line.

"Hello," he said, "how can I help you?"

"Hello," I said, and explained that I wanted to speak with Monk Frederik.

The monk passed the receiver to yet another monk, still not Frederik, and so it continued until I'd said hello to six monks. The last monk also said, "No problem." Then in the background I heard rapid steps and I knew they were Frederik's.

"Yes?" he said.

I gripped the receiver in both hands. "Hello," I said, and then nothing more.

"Hello, Luisa," Frederik said, and because it was so obvious, he understood right away that I didn't have an opening sentence. In the blink of an eye, he took over and simply pretended he had called me.

"Hello," he said, "it's Frederik. I just wanted to ask how Alaska is doing."

My hands stopped trembling. "Thank you," I said. "Thanks so much."

"No problem," Frederik said.

"Alaska's fine. Are things fine with you, too?"

"Things are always fine with me," Frederik said. "And you?"

I leaned my forehead against the window. "Can you see anything?" I asked.

"Yes, the sun is shining. I have a view of the wooden hut.

Its roof is covered with moss. Behind it are mountains. I can see the waterfall."

"I can't see anything," I said, "it's pitch-dark. What time is it?"

"It's ten in the morning."

"It's two in the morning here."

Frederik laughed and said, "We should find something to agree on."

I sat on the windowsill. The blank my mind kept drawing sat beside me and said in a voice like Marlies's: "Here I am. It'll never work. Get used to it."

"What can't you see?" Frederik asked.

"The fir tree outside the living room window," I answered. "The sumac next to it. Cows in the meadow across the way. The apple tree and the bridge."

The living room door that had been left ajar opened. Alaska came in and curled up at my feet. I stood up and stuck my hands in his old fur. I tried to look out the window again but only saw myself all blurry. I closed my eyes. If I can't get past this blankness, then that will be it, I thought, and life will take a wrong turn.

"Are you still there?" Frederik asked.

Things cannot disappear if you don't look at them, the optician had said, or something like that, and I wondered if they can disappear if you speak to them.

"Yes, I'm sorry. I'm just drawing a blank. I'm very blurry."

Frederik cleared his throat. "Your name is Luisa and I'm sure you have a last name, too. You're twenty-two years old. Your best friend died because he leaned against a door on the local train that wasn't properly shut. That was twelve years ago. Whenever your grandmother dreams of an okapi, someone dies soon after. Your father believes you can only become yourself somewhere far from home, so he's traveling. Your mother has a flower shop and is having an affair with the owner of an ice-cream parlor whose name is Alberto. The optician took a saw to the posts of the hunting blind in the meadow because he wanted to kill the hunter. This optician is in love with your grandmother but won't tell her. You're doing a bookseller apprenticeship."

I opened my eyes and smiled at myself in the windowpane. "The connection is very good," I said.

"Pretty good," Frederik said, "there's just a faint rustling."

I paced around the living room with the telephone. The cable followed me but the blankness didn't.

"Have you done your walking meditation yet today?" I asked.

"No, but I did my sitting meditation. Early. For ninety minutes."

I thought of the optician and his slipped disks from his sedentary occupation.

"Doesn't it hurt?"

"Yes," Frederik said, "it's very uncomfortable. But that doesn't matter."

"Why did you become a monk?"

"Because it seemed right. Why did you become a bookseller?"

"Things worked out that way."

"That's good, too, if that's how things work out," Frederik said.

"Do you always wear that black robe?"

"Almost always."

"Doesn't it itch?"

"No," Frederik said, "it really doesn't. Luisa, it's really nice to talk to you, but unfortunately I have to go now."

"More meditating?"

"No, I've got to climb onto the roof and clear away the moss."

I stopped in front of the section marked in red.

Frederik took up the opening sentence for me but not the closing one. I had to carry that one myself. I carried it until the very last minute of our conversation.

"All right, then, take care of yourself, Luisa," Frederik said.

I held one foot over the red-marked section. "I'd like to see you again," I said.

Frederik was silent. He was silent for so long, I was worried he had suddenly turned to stone and become a mountain named after him.

"You're very good at sticking your foot in the door at the last minute," he said. He suddenly sounded very serious. "I have to think it over," he said. "I'll give you a call."

"But how?" I asked, because he didn't know my telephone number, but he had already hung up.

When Selma opened the door wearing a flowered ankle-length nightgown and a hairnet to keep her hairdo safe during the night, I was still balanced on one leg with my foot hovering over the red-marked section.

"What on earth are you doing?" she asked, grabbing me by the shoulders and turning me around as if I were sleepwalking.

"I'm wide awake," I said. I held the receiver out to her. "Japan was on the line."

"That was certainly a highlight in this phone's life," she said, and took the receiver from my hand. Then with her shoulder she nudged me across the living room toward the sofa. I was as lively as if we were dancing a polonaise.

"He's going to think over whether we should see each other again," I said, and sat on the sofa.

"Maybe you should think it over, too," Selma said, and sat down next to me. The hairnet made her forehead look like it was barred.

"Why?"

"Because he's so far away," Selma said. We sat very close. We were dreadfully flowery.

"Almost everyone is far away," I said.

"Exactly, it would be nice to have someone nearby for a change. All I'm saying is that you should keep in mind the fact that it might not work out."

"It will work out," I said, "you can count on it."

And fourteen days later, a letter arrived.

The widow in the neighboring village brought it to Selma's on a Saturday. "I have an airmail letter for you, Luisa," she said. She spoke very loudly, and I wondered if it was a de-layed side effect of too much primal scream therapy. She held out a light-blue envelope as light as a feather. Beneath the many brightly colored, flowered stamps were lines in very even handwriting:

> *To*
> *Luisa*
> *c/o Selma (in the next village)*
> *c/o The House of Contemplation*
> *Fichtenweg 3*
> *57327 Weyersroth*
> ドイツ—*Germany*

"I must say, it's a rather bold address," the widow bel-lowed. "It's almost longer than the entire card. He writes that he has thought things over. He'll be back in Germany at the end of the year and you can see each other then. And he sends his best, this Mr. Frederik does."

"Did you open the envelope?" Selma asked.

"I didn't need to," she thundered, and turned the letter over, holding it up to the ceiling light. The envelope was so thin and the ink on the paper inside so black that you could read everything.

EXPIRATION DATES

My father came for a visit in September. As always, he suddenly appeared at the door with a deep tan and matted hair, wearing shoes that still had remains of an African desert or the Mongolian steppe stuck in their treads, and carrying a backpack with mold stains left by arctic snow. As always, before he'd even crossed the threshold he said, "I'll have to leave again tomorrow," as if it were a magic spell that allowed him to enter.

Now that he was constantly traveling, my father always wore two wristwatches. One showed the time in the country he was traveling in at the moment, the other was set to Central European time. "That way I always have you with me," he said.

He seemed larger than life when he stopped in to see us now and again, and he took up so much space that we had to rearrange ourselves like pieces of furniture that suddenly found themselves in a smaller apartment. We kept bumping into each other. We stood in corners while my father recounted his adventures with sweeping gestures and flashing eyes. He told them in a very loud voice as if he always had to shout over a stormy sea or into a desert wind for the last months.

Alaska was overjoyed to see my father. He didn't move from my father's side and suddenly looked younger. He leapt around my father and his tail never stopped wagging. Because Alaska was so big, his tail swept cups and newspapers off the coffee table and a flowerpot off the kitchen window-sill. "It's amazing what love can do," Selma said as we swept up shards and dirt behind Alaska. "I may be wrong, but I believe Alaska has grown a bit in the last half hour."

"And? How are things with all of you?" my father asked.

He said it with an undertone of regret, as if he weren't asking about our lives but the progress of a common cold or an especially boring village community meeting he had skipped.

"How are things with the Buddhist?"

"He's coming to visit soon," I said.

"Dr. Maschke swears by Buddhism," my father said, and pulled a plastic bag out of his backpack, "letting go and all that. You should talk to him about Buddhism sometime, Luisa, I'm sure he'd like that."

My father tipped the contents of the plastic bag onto Selma's kitchen table. There were presents wrapped in Arabic newspapers. Selma unwrapped a light green sequined caftan.

"How very nice," she said, and carefully pulled the shimmering caftan over her hairdo and down her long body. Her light brown orthopedic shoes peeked out from under the glittering material.

The optician received a jar of Tunisian honey and I got a saddlebag. "It's real camel leather," my father said.

"How practical," the optician remarked.

My mother wasn't there. Her gift lay unopened on the kitchen table.

That evening we sat on the front stoop. My father took up the whole bottom step, Alaska lay at his feet, and Selma, the optician, and I sat on the top step behind my father. My father smoked clove cigarettes, tilted his head back, and gazed at the stars. "Isn't it amazing that you see the same stars no matter where you are in the world? Crazy, isn't it?" he asked, and because it was a lovely thought, the optician swallowed the comment that this was not, strictly speaking, true.

Selma was not looking up at the stars but at my father's head. She adjusted her glasses and leaned so far forward that her nose touched the tips of his hair. "You have lice," she announced.

"Oh shit," my father said.

"I still have a lice comb from the children somewhere," Selma said, and went inside to look for the comb she had used to comb lice from Martin's and my heads.

I gazed up into the sky with my father. "Have you been to Japan yet?" I asked.

"No," he answered, "Japan doesn't interest me so much. But Dr. Maschke swears by Buddhism."

Selma came back with the lice comb, a bathing cap, and a plastic bottle. "I even found some lice shampoo," she said.

"Is it still good?" the optician asked. "It's at least fifteen years old."

My father took the shampoo bottle out of Selma's hand and looked it over. "There's no expiration date," he said.

"Well, then," Selma said, and unscrewed the top, because

she believed that anything without a listed expiration date can't expire.

Selma massaged the shampoo into my father's hair and combed it back. With his gleaming hair, he looked like Rock Hudson. He gazed back up at the stars. "It's crazy," he said.

"Hold your head straight, please," Selma said. "I'm going to pull the bathing cap on. The shampoo has to work overnight." It was Elsbeth's bathing cap, the purple one with frills that Selma had borrowed many years before and never given back. "Sorry, it's the only one I've got," she said.

"Go ahead," my father said.

Selma put her hands in the bathing cap to stretch it out and small tears immediately formed between the frills. The bathing cap had clearly passed its expiration date, even though there was none listed.

My father patted the cap on his head and turned to face me. "Well?" he asked.

I laughed. "Very fetching," I said.

"Where is Astrid?" my father asked. Selma, the optician, and I looked at each other. We didn't know if my father knew that my mother was in a relationship with the owner of the ice-cream parlor.

"She should be home soon," I said. "She's at the ice-cream parlor."

"She is?" my father replied, and we knew he didn't know.

When my mother drove up the hill a few minutes later and the glare from her headlights swept over us, Selma laid her hand on my father's shoulder and said, "Peter, my dear, it's like this. Astrid has, in the meantime, also let a bit of the world in."

My mother got out of the car and stopped abruptly when

she saw my father. Then she came toward us. She was carrying a small tray wrapped in paper. My father stood up.

"Hello, Astrid," he said.

My mother looked at my father in the bathing cap, then
at Selma in her caftan. "You two can wear absolutely anything," she said.

My father wanted to hug her, but she quickly held out her
hand. Then she unwrapped the tray, which held three cups
with three scoops of ice cream each, already starting to melt.

"That looks delicious," my father said.

"Unfortunately, I only brought three. I had no idea you
were here."

"You can have mine," I said to my father.

"No," my mother said, "please come upstairs with me,
Peter, I have something to tell you."

My father followed her into the house. We heard them
climbing the stairs to the upper apartment.

"Poor Peter," Selma said. "Let's hope he can handle it."

We left our ice cream to melt. The optician reached for
the crushed pack of clove cigarettes my father had left behind
and lit one. It tasted like he was smoking Astrid's flower shop.

Selma had known in theory that the optician smoked
since shortly after Martin's death, but he had never done it
in front of her. She watched him, fascinated, like a child seeing an adult pee standing up for the first time. The optician
did not enjoy the cigarette—not because it tasted like flowers
but because Selma was watching him with such fascination.
"Please don't stare at me like that," he said.

"I can't get my head around you smoking," she said, and
kept staring.

The optician sighed. "Well, I can't with you watching

me," he said, and put the cigarette out. Some things have to be kept secret from Selma, he thought.

After twenty minutes my father came back down and sat on the steps with us. He scratched his head under the bathing cap with his index finger. It was so tight, it didn't slip. "Good," he said, "good."

"What do you mean by 'good'?" Selma asked, and stroked my father's back.

"I mean because everything is taken care of, and that's good."

He reached for the clove cigarettes. I wondered if the news about my mother and Alberto had to sink in overnight. But that wasn't it. My father never mentioned Alberto again. He slept on Selma's red couch, washed the lice shampoo out of his hair the next day, and packed his freshly washed, still-damp clothes into his backpack. "I'm off again," he said. "It was nice here with you."

In the blink of an eye Alaska was once again as old as he actually was.

"Ah, here you are," Mr. Rödder said, and his eyebrows, as agitated as ever, drew together in a frown. "It's high time. Marlies Klamp came in again today and said that she didn't like your latest recommendations, either. It's a shame, Luisa, a shame. If things continue like this—"

"I've brought you something," I said, and handed the saddlebag to Mr. Rödder. His face immediately brightened.

"My goodness, Luisa, it's beautiful," he whispered, caressing the leather. "Is it really for me?"

"It's for you," I said. "It's genuine camel leather."

"I don't know what to say," Mr. Rödder said. "You know what? We'll hang it over the travel-writing shelves. How did you find this treasure?"

"Connections," I said.

When I climbed onto the stepstool to hang the saddlebag over the travel section, my mother suddenly appeared next to me. I put the bag onto a shelf.

"What are you doing here?" I asked. My mother was wearing a dark blue scarf with long gold fringes around her shoulders. Looking down at her head, I could see the gray roots in her dyed-black hair.

"It didn't make the slightest difference to him," my mother said, as if she had given my father an expensive present that didn't please him at all.

IVY FROM ELSBETH'S POINT OF VIEW

Luisa will have a visitor from Japan soon," Selma said to Elsbeth in October, and made her swear not to tell a soul, because she didn't know if it was all right with me for her to tell anyone. Elsbeth was able to keep the secret all the way to the general store.

Elsbeth had brought the shopkeeper one of my mother's Autumn Dreams because he liked to hang seasonal decorations in his shop. And she needed a mousetrap. The shopkeeper was just moving the alcoholic beverages next to the cash register to better keep an eye on them. The twins from the upper village had stolen schnapps more than once.

"If you burn dirt from the cemetery in a frying pan, the thief will bring back what he stole," Elsbeth told him. "Or you could just put mousetraps between the bottles. I need one, by the way."

When the shopkeeper brought Elsbeth a mousetrap and asked her how she was, it burst out of her. "Luisa is going to have a visitor from Japan, a Buddhist monk."

"Now, that's something," the shopkeeper said, and walked Elsbeth to the cash register. "Are they celibate?"

"No idea," Elsbeth said, and examined the mousetrap. It was the kind that broke the mouse's neck. "I am, at any rate."

"It would be good to know," the shopkeeper said, "in case Luisa is in love with him."

"Who's celibate?" asked Farmer Häubel's granddaughter, who had just walked into the store.

"I am," Elsbeth said.

"And the monk from Japan Luisa's in love with," the shopkeeper added, counting out the money for the Autumn Dream into Elsbeth's hand.

"He must be incredibly handsome," Elsbeth said.

"Then he certainly isn't celibate," Farmer Häubel's granddaughter said, and Elsbeth objected indignantly that it had nothing to do with looks.

"How do you know that?" asked the shopkeeper. "Have you seen him? Are there photographs?"

"No, unfortunately not," Elsbeth replied, "but that's what Luisa told Selma."

The optician came up to them carrying a package of frozen fish casserole, enough for exactly one person, and warm compresses for his back. "Listen to this," he said. "*When we look at something, it can disappear from our sight, but if we do not try to see this something, it cannot disappear.* Do you understand it?"

"That's the most inventive justification for shoplifting that I've ever heard," the shopkeeper said.

Elsbeth held the mousetrap out toward the optician. "Did you know that dead mice can actually help with eye complaints?" she asked. "I can bring some to you in your store if I catch any."

"Thanks, but no," the optician said.

"Luisa is in love with a Buddhist in Japan who is not celibate and is coming to visit in three weeks," Farmer Häubel's granddaughter said.

"I have no comment," the optician replied. "That's Luisa's business. Don't you have anything better to do than get involved in her business?"

"No," the shopkeeper and Farmer Häubel's granddaughter said in chorus.

"Unfortunately," Elsbeth said.

The optician sighed. "That she's in love with him is a bit of an exaggeration, she hardly knows him."

"But you don't need to know someone to love them," Elsbeth said.

"Do you know more?" Farmer Häubel's granddaughter asked.

"Of course," said the optician. He cleared his throat. *"Knowledge is living in unwavering serenity."*

The shopkeeper packed the optician's heat patches into a bag. "Now, that sounds a lot like celibacy," he remarked.

The optician walked around reciting his quotes and annoying everyone in the village every bit as much as Friedhelm had with his song about the lovely Westerwald.

The optician had been trying to use Buddhism to get the upper hand with his inner voices when they became insufferably loud, especially after ten o'clock at night. But it didn't work any better than trying to tame them with the smoky sayings on postcards from the county seat.

At ten o'clock, after setting his corduroy slippers on the bedside rug, the optician stretched out on his bed, which was big enough for exactly one person.

When the optician was a child, his mother had always told him that if he put all his worries into his slippers at night, they wouldn't be there in the morning. It had never worked, because his inner voices believed themselves better than mere worries that would be satisfied with slippers as lodgings.

The voices regularly reproached the optician for everything he'd done wrong or hadn't done at all. They chose random events from every period of his life and threw them at his slipperless feet. It didn't matter to them in the slightest that these were things he hadn't done precisely because the voices had advised against doing them; they reproached him with everything he hadn't done whether or not it was on account of them.

"When you were six you didn't jump over the Apfelbach River, even though everyone else did," they rebuked him, for example.

"But you told me it was a bad idea," the optician objected.

"That's completely irrelevant," they replied. It was always the voices and not the optician who decided what was relevant.

Their favorite topic was Selma. "How long has it been now, that you haven't dared tell her you love her?" they smirked.

"You know exactly how long," the optician said. "No one knows better than you."

"Tell us," they insisted.

"But you always advised me not to," the optician exclaimed.

When the voices were too lazy to come up with a concrete example—usually around midnight—they used words like *everything*, *nothing*, *never*, and *always*, with which they could easily jostle the optician, especially since he had grown old. *Always* and *never* are especially hard to shoo away at an advanced age.

"You've never been bold enough to do anything; you've never really dared," the voices said.

They were so clear and resolute that sometimes the optician could hardly believe the people around him, like Selma, couldn't hear them. The optician recalled Elsbeth's deceased husband, who had suffered from deafening tinnitus and, utterly worn out, had finally broken down in tears on my father's examination table and held his ear very close to my father's. "Can't you hear it?" Elsbeth's husband had asked in despair. "How is it possible that you can't hear it?"

"Shut up," the optician said tentatively, then turned onto his side and concentrated on his slippers, neatly lined up on the bedside rug.

"You've never really dared to do anything," the voices said.

"Yes, because you always told me not to!" the optician shouted, and the voices repeated that this was irrelevant: the results were what mattered. And so it went on, all night long. And so the following morning resulted in an ever more exhausted optician, eviscerated by his inner voices, slumped over on his examination stool, trying to lift the weight of *always* and *never* until he finally stuck his head into the arc perimeter. It was the only place the voices could not enter.

Now, ever since Frederik had appeared, the optician

kept a book on Buddhism on his night table, and when the voices started in on Selma and *never* and *always*, the optician opened it to one of the passages he'd underlined. "*I am the river*," he would say, "*and you are leaves floating by on my current*."

"Speaking of rivers," the voices replied, "the only thing we have to say is: Apfelbach."

"*I am the sky*," the optician said, "*and you are just clouds floating by*."

"Wrong, optician," they answered, "no one is the sky, and you're the cloud, a rather ragged one at that, and we're the wind that blows you around."

In early November, when I still didn't know that there would be a change in plans and Frederik would be there the next day, I went through the village with a list. I started with Marlies, to get the worst over with first.

"No one's home," Marlies shouted through her closed front door.

"Please, Marlies, it will be quick," I said.

"There's no one home, deal with it," she shouted back.

I walked around the house and looked in the kitchen window. Marlies sat at her table, as always in only a Norwegian sweater and her underwear. She was in her mid-thirties now but looked younger. Something preserved Marlies.

I leaned on the wall next to the slightly open window. "Marlies," I said through the gap, "I've got a visitor from Japan coming soon."

"I couldn't care less," Marlies said.

"I know," I said. "I just wanted to ask: In case you happen to meet my visitor, could you . . . could you be a bit more approachable? A little nicer? Just briefly. I'd really appreciate it."

I heard Marlies light a Peer 100, and soon after a puff of smoke blew toward me out the window.

"I'm not friendly, deal with it," she said.

I sighed. "Okay, Marlies. Otherwise are things all right with you?"

"Never better," Marlies replied. "And now, goodbye."

"So long," I said, then pushed off the wall and went to see Elsbeth, who was standing in her garden looking at an ivy-covered apple tree, her arms crossed below her enormous breasts.

It was the same tree she had tried to blow the leaves off of after Martin's death. When they fell on their own that autumn, Elsbeth had kicked the trunk and, tears flowing, had said that it was too late now, they could just as well have stayed on the branches.

Elsbeth pointed at the ivy. "I really want to get rid of the stuff, but I also really don't," she murmured. The pruning shears were propped up against the trunk of the tree.

"Why wouldn't you?" I asked.

"Sometimes ivy is an enchanted person, and when he reaches the top of the tree, he is freed from the spell," Elsbeth explained.

"Speaking of superstition . . ." I began.

"The question is, do I release the person or the tree?"

The ivy was already entwined around the top part of the trunk.

"I'd choose the tree," I said. "If it's a person, then he's already half free. That's more than can be said for the rest of us."

Elsbeth patted my cheek with her pudgy hand. "You

sound more and more like Selma," she said, and picked up the pruning shears.

"Elsbeth," I said, "I've got a visitor from Japan coming soon and I wanted to ask you if you could talk about superstition as little as possible."

"But why?" Elsbeth asked, and reluctantly started to clear the ivy. With each snip, she apologized to the person who the ivy might actually be.

"Because it's odd," I said.

"I'm sorry," Elsbeth said. "But wouldn't it be much odder if I *didn't* say anything about superstitions?" As she snipped, she said, "I'm sorry, dear possible person."

"No, I don't think so," I said. "You can talk about other things."

"About what?"

"About the turbulent preparations for the Christmas party in the community center," I suggested, "about the debate over holding it in the afternoon or the evening."

"That doesn't really sound very interesting," Elsbeth said. "But, fine. I won't say anything superstitious." She apologized to another ivy root. "I hope I won't forget. Here, take this."

She pressed the shears into my hand, closed her eyes, took two big steps forward and two back.

"What was that?" I asked, and Elsbeth said, "It helps against forgetfulness."

I found the optician with his head in the arc perimeter. Selma was there. She had brought him some cake and was perched on the edge of the table with the phoropter, with which Martin and I had believed you could see the future.

"It's just Luisa," she said when the bells on the door

jingled, so the optician would know it wasn't a customer and he could safely keep his head in the instrument and signal to the little dots that he had seen them.

"Could you take Alaska with you today?" Selma asked. "I'll be at the doctor's all day tomorrow." Selma's deformed hands shone with the pain relief ointment she had rubbed into them.

"Of course," I said. "I wanted to ask you two something."

"Shoot," the optician said.

"I wanted to ask you not to ask Frederik too many questions about Buddhism."

The optician took his head out of the perimeter and spun on his stool to face me. "But why not?"

"Because he won't be here on duty," I said, and thought of my father, who, when he was still a practicing doctor, was constantly being approached on the street, in the ice-cream parlor, and even in Dr. Maschke's waiting room, for advice on symptoms.

"What's that list you've got there?" the optician asked. I held my spiral notebook out to him, and he read out loud:

> Marlies: nicer
> Optician: no Buddhism
> Elsbeth: less superstition
> Selma: less skeptical
> Palm: fewer Bible quotations
> Mama: less absent-seeming
> Me: draw fewer blanks, less timid, less anxious, new
>   pair of pants

The optician pressed his hands against his lower back. "I thought Buddhism was about authenticity," he said.

"Yes," I said, "but not necessarily ours."

"New pair of pants is good," Selma said.

"Why no Bible quotations?" the optician asked.

"I thought that might irritate him, as a Buddhist," I said, as if Buddhism and Christianity were rival football teams.

"I thought he wasn't here on duty," the optician said, and Selma added, "And I thought nothing irritated Buddhists. But maybe I really should be a bit less skeptical."

"By the way, Buddhism is also about giving up control," the optician said, and stuck his head back in the perimeter.

"Come, let's go for a walk," Selma said to me. "It's almost half past six and I think you desperately need some fresh air."

We crossed the Uhlheck. It was blustery, the forest rustled. We had turned up our coat collars and the wind blew my hair into my face. Selma maneuvered her wheelchair over the soggy path.

Selma was no longer very steady on her feet, but she refused to give up her daily walk in the Uhlheck, so she had gotten herself a wheelchair with thick tires like those on mountain bikes. Selma would not let anyone push her. She would always bump along beside me in her wheelchair for a while, then she would get up and push it like a walker.

While Selma let her thoughts wander, she read mine, which, especially since Frederik's visit was approaching, refused to wander anywhere; they wrapped themselves around me and the surrounding tree trunks like garlands of letters.

"Why do you worry so much?" Selma asked. "Why are you so nervous?"

I looked at the wheelchair as it struggled through the mud and said, "Henry, the coach is breaking."

Selma looked at me from the corner of her eye. "I don't think so," she said.

"I'm scared he'll think we're all strange."

"But he himself is strange," Selma said. "He stumbles out of the underbrush and eats Mars bars."

The wheelchair got bogged down with one wheel in a mud puddle. Selma shook it free. "But that's not the only thing, is it?" she asked.

"No," I answered. Since Frederik's visit had been getting closer, I'd been eyeing my heart suspiciously, just as everyone in the village kept a suspicious eye on their own hearts after Selma's dreams. My heart was not used to getting so much attention, and so raced at a disturbing pace. I remembered that the onset of a heart attack is accompanied by a tingling in the arm, but couldn't remember which one and so both arms tingled.

"You're confusing things," Selma said.

Love befalls you, I thought, it arrives like the bailiff who recently appeared at Farmer Leidig's house in the neighboring village. Love comes in, I thought, slaps a seal on everything you have, and announces: "None of this belongs to you anymore."

"You're confusing things, Luisa," Selma said again. "That's not love, that's death."

She put her arm around me, and it looked like she was pushing me and the wheelchair through the mud. "And there's a slight difference between them," she said, and smiled. "A few people have returned from the kingdom of love."

While Selma and I were walking in the Uhlheck, the optician was checking the countless lenses in his phoropter. Naturally he couldn't see with this phoropter that Mr. Rödder would complain about Alaska the next day and lavishly spray the room with Blue Ocean Breeze. He couldn't see that

there would be a change in plans or that my defective, gar-
rulous answering machine would be speechless at the news
that Frederik was arriving early, that he was already as good
as here. The optician couldn't see that I would run to meet
Frederik or that on the landing we wouldn't know how or
whether we should hug each other. He couldn't see how
Frederik would laugh and say, "You're looking at me as if
I were the devil himself. It's just me, Frederik. We talked on
the phone."

And if he could see it, he didn't say anything.

FELICITÀ

"You're early," I said to Frederik when we met on the doorstep to my apartment building, and it was the dumbest possible opening sentence.

"I know, I'm sorry," he said, "something was rescheduled. You're shivering, you're trembling, even."

"It's perfectly normal. I do this all the time."

A salt dough wreath fell from one of the apartment doors across the hall and broke into a thousand pieces. Frederik looked at the shards, then back at me.

"Nothing's fastened very well here," I said.

Frederik was looking at me with an attention and friendliness that was almost unbearable.

"Come on in," I said, opening the door.

Two boxes filled with things from my father's medical office took up nearly all of my tiny entryway. He had spread his possessions widely. A few of his boxes were in Elsbeth's basement, a few were in my apartment, but most were at Selma's.

Alaska stood in the entryway, too, and it was as tight as

if we'd crowded into a closet. Frederik tried to bend down to Alaska but there wasn't enough room.

"What's that?" he asked, pointing at a clear plastic box on top of the cardboard boxes.

"Instruments for the ears, nose, and throat."

"Is there another room in your apartment?"

"Here," I said, pushing Frederik into my studio.

I tried to picture my studio the way Frederik was seeing it for the first time: the fold-out couch covered with a blanket for Alaska, the bookcase that had been in my childhood bedroom, the bed that was just a mattress on a slat frame, advance reading copies piled in a corner. Frederik glanced at the shelves and looked away quickly before heading determinedly over to a small photograph on the wall. The photograph was the only thing in the entire apartment I hadn't dusted.

"That's the way it is with guests," Selma had said once. "You clean your entire home and your visitor goes straight to the one spot you missed."

"That's Martin," I said. Martin and I were four years old in the picture. Selma had taken it at carnival. I was dressed up as a violet with Elsbeth's much-too-large violet hat on my head. Martin was a strawberry. The optician had draped artificial turf over his shoulders and was a convincing flower bed. He carried Martin in his arms.

"The bookcase is crooked," Frederik said without taking his eyes from the photograph.

"Are you hungry?" I asked.

"Very."

"I had an idea. There's a Japanese restaurant here that serves a dish called *Buddhist fasting meal*, so I thought—"

"To be honest," Frederik said, "what I really want are french fries. French fries with ketchup."

We walked through the county seat, Alaska between us, and I was amazed that people weren't staring at Frederik and his beauty, that there weren't car accidents, that people didn't crane their necks and run into lampposts, that a couple passing us, deep in conversation, didn't forever lose the thread of their thoughts. A few people looked at us out of the corner of their eyes, but only because of his cowl.

We went into a snack bar. There were two high tables and a slot machine. A television suspended over one of the two tables blared. The slot machine flashed and tootled. It smelled of old fat.

"It's nice here," Frederik said, and he meant it.

Frederik ate four servings of fries. "Would you like some more?" he kept asking after I'd finished my serving, holding out a fry speared on a plastic fork. "They're excellent."

Just then Al Bano and Romina Power appeared on the television overhead, singing "Felicità." "That reminds me: How are things with your mom and the ice-cream parlor owner?" Frederik asked, pouring another packet of ketchup over his fries.

"Good. But I think my mother still loves my father."

"Excellent. And your father?"

"He's traveling."

"And that optician? Did he tell your grandmother?"

"No."

"Excellent," Frederik said, shoving five fries into his mouth at the same time.

I smiled at him. "So, what do you eat in Japan?"

"Mostly rice with not much else," he answered, wiping ketchup from the corner of his mouth. "Is there any Coke left? Hang on, I'll get us another Coke."

Frederik stood up and went to the refrigerated case next to the register, passing the man at the slot machine, who didn't even turn to look at him. Suddenly I was glad we were going to go to the village. That way there would be people who could attest that Frederik had really been here. The man playing the slot machine and the snack bar owner were not reliable witnesses. They were, unbelievably, busy with other things than Frederik, busy with a gambling machine and a deep-fat fryer.

When Frederik was back at the table with me, he beamed at me with his light-colored eyes—which, as the optician would later tell me, were a shade of cyan blue—as if the Coke were some hidden treasure. He held a bottle out to me. I took it and noticed I was no longer trembling. How nice it is that you're here, I thought. Frederik laughed and leaned backward. "It's nice to be here," he said, in a relieved tone, as if he hadn't been at all sure.

We spent the night an arm's length away from each other; he was lying on the couch, I in my bed. The cowl lay draped over the chair like a ghost who had fainted. I'd been afraid that underneath it, Frederik might be wearing special Buddhist underwear that looked like a sumo wrestler's belt, but he wore what ordinary people do.

Frederik had moved the fold-out couch so he wouldn't have to look at the crooked bookcase. We both stared at the ceiling as if someone had announced that in a few minutes a prizewinning documentary would be shown on it. I didn't know how noticeably I was not sleeping until at some point Frederik said, "You need to sleep, Luisa."

"But I'm not making any noise."

"I can hear you not making any noise from here."

In the middle of the night, as Frederik and I were patiently waiting for the documentary to be screened on the ceiling, my mother woke with a start in Alberto's bed.

It was three o'clock in the morning. Alberto was not next to her. He often got up at night to compose new ice-cream sundaes in the parlor downstairs. My mother looked at the empty space next to her and the blanket that had been thrown aside. It took her a moment to realize that something else was missing besides Alberto.

It was the eternal question of whether or not she should leave my father. The question had disappeared, and my mother suddenly knew for certain that it would never come back, because in the moment that she had sat bolt upright, she had left my father.

She sank back on the pillows and looked at the dark, bare light bulb over Alberto's bed.

You can live for years with a gnawing question, you can let it hollow you out, and then have it disappear in a flash, in a single moment of waking with a start. My mother left my father; the fact that he had left her already some time before didn't change a thing. My mother was in a different time zone and so, from her point of view, she had left him first.

Naturally my father noticed. He noticed it far away in Siberia, and he called her from a pay phone the very second she woke with a start, but he didn't reach her because she was sitting in Alberto's bed, leaving him. My father was left in the Siberian phone booth listening to an endless ringing tone, and in the apartment below, Selma covered her head with her pillow because the phone on the floor above kept ringing and ringing and ringing.

After she had woken with a start, my mother could not get back to sleep. She got dressed and passed Alberto without a word on her way out of the ice-cream parlor and into the silent village. She looked at the closed faces of the houses she had known by heart for decades, and only then, for the first time, did they truly seem familiar to her. As she walked through the streets, the space she had gained with the question's disappearance began to expand around her.

My mother's fingertips, which had been cold for as long as she could remember, suddenly felt warm. My mother wasn't good at getting separated, but she was very good at being separated.

She walked through the village streets for a long time, longer than our village actually is, but she was so delighted with all the space she suddenly had, that at six in the morning she couldn't wait any longer. She went to the phone booth next to the village shop. The neon sign over the door was just flickering on; the supplier was parking his truck in front of the shop.

Frederik and I woke with a start when the telephone rang. I was alarmed because I knew that at such an hour the phone only rings for cases of unpostponable death or unpostponable love, and everything unpostponable about love was lying on my sofa right then. I thought: Someone has died.

"I'm sorry to wake you two, Luisa," my mother said,

"but I absolutely have to tell you something. I've left your father. I'm alone now." She said it with the excitement others say, "I've just met someone."

"Congratulations," I said.

"And I wanted to tell you . . ." My mother gave a heavy sigh. "I wanted to tell you that I'm very sorry I was never really there for you."

I rubbed a hand over my face. My mother could just as well have apologized for the weather. Because I didn't know what else to say, I said, "Well, that's how it was."

My mother looked at the delivery truck. The supplier was pushing a cart as tall as he was, stacked with boxes of groceries and covered with a gray tarp, into the store. He stopped halfway through the doorway to tie his shoelaces. And if Elsbeth had appeared just then and said, "Look, Astrid, it looks exactly like a monstrous gray wall of regret, before which we will all eventually kneel," my mother would have said, "Yes, that's exactly what it looks like."

"That's something I'll have to live with," my mother said into the handset.

"Yes, I'm living with it, too. I have been for a while. Everything's fine, actually."

"Get some more sleep, Luisy," my mother said, and I did want to sleep right then, very much, as did Frederik. We didn't want to wait for the documentary a minute longer, but as soon as I hung up, the telephone rang again. Once again it wasn't death but love.

"What is it now?" I asked.

"It's me," my father said.

"Did something happen?"

"No."

"Then why are you calling so early?"

"I can't reach Astrid and I wanted to tell you something."

"I'm very sorry that I was never really there for you," I said.

"What?" my father asked. "You've always been there for me."

"It was a joke."

"What? I can't really understand you. The connection's very bad. What I . . . what I wanted to tell you—"

"Are you drunk?"

"Yes. I wanted to tell you: I had to leave your mother back then. I didn't have a choice. You can't stay with someone who is always asking herself if she should leave you."

"Are you sure you haven't spoken to Mama?"

"No," my father exclaimed. "I told you, I can't reach her."

"And why did you want to tell me this?"

"Because I can't reach your mother," he said, crackling.

"I'm not very reachable at the moment, either, Papa."

"Just one more thing, Luisy. When people in Siberia go into the forest and then fan out alone, they call each other's names regularly and the others call back, 'Yes, I'm here.' That way they can all be sure that no one is being threatened by a Siberian bear. And now I can't reach Astrid."

"I have company right now, and not the company of a Siberian bear."

"Oh God, Luisa, I'm sorry. I forgot. Tell him hello for me."

I hung up and went back to my room. I stretched out on the bed, pulled the blankets up to my chin, and looked over at Frederik. "You look like the most exhausted person in the world," he said with concern.

"My father can't reach my mother because she left him after he'd left her because she was always asking herself if she should leave him," I said. "And he says hello."

"Can't they leave you out of it?" Frederik asked, and lay back down. "Give me your hand."

I scooted to the edge of my bed and stretched my arm out. It was just the right length for Frederik to hold my hand. We lay there holding hands.

"Shall we drive to the village tomorrow?" I asked.

"Yes, I'd like to," he answered.

We lay there like that until Frederik finally fell asleep and his hand slipped from mine.

SIXTY-FIVE PERCENT

Frederik and I sat in my car. It was pouring rain and the windshield wipers wagged furiously back and forth. "I can hardly see a thing," I said.

Frederik leaned toward me and wiped the windshield with his sleeve. He was humming a song I didn't recognize. I thought of the list I'd carried around the village in the hope that more of the points would be observed than just the new pair of pants, which I had, in fact, bought. I leaned forward, very close to the streaming, fogged-up windshield as if there were something on it to decipher. Alaska, asleep on the back seat, found it all very cozy.

"Breathe, Luisa," Frederik said, and cleared another patch for me to see through. The optician had been repeating this constantly since he'd started reading books on Buddhism.

"I've been breathing all my life," I said.

Frederik put his hand on my stomach. "Yes, but into here. You shouldn't breathe only with your upper body."

Selma was right. I'd been confusing two things. Frederik was bowling me over, but not like a bailiff or a heart attack, and, as directed by my list, I was not drawing a blank. Here it is, I thought, that famous here-and-now the optician was always talking about. Here I was, although I could hardly see a thing, right in the middle of the here-and-now instead of in my usual when-and-if. I took Frederik's hand and there was a loud bang. I was sure one of the bands around my heart had snapped, but it was a piston.

Frederik ran through the pouring rain to a phone booth, Selma's number in hand, to let her know that we would be late and to ask her to use the optician's German automobile club card to send a mechanic. Alaska and I waited in the car, and suddenly I noticed my feet were getting wet. I looked down. A deep puddle had formed around the clutch and the gas and brake pedals. I looked in the footwell of the back seat and saw water there, too. I got out and circled the car with Alaska, without knowing exactly what I was looking for.

Frederik returned soaking wet. Below his jacket, his cowl stuck to his legs. I opened the car door and pointed at the puddle. He leaned over the driver's seat. "How did that get in here?"

"I don't have the slightest idea," I said. "All of a sudden it was just there. I thought it was better to get out of the car, because of the electricity."

We stood on the shoulder in the November cold, completely drenched, and I thought of a passage the optician had read to Selma and me about finding beauty in every single moment. I tapped Frederik's arm and pointed at the asphalt. "Look at the beautiful colors in that puddle."

"I'm afraid that's oil," he said.

The mechanic came and was in a very good mood. "Is it

carnival already?" he said with a laugh, pointing at Frederik's cowl.

"It seems so," Frederik retorted, pointing at the mechanic's white raincoat, which looked like the gear of a forensics officer.

The mechanic examined the motor. "She's done for," he said. "Piston's galled."

"There's water in the footwell, too, even though the car is watertight," I said.

The mechanic raised his eyebrows and circled the car with a slowness that was not at all suited to the weather. He checked the windows, the roof, the doors. Then he slid under the car. Because I was thinking of the optician's Buddhist sayings, I didn't ask if he could hurry it up at all.

"Well?" Frederik asked when the mechanic slid out from under the car.

"To be honest, I can't figure how the water is getting in," he said in dismay. Apparently there usually wasn't much he couldn't figure out.

Alaska was shivering. I was shivering even more, and Frederik put his arm around me. He was shivering, too. Finally the mechanic shrugged. "Water finds a way," he said.

"Very true," Frederik agreed. "And now?"

"Now I'll tow you," he said, and attached my car to his truck.

Frederik got into my car, Alaska and I rode with the mechanic to show him the way. He had spread a tarp out for us to sit on so we wouldn't drip over everything.

"Water finds a way, no matter how well sealed something is," he said. The tree air freshener hanging from his rearview mirror was called Green Apple but smelled exactly like Mr. Rödder's Blue Ocean Breeze. It struggled against the smell of wet dog as assiduously and ineffectively as the wipers struggled against the rain.

I turned and waved at Frederik. He waved back.

"Humans are sixty-five percent water," the mechanic said.

I wiped the wet hair from my face. "Especially today," I said.

The village sign appeared. The mechanic and Frederik stopped at the bottom of the hill. Selma and the optician were standing in front of the house under an umbrella.

ONE THOUSAND YEARS AT SEA

They had come to meet us. Selma opened a second umbrella. The optician said, "Konnichiwa," and bowed deeply. Frederik bowed, too.

Frederik and Selma looked at each other for a very long time as they shook hands. "You don't look like Japan at all," Selma said. "More like Hollywood."

The optician and I thought of the several lives one has in Buddhism, because from the way Selma and Frederik looked at each other, they seemed to know each other from at least one previous life, and not just casually, but as if they had saved the world together or grown up in the same family.

"You also don't look the way I'd pictured you," Frederik said. "You look like someone on television, but the name escapes me."

And that was the moment we finally also saw the resemblance. My God, he's right, the optician and I thought, and we couldn't understand how it had never occurred to us before.

Selma frowned, because the optician and I were staring at

her as if seeing her for the first time. "Come inside, quickly," she said, and we went into the house.

"Careful, don't step there." From the foyer, the optician gestured toward the area in the kitchen circled with red tape. "The floor is too weak. I marked the area."

Frederik looked at the red outline from the hallway.

"It's been dangerous for a while now," the optician said. "I know it's no state to be in."

Frederik smiled and said, "Apparently it is," and took off his shoes. So we all did the same.

Selma went to get him towels and a bathrobe, then we all went into the kitchen. I tried to see it for the first time as Frederik would. The yellow wallpaper; the light blue credenza with gray pleated curtains in the glass doors; the corner bench; the old, scratched wooden table; and the gray linoleum floor with the round, red-outlined area near the window—Martin had once said that on the gray floor, that area looked like the eye of a whale, an eye completely encircled by an eyelid inflammation—and the water heater over the sink, still plastered with Martin's and my collection of Hanuta candy stickers: a grinning apple with a bite out of it that said, "Today, I had a bite"; an energetic walnut shouting, "Let's get cracking!" I tried to see with fresh eyes the macramé owl hanging on the wall, which the shopkeeper's wife had given Selma as a gift, and the white linen curtains that hung down precisely to the windowsill.

But I wasn't able. It was like trying to lose something on purpose.

Selma had a brussels sprout casserole in the oven; she always made it for first-time guests because a casserole never goes wrong. Through the fogged-up window we saw that it was raining even harder. The rain fell as if all the waterfalls in the world had decided that today, for a change, they would all converge and fall on our village.

On the kitchen table, next to a package of Mon Chéris, lay one of the optician's books about Buddhism. He quickly slipped it into one of Selma's cutlery drawers. "May I?" Frederik asked, pointing at the package of Mon Chéris.

"Of course," Selma replied.

"Delicious," he said, nodding gravely, and Selma nodded back just as gravely, as if Mon Chéris were a highly specialized science known only to a few experts in all the world.

"You two are dripping," Selma finally said.

"Oh, I'm sorry," Frederik said, and picked up the bathrobe and a towel in one hand and a second Mon Chéri in the other.

The optician started to clear the table and Selma to stir the sauce on the stove. As soon as the bathroom door closed, they spun around and hurried to me.

"Is everything okay? Any tingling in your arms?" Selma asked.

"How often is your mind going blank?" the optician asked.

They peered at me as if I were a patient in the emergency room.

I stroked Selma's hair, which we had finally recognized as Rudi Carrell's. "Everything's fine," I said, "hardly any blanks; condition stable."

"Then all's well," Selma said, and Frederik returned wearing her bathrobe and with his sopping-wet cowl over his arm. I went into the bathroom with one of Selma's dresses.

While the casserole was baking, Frederik sat on the radiator in the living room, in the exact spot from which the blank and I had talked to him on the phone for the first time.

The living room was even neater than usual at Selma's. There wasn't a speck of dust on the perfectly straight book-shelves. The stack of magazines on the coffee table was exactly aligned. The cushions on the red sofa looked like no one had ever leaned on them.

Frederik watched Selma hang our wet things on the dry-ing rack. "May I help?" he asked, but Selma waved him away.

"Not at all," she replied. "You can start by drying out, you sopping-wet monk."

Selma hung our clothing up to dry as carefully as if it were going to hang there forever, as if future generations could learn valuable lessons about hanging laundry from it.

"You're a good Buddhist," Frederik observed.

Selma clamped a final clothespin on my pants and turned to face him.

"Nice that someone finally noticed," she said.

After each of us had eaten two helpings of casserole and Frederik four, the optician laid his silverware on his plate and cleared his throat.

"I wanted to ask you a quick question," he said, giving me a sideways glance. "Is it true that something can disap-pear if we try to see it, but can't disappear if we don't try to see it?"

I kicked the optician's shin under the table.

"I'm not at all interested in this from a Buddhist point of view," he added quickly, "but purely for professional reasons."

Frederik wiped his mouth. "I don't know," he said, "I'll have to think about it."

Selma pointed at the window through which we could see three silhouettes with umbrellas climbing the hill: Elsbeth, the shopkeeper, and Palm.

Selma opened the door.

"Hello," Elsbeth said, handing her a blender. "I wanted to finally return your blender. I happened to be in the neighborhood."

"That's right. We brought ice cream, too," the shopkeeper said, standing behind Elsbeth with an enormous wrapped tray.

Selma stepped aside and the three came into the kitchen one after the other. I scooted closer to the optician and no longer felt sure that it really was a good idea to let more of the world in. The optician smiled at me.

"Buddhism is also about unconditionally accepting every experience life brings," he whispered.

Elsbeth was dressed to the nines. She wore a black dress with enormous purple flowers and a purple hat with a little black veil and a bunch of violets on the brim. Frederik stood up and Elsbeth offered him her hand.

"So there you are," she said, beaming. "We've all been eagerly waiting to meet you."

"Thank you," Frederik said. "What a lovely hat."

Elsbeth blushed. "You think so?" she asked, and put her hand on the violets. "By the way, did you know that smelling violets either gives you freckles or makes you crazy?"

"Elsbeth, please," I whispered, and she flushed even deeper.

"At least, that's what some people say," she added quickly. "Personally, I would never, that is, I think it's . . ."

Elsbeth looked around, hoping that someone would help her get out of the sentence, but no one knew how.

"Aside from that, we're experiencing a lot of turbulence with the preparations for the Christmas party in the community center. We're wondering whether it would be better to hold it in the afternoon or the evening. It's all . . ." Elsbeth looked as if she were trying to remember something learned long ago by heart. "Really very interesting."

Frederik bent forward and sniffed the bunch of violets.

"I'm hoping for freckles," he said. "What's in that package?"

"Good afternoon," the shopkeeper said, and pushed past Elsbeth. "I'm the shopkeeper."

He unwrapped the cardboard tray, which held seven sundaes decorated with paper umbrellas.

"These are from the ice-cream parlor. We have four medium Secret Loves, one Hot Desire, and one Flaming Temptation," he announced as he lifted the respective sundaes from the tray and placed them on the table. "And here we have a special treat: Alberto's latest creation, Astrid's Tropical Cup. She'll be here in a moment."

"Delicious," Selma said.

She pulled out the table. We squeezed together around it. On the far end sat Palm, who still hadn't said a word, like a shy ten-year-old. A strand of hair stood straight up on his head. For reasons of space, the optician extended his arm on the back of the kitchen bench behind Palm, careful not to touch him.

"This is Mr. Werner Palm," Selma said, and Frederik extended his hand across the table.

"Pleased to meet you."

Palm, still silent, smiled and nodded.

"So, tell us," Elsbeth said, "what's it like living in a monastery?"

"Why did you choose to become a Buddhist?" the shopkeeper asked. "Did you never consider an occupation that requires training?"

"Is there a Buddhist woman in your life?" Elsbeth asked.

"Personally, I'd like to know how flaming temptation and hot desire can be reconciled with imperturbable equanimity," the shopkeeper said. "Are you celibate?"

"Our optician told us that sometimes, during meditation, a monk is beaten by other monks," Elsbeth said. "Is that really true?"

"Can you say something in Japanese?" the shopkeeper asked.

"Could you please all be quiet?" I shouted, and everyone looked at me as if I'd made an extremely inappropriate remark it was best to ignore, then they all turned back to Frederik. He set his spoon down next to his Hot Desire and said that for the most part it was very quiet in the monastery and that Buddhism actually does require training. And no, he added, there was no Buddhist woman in his life, at least none that would get in the way of celibacy, and, in fact, one was sometimes struck with a stick while meditating, but with a very well-placed blow that relaxed the muscles on the back of the neck. Then he said, "Umi ni sennen, yama ni sennen."

"What does that mean?" Elsbeth asked.

"One thousand years at sea, one thousand years in the mountains," Frederik translated.

"Oh, how nice," Elsbeth said, reaching across the table to pat my hand. "That sounds like your father."

They all smiled at Frederik as if he were a prizewinning documentary. Frederik gave them an embarrassed grin.

"You're all very kind," he said.

"That's true, isn't it?" Elsbeth said, sitting up straight.

Frederik stood up.

"I'm just going to put my robe back on," and we nodded, astonished. We'd all thought it was a cowl.

As soon as Frederik stepped out of the room, they all turned toward me.

"He's a good man," the shopkeeper said.

"He's fantastic," Elsbeth said. "He's not as handsome as you said, but he is incredibly smart."

They said these things as if I had invented him. Palm nodded without a word, and the optician said in a solemn tone: "Bioluminescence."

"What on earth is that?" Elsbeth asked.

"It's a substance that makes animals glow from inside," he explained.

Selma said nothing and stroked my hair.

Frederik and I went to the Uhlheck with Alaska. Frederik wore the optician's yellow raincoat over his robe and I was still wearing Selma's dress with her yellow raincoat over it.

"We're a symphony in yellow," Frederik said. We wore rubber boots. Selma had rubber boots from every era and in every size. He held Selma's umbrella over both of us. Rain pattered down on it.

"Werner Palm doesn't say much," Frederik said, and I

explained that he said next to nothing unless he was explaining verses from the Bible. He was always there and that was exactly the point, that Palm was there, that he was sitting at the table with us and not at home alone.

"You don't say much, either, Luisa," Frederik observed.

I didn't tell him that I had my hands full just with him suddenly sitting at the table, with the world that had been let in, and with the world in the form of Selma, the optician, the shopkeeper, Elsbeth, and Palm. I didn't mention the list in my pocket, with items that not a single one of them respected, and that under these circumstances it's hard to say much and far better just to watch.

"Rudi Carrell," I said.

Frederik looked around. "Where?"

"Selma," I replied. "She looks like Rudi Carrell."

"Exactly," Frederik cried, "exactly like him, that's what I was thinking."

The rain was so heavy, you could hardly see a thing. The path and the fields had long become indistinguishable, and the rain had diluted the beauty of the landscape, which today, for once, I wouldn't have walked past without noticing, and which I would have liked to show to Frederik as if it were my own invention. I held tightly to the edge of the umbrella, which threatened to collapse under the mass of water.

Frederik shut the worn-out umbrella and took my hand as if there'd been a time shift, as if many years had passed since he held my hand for the first time last night, and as if it were completely natural for us to hold hands.

We ran home, as I had run only as a child, only with Martin, when we were convinced that a hellhound or a death that didn't exist was chasing us. Alaska ran alongside

us, laboriously, because all the rain had made his fur even
heavier than it usually was.

The optician drove Frederik and me back to the county seat.
Palm had, in fact, not spoken a single word the entire visit.
Only at the very end, when they were all standing by the
door to wave a lengthy goodbye, did Palm step forward, take
Frederik's hand, and say, "I wish for you God's bountiful
blessings."

"I wish them for you, too," Frederik replied, and bowed
so deeply that Palm reached out his hand to catch Frederik in
case he lost his balance, but it wasn't necessary.

When we had already reached the village border, in front of
Marlies's house, my mother came running toward us. She
held a long bouquet wrapped in cellophane over her head.
The optician braked and rolled down the window. The rain
was still pouring down. My mother stuck her dripping head
through the window.

"Dammit, once again I'm too late, I'm sorry." She reached
past the optician and shook Frederik's hand. "I'm Astrid, her
mother. I'm also now Luisa's father's ex-wife."

"Good evening," Frederik said.

My mother pulled her head back. "This is for you," she
said, and stuck the bouquet of very long-stemmed gladiolas
through the window.

"Oh, thank you. They're beautiful," Frederik said, and
awkwardly stowed it between his knees. The flowers touched
the car's ceiling. My mother knocked on the back window and smiled at me. She looked happy and very young. I

WHAT YOU CAN SEE FROM HERE

nodded at her and, behind her, saw something move in Marlies's darkened living room window. My mother held her bag over her head even though it made no difference and hurried away. I opened the car door and went up to Marlies's house.

"Marlies, it's me," I called. "Do you want to come say hello?"

Nothing moved.

"You don't need to be approachable. It was a very dumb idea."

Marlies opened the window a crack. "Leave me in peace with your stupid visit," she called.

"Fine, then, take care," I said, and got back in the car.

Frederik turned and looked at me. "Anyone else coming?"

"No," I said, "no one else."

THE BLUE WHALE'S HEAVY HEART

The optician's car was an orange Passat station wagon from the 1970s and it, too, could have been used in an experiment to find the secret of immortality. The optician had driven Martin and me to school in this Passat when the local train was canceled because of too much snow, and he had driven me to school every day for six months because I refused to get in the train after Martin's death.

"Why didn't the train door on my side open?" I'd asked the optician from the back seat two months after Martin's death.

The optician pulled over on the shoulder. He put on the hazard lights and looked at me for a long time in the rearview mirror. I was sitting on two cushions so that the seat belt lay properly over my shoulder. Ever since Martin's death, the optician buckled me into the back seat.

He turned to face me. "Do you remember how I taught you to tell time and explained how time zones work?"

I nodded.

"I also taught you capitalization, the ß, and arithmetic.

And all about deciduous and coniferous trees. And about animals on land and in the water."

I nodded again and thought again of how the optician could find connections between completely unrelated things, so he'd surely be able to draw one between arithmetic and the doors of a local train.

"And when you're older, I'll explain many more things. I can teach you the structure and function of the human eye and how to drive and how to mount a dowel. I can explain geopolitics and identify all the constellations. I can even explain things I don't understand. If you want to know something that I have no idea about, then I'll read everything there is on the subject and explain it to you. I am at your disposal for any topic, for this question, too," the optician said, reaching back and stroking my cheek.

He got out, circled the Passat, and sat next to me on the back seat.

"I've never sat here before," he said, looking around. "You've got a nice spot here, Luisa."

He looked at his hands as if the question were lying there, as if he were holding it so that he could examine it from every angle.

"There's no answer to your question," he said, "not anywhere in the entire world or anywhere else, either."

"Not even in Kuala Lumpur?" I asked. That's where my father was at the time.

"Not even there. Looking for an answer to that question is like Vasily Alekseyev trying to lift one hundred thousand kilos."

"No one can do that."

"Exactly. It's anatomically impossible. And the answer is also anatomically impossible."

He placed his hand on mine. My hand disappeared under the optician's large one.

"There will be times in your life when you'll ask yourself if you've done even one thing right. That's perfectly normal. It's also a very heavy question. Around a hundred and eighty kilos, I'd say. But it's one that has an answer. Mostly it comes late in life. I don't know if Selma and I will still be around then. So I'm going to tell you now: When the time comes, when the question arises and you can't find an answer right away, then remember that you made your grandmother and me very happy, you brought us enough happiness for an entire life from beginning to end. The older I get, the more I believe that the two of us were only invented for you. And if there ever was a good reason to be invented, then it's you."

I leaned against the optician's shoulder and he rested his cheek on my head. For a while we listened to the ticking of the hazard lights.

"Now someone has to drive me to school," I said.

The optician smiled. "That someone is me," he said, then kissed the top of my head and got into the driver's seat.

For a while Frederik kept trying to straighten the crackling, expansive gladiola bouquet, then he gave up. He leaned his head against the car window in order to see around the flowers. The optician glanced at him now and again, but the bouquet kept Frederik hidden.

Alaska slept. He took up almost the entire back seat. His head lay on my lap. The only sounds were the patter of raindrops outside, the windshield wipers struggling, and now and again the crackling of the cellophane.

I touched the top of the closed window where the water

ran down diagonally outside. This ancient car is still water-proof, I thought.

"May I confide in you?" the optician suddenly asked without taking his eyes off the road.

"Of course," Frederik said from behind the bouquet.

The optician gave me a quick look, cleared his throat, and then spoke softly as if hoping that the sound of the rain would cover his voice.

"You talked about blows from a stick," the optician said. "I've read that you are also struck when your thoughts are straying during meditation. In my case, it's the thoughts that pummel me. And I'm made up of much more than sixty-five percent thoughts."

The optician told Frederik all about the voices that jostled him and made him stagger, that taunted him about everything he hadn't done because of them. He told how he had tried to cope with the voices using inspirational quotes on postcards and Buddhism, and that he had tried to pass himself off as the sky and as a river before them. Frederik said nothing. His head rested against the window; the streetlights blurred in the downpour and formed trails of light.

"You must think I'm crazy," the optician said. "I'm sure you think I urgently need a doctor."

He wiped the windshield with his sleeve.

"I've already seen a doctor. He gave me an electro-encephalography."

The optician looked over at Frederik, at the silent gladiolas.

"I'm sure you think I should go to a doctor who doesn't use machines or instruments. I'm sure you think I should see a psychologist. But I don't want to see a psychologist," he said, and blinked. We had almost arrived. "Psychologists creak and send their patients out into the world. I don't want that. I'm too old for the world."

You're as old as the world, I thought on the back seat.

"I've never told anyone all this," the optician said to the windshield wipers, to the rain, to the cellophane, to Frederik. "I hope I haven't made you uncomfortable."

He stopped in front of my building and Frederik finally spoke. "Are we there already?" he asked.

"Come in for a bit," Frederik said at my front door. The optician looked at me. I nodded.

"But only for a minute," he said.

In my apartment the optician walked around the opened fold-out bed and took the framed carnival photograph from the wall.

"There we all are," he said. "I think I look good as a flower bed."

Frederik lingered in the doorway.

"That bookshelf is impossible," he said before disappearing into the kitchen.

"What's wrong with the bookshelf?" the optician asked in a whisper.

"He says it's crooked," I replied.

The optician took a step back and looked at the bookshelf for a long time.

"It's true, now that you mention it."

"Could you both come here for a second?" Frederik called from the kitchen.

He was sitting on one of my chairs and pointed at the other. My father's otorhinolaryngological instruments were spread out on the table.

"What do you have in mind?" the optician asked.

Frederik said, "Please take a seat."

The optician gave me a questioning look. I shrugged, and the optician sat down. Frederik was wearing my father's head mirror. My father's head was bigger than Frederik's because he had hair, so Frederik had to hold the mirror with one hand. With the other he picked up the silver nasal speculum. The optician looked at Frederik.

"I'm going to examine the voices," Frederik said.

"Please," the optician objected, "that's not even possible."

"Yes, it is. It's a new method. From Japan."

The optician looked at Frederik as if he were the one who urgently needed a psychologist.

"Please look straight ahead and keep still," Frederik said. He leaned forward and looked into the optician's ear with the speculum.

"That's actually an instrument for the nose," I pointed out.

Frederik glanced up at me; the mirror sat just above his eyebrows. "Not in Japan," he said before immersing himself in the optician's left ear.

Alaska came in and sniffed at the case that held the rest of the instruments. He looked happy; perhaps it smelled of my father.

"And?" the optician asked after a while.

"I can see them very clearly," Frederik said.

The optician held very still. He suddenly remembered visiting a doctor in the neighboring village when he was five years old. He'd had the chicken pox. He was covered with red pustules and had a high fever and chills. The fever gave him bad dreams, day and night, and so the optician cried a lot, even after he had been awake for a long time.

He had been afraid of going to the doctor. Afraid the doctor would tell him, "Stop your crying," afraid of the cold stethoscope. But the doctor had said in a very friendly voice, "Please have a seat, my spotted young man," and rubbed his hands to warm them and breathed on the stethoscope so it wouldn't be too cold. He'd explained to the optician that with the syrup and the ointment he was going to give him, countless tiny boxing champions were going to slip inside him. They were too small to be seen with the human eye, but they were very strong and were only invented to knock out the chicken pox. The optician immediately felt better because of the invisible boxing champions inside him, fighting on his side to smash the fever and the dreams, too.

Naturally the optician didn't believe for a second that Frederik could see the voices. But the child the optician once was believed it happily.

"Really?" the optician asked. "You can see them?"

"Clear as day. There are at least three of them. They really are . . . they're really very ugly."

"They are, aren't they?" the optician said, and smiled at Frederik.

"Please hold still," Frederik said, and the optician quickly straightened his head.

"Very ugly," Frederik repeated. "And it looks like you caught them a very long time ago."

"That's true," the optician said, "that's very true."

Frederik adjusted the head mirror and clamped the speculum between his teeth. He grabbed his chair leg with his free hand and scooted to the other side of the optician.

"I'm going to look into your right ear now," he said. "Ah, now I see them from behind."

The optician looked straight ahead at the tiles over my sink with great concentration.

"Some people give their voices names," Frederik said, "but that hasn't helped me."

The optician spun around and stared at him. "You have them, too?"

"Of course. Now please look straight ahead again."

"Is there anything that can be done for it?" the optician asked without moving.

"To be honest, no. These voices will probably stay." Frederik tapped the optician's ear with the nasal speculum. "Where are they supposed to go? They don't have anyone besides you. And they never learned how to do anything other than harangue you."

The head mirror slipped over Frederik's eyes. He pushed it to the back of his head. "And stop reading to them. No postcards and no Buddhism. They're so old, they know it all already."

He put the speculum on the kitchen table and looked at the optician. The optician picked up the speculum and examined it for a long time.

"Amazing what you can do with modern technology," he said, smiling.

The optician drove home. There, he dropped facedown on his bed, the bed that was just the right size for one person, feeling at least as heavy as the heart of a blue whale, as heavy as something that seems anatomically impossible. I've got to tell Selma that it's possible to be that solid and that heavy, he thought before falling asleep, in case she doesn't know.

Naturally the optician's inner voices were not going to leave him in peace just because someone claimed to have seen them. It wasn't that easy, but it did gradually become less difficult.

The optician stopped reading to the voices. He stopped pretending he was a river or the sky, which had never been hard to disprove in any case. He no longer professed anything. He never said anything to them at all anymore. In time the voices' hiss softened to a lisp, their wails turned to whines. The optician didn't lose the voices, but over time the voices lost the optician. When they said something, which they continued to do often, they spoke more and more into the void, as if to a broken answering machine.

BIOLUMINESCENCE

haven't talked this much for a very long time," Frederik said. We sat on the windowsill, looking at my sofa and my bed, where Frederik and I were separately not sleeping. Between us was a bowl of peanuts that Frederik had already emptied and filled again.

"I'd really like to stay longer, but I have to go back tomorrow," Frederik said.

I looked at him, and he could probably see clearly that I thought this was terrible.

"Is that bad?" he asked.

I thought of the authenticity valued in Buddhism and how I had forbidden it to everyone. It had still found its way, and it hadn't been so bad. Authenticity, I thought, come on, Luisa, one, two, three.

"No," I said. Dammit, I thought. "No, it's not bad."

A book that had been stuck at an angle on top of the others on the bookshelf fell to the floor. *An Outline of Psychoanalysis*. My father had given it to me.

"Around you, things are often falling," Frederik remarked.

I looked at him from the corner of my eye, the way you look at someone you love far more than you're prepared to admit. He looked tired. I was wide awake but pretended I had to yawn.

"It's very late," I said. "I'm going to go brush my teeth."

"Do that," Frederik said, and I went to brush my teeth. Then I came back and sat next to him.

"I'm going to go brush my teeth, too, then," he said.

"Yes, do that," I said, and went into the kitchen, where Alaska had already curled up on his blanket under the table. I stuck his evening pill in a ball of liverwurst, put it in front of him, went back, and sat down next to Frederik.

"What's wrong with him, actually?" he asked.

"Hyperthyroidism and osteoporosis," I said.

I thought about what else to do.

"I'm going to give Selma a quick call to ask if it's still raining so hard."

"Yes, do that," Frederik said.

How can anyone be so beautiful? I wondered, and I thought about the importance of nonaction in Buddhism.

"You know, what I'm doing this whole time is not kissing you," I said, standing up quickly to go to the telephone. Frederik grabbed my wrist.

"I can't anymore," he said, putting his hand on the back of my neck and pulling my face toward him. "This has got to end at some point."

And so it began. Frederik kissed me and I kissed Frederik as if we'd been invented precisely for this.

Frederik pulled his robe over his head like a sweater that was much too long and then he started unbuttoning Selma's dress.

He undid the buttons with intense concentration, as if

future generations could learn valuable lessons from this method of unbuttoning. It took an enormously long time, as if Frederik were unbuttoning the entire stretch between Germany and Japan, and this gave the blank my mind was drawing time to settle down comfortably next to us. Because of the blank, I thought of how I'd never stood quite so naked as I would soon stand before Frederik as soon as he'd unbuttoned the entire stretch. I also thought about how I'd always made sure that my nakedness was unlit and covered with a blanket, for good reason, I thought, but luckily I also thought about how things can disappear when you acknowledge them.

"I'm not half as beautiful as you are," I said.

Frederik had undone the last button. The button at the very bottom of Selma's dress. He stood up and slipped the dress from my shoulders.

"You're three times as beautiful," he said, then lifted me up and laid me on the bed. My blank stayed where it was on the windowsill.

And everything Frederik then did, he did with as much assurance as if he'd already studied a map of my body for years, as if that map were hanging on Frederik's wall in Japan, as if he had stood before it and memorized all the routes.

I had no map of Frederik's body. I didn't know where to start and fluttered my hand over his chest and stomach.

Frederik took hold of my hands and said, "You don't need to do a thing." He took my shoulders and pressed my upper body onto the mattress.

"Frederik?" I whispered when he was far below, concentrating on topology with his mouth and hand, which didn't need to look for the way.

"Yes?" he murmured, as if I were knocking inopportunely on his door when he was in the middle of a revolutionary invention.

"Your . . . your precision is incredible."

Frederik looked up at me.

"Isn't that the sort of thing one says about electric razors?"

He smiled at me. His eyes were no longer cyan blue or turquoise, but almost black. I remembered what the optician told me about pupils when I was a child: that darkness or joy makes them dilate.

Frederik came back up and laid his head at my throat and his hand on my breast, under which my heart hammered like someone outside not being let in. My heart doesn't have anything in common with the heart of a blue whale, I thought.

"Why are you so calm?" I asked.

Frederik kissed me and said, "I'm so calm because you're so nervous."

He stroked my neck with the back of his hand.

"I did tell you that you didn't need to do anything," he whispered.

"But I'm not doing anything."

"Yes, you are. You've been thinking the whole time."

I turned my head toward him. My mouth touched his forehead.

"You're not thinking at all?"

"No," Frederik murmured into my throat, and laid his hand on the hollow between my ribs and my hip, "not right now. I probably will tomorrow." He laid the flat of his hand below my navel, and that was the end of my not doing anything. I wrapped my arms around him. "I'll do a lot of thinking tomorrow," he whispered, pushing my legs apart with his, "but not right now, Luisa."

I'd already stopped listening.

Around three in the morning I woke up. Frederik lay asleep next to me, on his stomach with his face turned toward me, his arms folded under his head. I watched him for a while, then stroked his rough elbow with my finger.

"Remember all this well," I said softly to myself and to the blank far away on the windowsill.

I sat up on the edge of the bed. At first I thought the rain had leaked in during the night, but the puddle in the middle of the room was just Frederik's robe.

My comforter was on the floor. It had slipped off the bed a long time ago. I pulled it up like a very old fisherman hauling in a net. It took a while. My arms were ninety percent water. I was enfeebled by love.

While I was hauling in the comforter, the heavy optician slept facedown on his bed, not moving once over the course of the night. At the same time, Elsbeth and Palm slept sitting upright on Elsbeth's sofa. Elsbeth had fallen asleep first and then started awake. "I'm sorry, Palm, but you make me so tired with all those Bible passages and explications."

Palm had smiled at her and said, "But that's no problem at all, my dear Elsbeth." Elsbeth had fallen asleep again and Palm continued his explication until he, too, nodded off. At the same time, Marlies was not sleeping. She stood at the window, eating peas from the can. She stood right in front of the window, something she could only do at night because no one came by to bother her then. She shoveled the peas in reluctantly because her body had shyly reminded her that once again she'd eaten nothing all day. The juice from the peas ran down her chin and she wiped her mouth. At the same time, my father was standing in front of a telephone booth in Moscow. He checked the wristwatch that was set to Central European time and hung up the receiver. At the same time, my mother, lying next to Alberto in the apartment over the ice-cream parlor, had the hiccups. A few hours earlier, Alberto had asked my mother if she wanted to move in with him and she had laughed longer and louder than she had for an eternity, as if moving in together were the funniest joke in the world. Alberto, rightly, was offended.

"Fine," he said, "now pull yourself together."

But my mother couldn't stop laughing. "I'm sorry," she said, "it has nothing to do with you." Tears streamed down her cheeks. "But it's hilarious, I don't know why, either."

She tried to fall asleep, but the hiccups continued, and whenever she thought of the words "move in together," she burst out laughing again, until Alberto said, "I've had it. I'm sleeping on the sofa."

At the same time, Selma lay in bed under her flowered quilt and luckily only nearly dreamed of an okapi. At the very last moment, she realized it was just a misshapen cow standing next to her in the twilight in the Uhlheck.

ANIMALS CAN SENSE THESE THINGS

I slept until late morning and woke up to the sound of the doorbell. Frederik had disappeared. Only his robe and his suitcase were still here. I stumbled to the door still half asleep and answered the intercom.

"Please come down and help me carry something," Frederik said.

Because I had no bathrobe, I pulled on Frederik's robe and ran down the stairs. He stood at the entrance, surrounded by six boxes.

"You look like a burnt gingerbread man," he said.

"And you look perfectly normal," I said, because Frederik was wearing jeans and a sweater, like an ordinary person.

I pointed at the boxes. "What's all this?"

"The crooked bookshelf has to go," he said. "I bought you a new one."

We carried the boxes into the lobby and up the stairs, Frederik behind me.

"How did you get them all here?" I asked.

Frederik stopped.

"He who brings home all of life's gifts, one by one, will achieve enlightenment," he said.

I turned and looked at him.

"It was just a joke. Furniture delivery."

Upstairs he looked at his watch. "I have to go," he said. "You'll have to assemble it yourself." Neither of us knew that I wouldn't do it for another eight years.

The airport teemed with carefully concealed truths wanting out at the last minute. Everywhere there were people hugging each other one last time, and I hoped they were hugging because a truth had come to light and proved not to be as terrible and terrifying as they feared. Maybe they were hugging each other as tight as they could to keep a silenced truth from slipping out and spreading an awful stink and a great commotion in the last few meters.

We stood in front of the departure display panel. Frederik put down his suitcase and looked at me.

"I'll give them back," he said. "I'll mail them to you."

He was talking about one hundred and twenty marks.

We'd remembered very late that we didn't have a car anymore and took a taxi.

"Does that enormous, ugly beast have to come?" the driver complained.

And Frederik replied, "Yes, it does. The enormous, ugly beast always has to come with us."

We sat in the back seat, Alaska between us, half on the seat, half in the footwell. Frederik had said he'd have a lot of thinking to do, and he was thinking now. I watched him.

We kept silent the entire drive. Only at the exit to the airport did Frederik put his arm around me, which mostly meant putting his arm around Alaska.

"Why are you so calm?" he asked.

"I'm so calm because you're so nervous," I replied, and it was true. I wasn't nervous, not yet. I only became nervous once we were standing in the departure hall.

"No," I said, "don't pay me back. You gave me the bookshelf, after all."

We looked up at the giant display panel when it started to update noisily. The letters clattered over each other and blurred into a white-and-black mass. We and everyone around us waited for the letters to calm down. We looked up, spellbound, as if hoping the display panel were about to reveal what life had in store. The letters slowed and the display panel did, indeed, reveal what life had in store, at least for the next five minutes, in its laconic display panel way.

"Gate Five B," Frederik read.

As we crossed the departure hall, Alaska strained at the leash so hard I almost lost my balance.

He pulled toward a man who came running up to us. I squinted. I'd never seen this man before, but I immediately knew who he was.

"Excuse me for addressing you like this," he said to Frederik, "my name is Dr. Maschke. I'm a psychoanalyst. You're Buddhist, aren't you?" He offered Frederik his hand. His leather jacket creaked.

"Yes, I'm Buddhist," Frederik replied and glanced at me. "At least I think I am."

"I'm very interested in Buddhism. Do you practice zazen?"

Frederik nodded, and Dr. Maschke couldn't take his eyes off him. He looked at him as rapturously as Mr. Rödder had looked at the saddlebag.

I stared at Dr. Maschke. He had reddish hair and a short reddish beard. He wore wire-rimmed glasses and was about the same age as my father.

"My name is Maschke," he said to me, giving my hand a cursory shake. He wanted to turn back to Frederik, but his gaze lingered on my face. "You remind me of someone."

"Of my father," I said.

"Unbelievable! You're Peter's daughter! You look exactly like him. How nice to meet you."

Alaska was overjoyed, probably because he had been Dr. Maschke's idea.

"Alaska was Dr. Maschke's idea," I explained to Frederik. "So was the trip around the world."

"No, the opposite is true," Dr. Maschke objected. "I repeatedly tried to talk him out of it. I urged him to stay home with you." He turned back to Frederik. "But tell me . . . I have a question about Yogācāra Buddhism."

"But that's simply not right," I said indignantly, "it was all your idea." I realized, as I was speaking, that there wasn't the slightest proof that Dr. Maschke had sent my father around the world. Selma and I had just assumed it to be the case, and the opposite could well be the case.

"Then shoot," Frederik said.

Dr. Maschke cleared his throat. "To be more precise, I have a question about the eight vijñānas."

"What's going on with Alaska?" I asked, because he was still overjoyed at seeing Dr. Maschke.

"We spent a lovely day together," Dr. Maschke said, giving Alaska a creaking and absentminded pat on the head. "My question, in fact, is about ālayavijñāna."

"Storehouse consciousness," Frederik said.

"Exactly." Dr. Maschke beamed.

"What do you mean, you had a lovely day together?" I asked.

"Alaska visited me this summer, we spent the entire day together."

I thought of the day Alaska had disappeared and Frederik had appeared.

"He was with *you*?"

Frederik looked at me. "So that was Alaska's adventure. You look pale. Are you all right?"

I was pale because you always change colors when the opposite is suddenly the case. "Why did he run to you, of all people?"

"Because he missed Peter, I assume," Dr. Maschke said. "And I'm very close to your father. Animals can sense that kind of thing."

"I'm very close to my father, too," I retorted.

"Yes, but you know, psychoanalysis brings a different kind of closeness."

Frederik laid his hand on my back. "Go away," I thought fervently in Dr. Maschke's direction.

"Unfortunately, I have to go now," Frederik said to him.

"But about ālayavijñāna . . ." Dr. Maschke said. "When does your flight leave? Mine's not for a half an hour yet."

I elbowed Frederik discreetly in the ribs. He looked at

me. "Before my flight I need to instruct Luisa in the noble truths. If you know what I mean."

Naturally Dr. Maschke knew what he meant. "It's an honor for me to meet a pro like you. It's marvelous that you've decided to follow this path."

"Now pull yourself together," I said, pretending I was talking to Alaska, who was still fawning over Dr. Maschke and pulling hard on his leash in the direction the doctor was disappearing.

We watched him go. "The opposite is true," I said softly. "I can't believe it."

We ran to security, through which only Frederik could go. Dr. Maschke and storehouse consciousness had stolen a lot of our time. We only had a few minutes left.

"You know what," Frederik suggested, "when the opposite is true, it may apply in a few other cases as well."

"For example?"

"Maybe you were made to travel the seven seas."

"Thanks again for the bookshelf," I said.

And Frederik replied, "Breathe, Luisa."

"Where, again?"

"Into your belly."

"Speaking of which," I said, pulling a bag out of my purse. I'd packed a lot of peanuts.

"Thanks," Frederik said.

He rubbed a hand over his head as if he'd forgotten he had no hair.

"I know there are a lot of open questions, Luisa."

I couldn't see Frederik's open questions. Mine lay at my feet like dangerous spots outlined in red. *Where do we go from here?* was one of them, for example. *What do we do now?* was another.

"I don't have any answers right now," he said. "Unless you'd like to ask me about Yogācāra Buddhism."

He smiled and took my face in his hands.

"You're all blurry again, Luisa."

I wanted to tell him that I wasn't remotely made to travel the seven seas, no matter how many opposites were true, but instead was mostly made for him. However, that, too, was outlined in red.

"You have to go now," I said.

"Yes."

"Go on."

"First, you'd have to let go of my hand," Frederik said, and I let go.

"Now you can," I said, and Frederik walked through the glass door. It shut behind him before I had a chance to stick my foot in it, which is impossible anyway when you're made of ninety-nine percent water.

Frederik hurried on, and I tightened my grip on Alaska's leash because he was pulling on it again. Frederik turned and waved. His face suddenly filled with a look of astonishment. He was looking just over my head as if a storm front had built up behind me. I turned around. Dr. Maschke was standing right behind me.

"He'll be back," he announced, as if he were a celebrated scientist revealing a sensational discovery to the world. He said it so solemnly that for a moment I was unsure if he was, in fact, talking about Frederik or someone else for whom a return was anatomically impossible, like my grandfather or Martin.

"Go away," I said. I'd never said this to anyone and

thought of Marlies, who never said anything else from morning to night.

Dr. Maschke gave me a soothing smile.

"Express your anger freely," he said. "Self-actualization is impossible without experiencing anger."

"Go away and stop getting on everyone's nerves with your creaky leather jacket," I said.

And it worked.

For 140 marks, Alaska and I took a cab back to town, straight to the bookstore. I paid the driver—it was the most expensive day of my life. I thought of the bailiff who had gone to Farmer Leidig's house, put seals on everything he owned, and announced: "None of this belongs to you anymore."

SEE ABOVE

The well-planned Christmas party in the community center took place in the afternoon and without the slightest turbulence. Palm had remained silent almost the entire time despite the many Bible quotations that would have been fitting. The entire afternoon he had only said two words: "To Martin."

At the end of every Christmas party in the community center, the optician raised his glass. "To Martin," the entire village said in chorus, and looked up at the wood-paneled ceiling. High above, Martin sat on a cloud in heaven, within earshot of the Lord, waving at us. That was how Palm, who toasted with currant juice instead of wine, had explained it to us.

Afterward, the optician, Palm, and Elsbeth came over to Selma's. My mother had decorated the entire apartment with wreaths and branches. It smelled like the forest. We'd tried everything, but the Christmas tree would not stand straight. So the optician put on gardening gloves and held it tight. As long as we sang, he gripped the tree just beneath its peak with his arm outstretched, as if he were holding a newly apprehended criminal who was a flight risk.

We sang "Oh How Joyfully." Palm had requested it and sang, his voice loud and deep, of a world that was lost. My father was on the phone from Bangladesh. The receiver lay next to us on the coffee table and he sang along.

When we had finished singing, blown out the candles, and propped the Christmas tree against the wall, the optician suddenly announced, "I have something to tell you. I can't keep it to myself any longer."

Selma had just pulled the roast out of the oven, Elsbeth was carrying six plates to the table, my mother and I, on the couch with Palm, were about to toast each other with Selma's eggnog. We all froze as if a spell had been cast on us. Now, we thought, he's finally going to reveal what we've always known.

Selma stood rooted to the spot, holding the roast, and looked as if she regretted having stepped clean over the area outlined in red instead of stepping right in the middle of it and sinking through the floor.

The optician went up to Palm, who stared at him, eyes wide.

"Me?" he asked.

"Yes, you."

Palm stood up. Apparently we could move again.

"Werner Palm," the optician said, his hands trembling, "I sawed the posts of your hunting blind. I wanted to kill you. I'm terribly sorry."

Selma exhaled; the whole of her thin body was one exhalation.

"But nothing happened," Elsbeth quickly interjected. She still had all the plates in her hands. "And that was twelve years ago."

"Still." The optician looked at Palm. "I ask for your forgiveness."

The optician was shaking. We hadn't known what a heavy burden he had been carrying.

Palm looked up at the optician. He squinted as if trying to decipher him.

"It doesn't matter," Palm said. "I even understand."

Now the optician exhaled. Now the whole of his tall, thin body was one exhalation. Even though it wasn't allowed, he was about to hug Palm, but Palm raised his hands and said, "I have something to tell you all, too."

Selma set the Christmas roast on the windowsill.

"That is, I have something to tell *you*, Selma."

He clasped his hands behind his back. The rest of us, still anticipating a declaration of love, briefly wondered if love would suddenly be launched at Selma from an entirely unexpected direction, if it were ultimately revealed that Palm secretly loved her, and what Selma would do if Palm declared his love for her. After all, since Martin's death, Selma had been unable to refuse him anything, except the deer.

I put my eggnog on the coffee table and took my mother's hand.

"I wanted to murder you, Selma," Palm said softly, looking at his feet in his Sunday shoes. "For Martin's death." He looked up briefly. "Because of your dreams. I thought that would be the end of it and no one else would die."

We all stared at Selma. We couldn't tell if she would let it pass or if she would suddenly deny him everything, all her affection and all his explications. It was clear that that's what Palm expected.

She let it pass.

"You didn't do it," she said, and went over to Palm.

"I'd loaded the gun," he whispered.

Selma wanted to stroke his shoulder, but since that wasn't possible, she stroked the air a few centimeters above his shoulder.

"It was nice of you not to shoot me."

"I was so stupid," Palm said with a sob. "Only God is immortal."

"The roast is getting cold," Selma said. "Any more attempted murders, or should we eat?"

"By all means, let's eat," my mother said. "By the way, Peter's still on the line."

"Oh God," Selma cried, and ran to the phone.

"I didn't understand a thing, the connection's so bad," my father said. "Are you done singing?"

"Yes," Selma replied, "everyone's done singing."

Later that evening, I went out for a walk with Alaska and took a piece of the roast, wrapped in tinfoil, to Marlies's house. Before, she used to join us at least on holidays, but now she refused to come at all.

The night was very clear and very cold.

"Look how beautiful it is here," I said to Alaska, "a symphony of clarity, cold, and darkness."

Friedhelm waltzed past, softly singing "Every Year Again." He tipped his hat and I nodded at him. I wondered if the shot my father had given him for his panic attack twelve years ago was a depot injection that gradually released happiness and satisfaction over the decades.

Because Marlies wouldn't open the front door anyway, I went right around the house to the kitchen window she always left ajar.

"Happy holidays, Marlies," I said. "Here's some of the roast. It's excellent."

"I don't want it. Go away."

I leaned against the wall next to the window.

"You missed something tonight," I said. "Palm almost murdered Selma, and the optician almost murdered Palm."

There was the noise of a kitchen chair being pushed back.

"What?" Marlies asked.

"That is, not tonight, but a while back."

Marlies said nothing.

"Do you remember my visitor from Japan?" I asked. "From a few weeks ago. I haven't heard a thing."

Marlies said nothing.

"I'll have to come to terms with it," I said. "Oh, and by the way, I passed my trial period. Even though you complained so much."

"Your recommendations are shit," Marlies said.

"That's probably why I haven't heard a thing from Japan," I said.

I put the slice of roast on the windowsill. The tinfoil glistened like moonlight reflected in a bowl.

In January, the optician, Selma, and I drove to the doctor's office in the county seat. Selma's joints were becoming increasingly deformed and, in order to verify what everyone could already see, her hands, her feet, and her knees were put in an X-ray machine, one after the other. She had to hold still, which she did with her eyes closed, not opening them even when someone came in now and again to rearrange her limbs for the next image. Selma sat there and looked at the black-and-white afterimage on the inside of her eyelids.

She saw Heinrich with a frozen smile, turning to wave one very last time. Meanwhile, the X-ray machine took grayish-white pictures of Selma's frozen body, and Selma, looking at Heinrich, tried not to twitch when the machine took the images.

The optician and I sat outside the X-ray room.

"A letter from the other end of the world takes time. He'll be in touch," the optician was saying when Selma appeared, holding something that looked like a cross between a shoe-horn and a fork.

"Look what they gave me," she said happily.

Lately, it had become difficult for Selma to raise her arm to touch her head, and what she had in her hand was a long-handled comb.

"Besides, *you* could write, too," Selma said later in the opti-cian's car. And because she was right, I told Mr. Rödder the next day that I was going to tidy up the back room. Mr. Röd-der nodded, and I leaned against the door, climbed over all the broken objects, sat down at the folding table, opened a bottle of hazelnut liqueur a customer had given us, drank half a coffee cup's worth for courage, and wrote Frederik a letter.

I wrote that the letter I was sure he'd written had unfor-tunately not arrived yet. Then I explained in many, many sentences why it was, in fact, impossible for a letter from Ja-pan to ever make it all the way to the Westerwald, given all the pitfalls and all the conceivable human errors that would plague such a letter on its voyage. Surely, I wrote, Frederik's letter from the summer was the only one ever to have made it all the way here from Japan.

Then, after drinking a third half coffee cup of hazelnut

liqueur, I started in with *never* and *always*. I wrote Frederik that he had upended my entire life and that I'd loved him from the moment I saw him and that nothing could ever get in the way of my love. I wrote that Buddhism is not very well thought out because it's perfectly clear that things disappear even when we aren't trying to see them, which is proven by the fact that for several weeks now I hadn't been trying to see him, but he had still disappeared completely. Because of the hazelnut liqueur, this sentence struck me as exceptionally lucid. I wrote, "Selma, Elsbeth, and the optician also send their very best, of course." I wrote that yesterday the optician had yet again resolved to reinforce the weak spots in Selma's floor with Palm's help. "This is an impossible state of affairs," the optician said, even though it had been possible for years. I wrote that Frederik not writing was also an impossible state of affairs, and moreover, I wrote that perhaps the opposite was true and he may well have already written seven letters, not one of which, unfortunately, had arrived because of the above.

I screwed the top back on the bottle of liqueur, put it under the table, and slipped four violet pastilles into my mouth. Mr. Rödder had hidden small stashes of violet pastilles everywhere, even in the pot of a discarded coffee maker.

I pried open the door and steered clear of Mr. Rödder as he unpacked the new releases. At the counter, I found a book of stamps. I had no idea how much the postage for a letter to Japan cost, so for good measure I covered the entire envelope with stamps.

The optician entered the bookstore. He had only come to pick me up, but still he held up a book on home repair I had ostensibly recommended to him and which had changed his life.

"Yes, fine, I get it," Mr. Rödder called from the back of the store.

"You're completely disheveled," the optician said when we were in the car. "Have you been drinking? You smell like, I don't know, like violet liqueur."

"Stop at the mailbox," I said as we drove into the village. "I've written to Frederik."

"Just now? In your condition?"

"Absolutely."

"Maybe you should sleep on it," the optician suggested, "or show it to Selma first."

We always showed important letters to Selma before sending them. When the optician had to send payment reminders to his customers, he always showed them to Selma and asked, "Is it too brusque?"

"It's much too nice," Selma replied in most cases.

"Nonsense," I said, "I'm mailing it now. Enough with the careful precautions already."

I put my arm over the optician's shoulders like a self-important driving instructor.

"Spontaneity and authenticity are the alpha and the omega," I said, and realized too late that I should have chosen two words that were easy to pronounce even after hazelnut liqueur.

Then I got out of the car and mailed the letter.

At seven o'clock the next morning, I was standing next to the mailbox. The mailman opened the emptying flap and attached his mailbag under it.

"Please give me my letter back," I said.

The old mailman had retired the year before. The new one was one of the twins from the upper village.

"Nah," he said.

I had already waited a half hour next to the mailbox. I was cold and had a headache. I imagined how nice it would be to have Palm's rifle at hand. "Hand it over, jackass," I'd say, pointing the gun at him, "I'm the one who calls the shots."

"Please," I said.

The mailman grinned. Little puffs of mist came from his mouth. "What's in it for me?"

"Everything I have."

"And that is?"

I pulled out my wallet. "Ten marks."

The mailman plucked the bill from my hand and shoved it in his pocket. He opened the bag and held it out. "Help yourself."

I bent over the bag. It was much too large and much too deep for the few letters it held. I rummaged in it with clammy fingers.

"Happy New Year, Luisy," the mailman said.

The next morning, there was a letter from Frederik in my mailbox. It was a blue airmail envelope. I held it up to the hall lamp. This time the letter was written on thicker paper and you couldn't make out any of the writing. The words were blurred like the letters on the display panel in the airport when the flights are updating.

Dear Luisa,

Please forgive me for not writing earlier. I had so much
to do (that's probably hard to imagine, but it's true).
At this time of year, there are always a lot of guests for
whom I'm responsible. I explain everything to them.
How to eat in the monastery, how to sit, how to walk,
when to be silent, and how long to sleep. When guests
come to the monastery, they have to learn everything
anew. Like after a serious accident.

I've thought about you a lot. It was so nice to be with
you. Stressful, too. I'm not used to being with so many
people for that long. There's not much talking here on
the other side of the world.

And as you can imagine, I'm also not used to being
so close to anyone as I was with you.

Being close is a tricky thing. You're a mystery to me,
Luisa. Sometimes you seem very forward and stick your
foot in a door that is trying to close. Other times you
seem very blurry. In those moments, I have the feeling
that you're behind a fogged-up pane of glass, and I can
only guess at what's hiding on the other side.

When I was with you, with you and your family, I
kept falling in love with you, at least with what I could
see of you (see above, pane of glass).

But this infatuation has to be transformed because,
Luisa, we aren't made to be together. I've chosen this life
at the end of a long process for which I had to summon
all my courage.

And as unromantic as it may sound: I don't want
to confuse everything. It's very important for me that
everything be in its place.

And my place is here, without you.

I don't know what you think about all this, that is,
about us. Can you affirm the fact that we're not made
for each other?

Yours,
Frederik

I held only this letter in my hand, but when I opened the
front door and walked slowly into the bookstore, it felt like I
was carrying a very heavy suitcase.

Behind a pane of glass, I thought. Field, meadow. Crazy
Hassel's farmhouse. Pasture, forest. Forest. Hunting blind
one. Field. Forest. Pasture. Meadow, meadow.

I carried the letter around all day. I carried it out of the
bookstore and along the main street, where I'd agreed to
meet the optician in front of the gift shop. Because the only
things I could see were Frederik's words, I ran right into
Dr. Maschke, who was suddenly standing in front of me on
the sidewalk.

"Oops," he said. "How nice it is to see you."

He put his hands on his hips and examined me as if he
had just fabricated me.

"It's unbelievable, you're the spitting image of your
father."

I looked over at the gift shop. The optician was already
waiting for me. Smoke wafted up from behind the postcard
display rack.

Dr. Maschke started listing all the questions he wanted
to ask Frederik. He talked about "non-action" and "non-

attachment" and "not one" and "not two." This place is swarming with negatives, I thought, hardly listening to Dr. Maschke. I felt like I really was behind a fogged-up pane of glass and was amazed there hadn't been a clinking sound when I bumped into him.

I repeated several times that I had to get going, but Dr. Maschke kept talking. He talked and talked, until Marlies suddenly appeared at the corner.

"What are you doing here?" I asked. "Did you have another complaint?"

Although it wasn't very cold, Marlies wore a cap pulled down low over her forehead, and a scarf covered the lower half of her still-youthful face.

I wondered what it was that preserved Marlies so well. Maybe she didn't age because all her days were exactly the same, so time thought it should leave her face untouched.

She was carrying an elongated package, which she pointed at Dr. Maschke like a rifle. "I bought a bar lock for my door."

"You already have one," I said.

Marlies had four locks on her door already. I asked myself how one door could have so many locks. I thought of Frederik's letter, and a door collapsing under the weight of its locks struck me as such a sad image—I almost started to cry.

"You can never have enough locks," Marlies said. "And now I'm going home."

Dr. Maschke was fascinated by Marlies, as if she were a masked beauty.

"Do that," he said to her. "Blaise Pascal once said: *All of humanity's misfortune stems from one thing: not knowing how to sit quietly in a room*."

Marlies squeezed the package under her arm and smiled.

Not once in my entire life had I seen her smile. I didn't even know that it was anatomically possible.

"That's right," Marlies said. Not once in her life had she said that something was right.

"I've got to go, too," I said.

Dr. Maschke held me by the sleeve. His leather jacket creaked.

"Speaking of staying at home, do you know why your father is always traveling?"

I looked over at the postcard display rack, behind which the optician had lit another cigarette.

"Are you allowed to speak about your patients with people you don't know? Isn't that forbidden?"

"I consider your father more of a friend than a patient," Dr. Maschke replied. "But far be it from me to impose my insights on you." It wasn't so far after all, though, because he pushed his wire-rimmed glasses up on his nose and continued undeterred. "He's always traveling because he's searching for his own father."

"Hunh?" Marlies said. "But he's dead."

"Which is very practical," Dr. Maschke said. "That way he can be searched for everywhere."

He looked at us the way Martin used to look at me when he was waiting for applause after pretending to be a world champion weight lifter.

Behind the postcard rack on the other side of the street, the smoking stopped and the optician's foot appeared, crushing a cigarette butt.

"I really have to go," I said. "Would you like a ride, Marlies?"

"That'll be the day," she said. She shouldered her package and walked off.

"Could you give me your Buddhist's address?" Dr. Maschke asked.

"That'll be the day," I said, and ran across the street with my letter and fell into the optician's arms.

Late in the evening Selma, Elsbeth, the optician, and I sat on the front stoop. We had spread the blanket from Selma's sofa on the steps. The optician had read that there would be an especially high number of falling stars tonight.

Selma, the optician, and Elsbeth had put on their glasses and bent their heads together over Frederik's letter for a long time, as if it were difficult to decipher.

"I don't want to affirm anything of the sort," I said. "That's just stupid. And I can't transform it, either. What on earth is he thinking?"

The optician stood up and grabbed one of his books on Buddhism from the kitchen; he hoped to find guidance in it for situations where affirmation is withheld.

He put on his glasses, leafed through the book, then read aloud: *In life, one thing is important: establishing intimacy with the world.*

"Intimacy with the world," he repeated, "isn't that beautiful?" He underlined the sentence again, even though it was already underlined.

Elsbeth stuck a Mon Chéri in her mouth.

"We could try tricking him into love," she said, because she figured that since love can't be transformed, then we'd have to transform Frederik. "There are a lot of ways to do it. For example, fingernail scraps stirred into his glass of wine will make whoever drinks it absolutely mad with love. You get the same effect by secretly mixing a rooster's tongue into his food. Or by hanging a chain of owl bones around his neck." Elsbeth pondered. "It might work with canary bones, too. I think Piepsi would understand."

Elsbeth's canary, Piepsi, had died that morning.

"Or"—Elsbeth took another Mon Chéri—"you could give Frederik a piece of bread you've found. Then he'll lose his memory. He'll forget that he doesn't want to confuse everything."

I imagined tricking Frederik into love the way we tricked Alaska by hiding his medicine in a ball of liverwurst.

"You could carry some verbena dug up with a silver spoon," Elsbeth suddenly remembered, "then everyone will love you—including a specific person."

She looked at the many crinkled, dusky pink wrappers on her lap.

"The problem, of course, is that he needs to be here for all these to work. But we can manage that, too. If you put three brooms in the oven, you'll have visitors. That is: specific visitors, too."

"A shooting star," Selma said, and we looked up.

"All that about shooting stars is nonsense, by the way," Elsbeth said. "They're no help at all."

"I think there's only one thing to do," Selma said. "Whether or not you're willing to affirm it, you'll still have to tell him goodbye."

The optician cleared his throat. "Frankly, I don't think we've heard the last of this matter," he murmured.

"And we all love him," Elsbeth added.

"True, but nevertheless," Selma said.

"Did you know," the optician asked, looking at his book, "that we're all just ephemeral protrusions in time?"

"What does that have to do with this?" Elsbeth asked, putting all the wrappers in an empty flowerpot.

Then no one said anything. We sat in silence, looking up at the sky, in which five more useless shooting stars fell toward us.

Only Elsbeth was not looking up. She looked at me and saw that tears were filling my eyes again because of the stupid affirmation, because of the unimaginable transformation.

We can do all sorts of things with love. We can hide it more or less well, we can drag it behind us, we can lift it over our heads, we can bury it in the ground and send it up to heaven. And love always cooperates, forbearing and amenable as it is. But we cannot change it.

Elsbeth gently swept a lock of hair from my forehead. She put her arm around my shoulder and softly said, "If you eat a bat's heart, you'll no longer feel pain."

Then she stood up.

"I have to go. I've got to leave for town very early."

Plump & Chic's clearance sale was starting the next day.

"See you tomorrow," we said as Elsbeth, an ephemeral protrusion in time wearing worn-down pumps, turned and left.

"Maybe I can find a rooster tongue," we heard her murmur.

Selma stroked my back. "You should probably cut and run, Luisa."

Selma and the optician looked at each other over my head. They were well versed in the unchangeable nature of love.

NO NEW INFORMATION

All night I found it impossible to give my affirmation and I wondered how one cuts and runs. The next morning, in the bookstore, I was still wondering how exactly you cut and run even as I alphabetized the special-order books by customer name. Mr. Rödder tapped me on the shoulder. "Since when does *F* come before *A*?" he asked. Then the front door was thrown open and the optician rushed in.

"Elsbeth has had an accident," he said.

Time stopped for a moment after he said this, and then it began racing. It raced alongside us as Selma, the optician, and I drove to the county hospital. Then it braked and passed infinitely slowly as we sat in the hospital corridor and waited with beige-colored coffee cups not one of us could hold straight.

Doctors came and went constantly. Their footsteps on the linoleum sounded like a child's hiccups. Again and again the three of us jumped up, and each time we were told there was no new information.

"Incidentally, I didn't dream of anything at all last night," Selma said, answering the question the optician and I had been avoiding for hours. I thought, It can't be all that serious, and tried to believe it. This wasn't easy, because Elsbeth had been hit by a bus, the county seat's public bus. How could it not be all that serious?

The frantic bus driver had said that Elsbeth appeared out of nowhere, right in front of the bus, which was going at full speed. Bystanders said she'd just walked into the street without looking to her left or right, completely focused on a piece of paper she was holding. One of the bystanders had picked up the piece of paper, which had fluttered onto the asphalt far from Elsbeth. It was a list, written in Elsbeth's shaky handwriting.

> Wine
> Ask Häubels re rooster tongue
> Boil Piepsi's bones
> Verbena
> Bat heart
> Brooms

When night fell and there was still no new information, the optician stood up.

"I'm going to call Palm," he said abruptly and decisively, as if he had just realized that Palm was a celebrated doctor.

Selma gave him a questioning look.

"So he can pray for Elsbeth?"

"No," the optician said, "because he knows about animals."

After the call, Palm got right into his car. He drove a long way, to the large, weather-beaten fortress he had visited a few times with Martin, on the few days he hadn't been drunk.

And while Selma and I clutched our mugs and the optician smoked one cigarette after another in front of the hospital door, Palm parked his car, took his flashlight from the trunk, and shoved it in under his belt. Palm's lights were always good, he knew about illumination.

He looked for an unlocked door but couldn't find one. The low door on the back of the tower looked very weatherbeaten, but its padlock was sturdy. Palm started to shake the door.

After Martin's death, Palm was drained of his rage and, with it, his strength, because the two always went together in Palm. He looked around and cleared his throat.

"Please open, door," he said, and shook it, but the door was a good one that could not be so easily shaken, despite its worn-down appearance. "Is this the best you can do?," it seemed to be taunting him. "It's going to take more than this, you feeble hunter." Palm started to shake the door harder and harder. He shook the door like a *Tatort* detective gone mad shaking the shoulder of a criminal who won't reveal where he hid his kidnapping victim. Palm became heated.

"Open up, you goddamn piece of shit," he croaked more than shouted; his voice was no longer used to being loud. "Or I'll blow you away," he added for good measure.

The padlock held, but the door burst in two.

Palm exhaled and wiped his forehead with his sleeve.
He turned on his flashlight, stepped over what was left of
the door, and climbed the flight of stairs that led all the way
to the top of the tower. He reached into his pants pocket to
make sure he'd brought the sharpest knife he owned.

We were still waiting as Palm ran up the hospital corridor
toward us an hour later. At the same time a doctor came toward us from the other direction. He was in no hurry, walking slowly to gain time before it abruptly stood still.

The winded Palm and the unhurried doctor reached us
simultaneously. Selma, the optician, and I stood up, because
an invisible person said, "Please rise."

"She didn't make it," the doctor said.

Selma put her hand over her mouth, the optician fell back
into his chair and buried his face in his hands, and Palm
opened his fist, which we now noticed was covered with
blood.

A small piece of meat fell onto the linoleum. It fell right
in front of the doctor's white shoe, which made a strange
noise, a kind of squeak.

"What in heaven's name is that?" the doctor shouted.
How could he have known: Who recognizes a bat's heart at
first glance?

It was raining on Elsbeth's funeral. It rained as hard as it
had on the day Frederik visited me, and from above, all the
unfurled black umbrellas huddling around Elsbeth's grave
looked like a giant ink blot.

I held Selma's hand in mine. Her shoulders shook with sobs.

"Elsbeth told me that it's good for the person being buried if it rains on the coffin," I whispered into Selma's ear.

Selma looked at me. Her face was swollen and wet. "But not this hard," she said.

The raindrops pelted the ornaments on the coffin lid. Selma had insisted we buy a lavishly decorated model, given that Elsbeth had always cultivated a lavish appearance. When the funeral director had named the price and the optician asked if it wasn't possible to reduce the price somewhat, the funeral director announced triumphantly that one shouldn't haggle over the price of a coffin or the person being buried would never find rest. "I know because Elsbeth told me," he said.

Strictly speaking, Elsbeth's house had not been hers for a long time. It was owned by a bank in the county seat, and now that she was dead, the house had to lose all traces of her as quickly as possible.

My father helped us empty it. He had just returned from some desert and was about to leave for another. Alaska impeded our work because he kept jumping around my father to get him to put down the cartons he was carrying and pet him.

While packing, I found Elsbeth's photo album with black-and-white pictures of young Elsbeth, Heinrich, and Selma. I knew these pictures by heart; Elsbeth had often shown them to Martin and me. One was of Selma and Heinrich pointing to an empty lot on which our house would be built. Martin and I were never able to understand how Elsbeth and Selma had ever been so young or how my grandfather had once been in this world and our house had not.

My mother also helped us, and it was as if my parents had decided to stage a box-carrying competition. If my mother saw my father carrying two boxes at once, she picked up three. If my father saw my mother with three boxes, he lifted four. When my mother finally tried to carry five boxes at once, the top one fell in the garden and burst open. Sunflower-yellow notebooks were scattered on Elsbeth's lawn and one had fallen open.

The shopkeeper set down Elsbeth's iron and picked the notebook up. "*Sex with Renata blows my mind*," he read. "What on earth is this?"

The optician took the notebook from his hand and snapped it shut.

"Nothing," he said, "it's nothing."

He gathered the notebooks into a pile, added some dried leaves, took his lighter from his jacket pocket, and lit it on fire. While the flames licked at the sunflower-yellow covers and the pages filled with writing, the optician looked up at the sky.

"Look, Elsbeth," he whispered. "Renata will soon be just a dusting of ash."

Selma came out of Elsbeth's house. She had kept her composure all day long and, to the extent she could, had impassively helped pack things up and carry them outside. She only lost her composure when putting Elsbeth's slippers, standing under the telephone side table as always, in a plastic bag.

Selma pushed her wheelchair, its seat covered with glass jars full of herbs and powders, the uses of which were a complete mystery to us. Selma thought for a moment and then tipped it all onto the small fire at the optician's feet, all the cures for a broken heart, for constipation, for people who refused to die after their deaths, for toothache, sweaty feet, bankruptcy, and gallstones, all the aids for easy births, for restful sleep, and to make someone fall in love with a person he could not love.

"Without Elsbeth, none of this is any help," she said.

Selma kept Elsbeth's photo album. She kept the piece of carpet Elsbeth always stuck between her stomach and the steering wheel when driving, and her slippers. She put Elsbeth's slippers under the living room sofa, on which I lay awake all night after Elsbeth's funeral.

I turned on the light and picked up one of the slippers. It was impossible to guess what the original color had been. I looked at the landscape that had formed on Elsbeth's slipper over the years. The uneven, furrowed rubber sole, the inner hollows caused by her bunions, the glistening black hollow made by her heel.

I didn't cut and run. I put Elsbeth's slipper back under the sofa, next to the other one. I took a piece of paper and wrote: "I hereby affirm that we are not made for each other." I wrote it as solemnly as other people sign a marriage certificate.

PART THREE

ENDLESS EXPANSES

Ever since my father started traveling, he would give Selma a book of photographs of whatever country he happened to be in for her birthday. Selma no longer shelved these books without looking at them, as she had before; now she studied them carefully. She wanted to form a picture in her mind of what her son was seeing.

After the birthday guests were gone, Selma sat in the armchair with her new book of photographs and the optician settled down on the red couch opposite her. The captions in the books were usually in English, and for that the optician was considered the resident expert—ever since he had translated song lyrics for Martin and me. He watched Selma as she read or he looked at the old fir trees outside the window, their branches swaying in the wind that always blew here. And he waited. He waited until Selma looked at him over the top of her reading glasses and asked about English words she didn't know. He knew them.

On her seventy-second birthday, Selma sat with a book

of photographs of New Zealand on her lap, and it seemed to her that she had just unpacked her last birthday book a few days before.

It's true that time goes faster the older you are, Selma thought, and felt that this wasn't a very good arrangement. Selma wished that her sense of time would grow old with her, that it would develop a limp, but the opposite was true. Selma's sense of time behaved like a racehorse.

"What does *New Zealand's amazing faunal biodiversity* mean?" Selma asked.

"Astonishing variety of animal species," the optician explained.

In the village below, the shopkeeper was moving the cartons of milk from the back shelf on the right to the back shelf on the left. My father came to visit us. He brought shawls of Genoan velvet. I wrote Frederik. Frederik wrote me. One of the mayor's pigs escaped and the optician caught it.

Meanwhile, the trees in the Uhlheck lost the green from their leaves and let them fall. Not much later, the shopkeeper's warehouse roof collapsed under the weight of a heavy snowfall that, heavy as it was, nonetheless melted in an instant, according to Selma's sense of time. Then, in the twinkling of an eye, the trees in the Uhlheck grew new leaves and in the same twinkling of an eye, Selma was celebrating her seventy-third birthday with a book of photographs of Argentina on her lap.

"What does *untamed nature* mean?" she asked.

And the optician replied, "Uncontrolled wilderness."

I wrote Frederik. Frederik wrote me. We wrote each other despite or perhaps even because of my affirmation, and even though our letters had to travel halfway around the world, even though they were prey to all sorts of technical and human error, they dependably arrived at their respective destinations, albeit with a certain delay.

"The twin from the upper village, the one who's the mailman, put newborn cats in a bag and drowned them in the Apfelbach," I wrote Frederik.

Two weeks later his answer arrived. "Drowning cats brings very bad karma."

"Couldn't we talk on the phone sometime?" I asked in a letter, and, as expected, he answered that phone calls were very complicated.

Even though it wasn't anatomically possible, I tried to transform love, at least into something modest and manageable. That, too, was complicated, but because I didn't see Frederik and never spoke with him, it wasn't hard to pretend, with time, that it was manageable.

The optician often asked how things were with Frederik. "We write," I said, and the optician found that wasn't an adequate answer to his question.

"But you love him," he said as I sat on his examination stool for a vision test because my eyes always hurt whenever I read fine print.

"No," I replied, "not anymore."

The vision chart behind the optician fell to the floor. He went into the back room to get another.

"I made this one just for you," he said.

It read:

You cannot always
choose
which
adventure
you're made for

I leaned forward. "I need glasses," I said.

Mr. Rödder sprayed Blue Ocean Breeze on Alaska, Marlies complained to the shopkeeper about the frozen vegetables, and my father came to visit. He looked more and more like Heinrich. Little by little my father's facial features had started to shift like a landmass slowly sliding toward his father's face.

"How strange," he said, grabbing his nose, "and yet I'm much older than he ever was."

On my twenty-fifth birthday, when the candles stood close together on my cake, the optician said, "Happy birthday. Be glad that they all still fit on one cake. For me, we'd need half the bakery."

"Close your eyes," Selma said. She put a chain of blue gemstones around my neck.

"The stones are cyan blue, by the way," the optician said.

"Thank you," I said.

"Happy birthday, dear Luisa," Frederik wrote. "I have the feeling that someone who hopefully means well has seated us at opposite ends of the same table. However, it's a table that is 9,000 kilometers long (with those dimensions I think we could call it a banquet table) and although we can't see each other, I know you're at the other end."

The optician looked at me steadily. "The stones are *cyan blue*," he repeated.

"Yes, thanks, I got it," I said.

"What does *the impressive Greenland ice deposits* mean?" Selma asked on her next birthday, and the optician translated it for her.

Palm quoted Bible passages, the optician thought up connections between things that had nothing to do with each other (gravel and hairdos, orange juice and Alaska), and Marlies covered the already opaque window in her front door with packing paper. I moved the still-unpacked bookshelf Frederik had given me four years earlier from one corner of the room to the other. The mayor's daughter and Farmer Häubel's great-grandson had their sixth child, and I got my first pair of glasses. Then came a total solar eclipse.

The optician had never had so many customers in his life. People came from the county seat and the surrounding villages, where the solar eclipse glasses had sold out immediately. I helped the optician at his store; he had bright red cheeks and a hoarse voice from so many customers. The twin from the upper village, the one who was not the mailman, tried to resell his pair for eighty marks, but no one was interested.

We watched the eclipse from the Uhlheck. The entire village was there; the mayor took a group photograph. When the sun was completely blacked out, Palm took off his glasses and looked directly at the circular blackness unprotected. "What are you doing?" Selma cried in alarm, and put her hand over Palm's eyes.

"The glasses don't let any light through," Palm objected.

"That's the whole point," Selma explained, but because

her fingers were so crooked, Palm could see through them. Then time shifted to a new millennium.

"To think I lived long enough to witness this," Selma said. "But if time keeps racing this fast, I may well see the next millennium."

"I worry that gravity will disappear with the change to the new millennium," I wrote to Frederik.

We celebrated the new year in the community center. The optician and the shopkeeper spent the entire evening setting off fireworks; from above, our village looked like a ship in distress. Behind the building, near the toilets, I drunkenly kissed the drunken twin from the upper village, the one who was the mailman. I kissed him despite his bad karma and because everything was spinning from the sparkling wine, but I stopped as soon as he said, "Luisa, you're as hot as a Roman candle."

Gravity did not disappear. Nothing changed except for the actor who had played Melissa in Selma's television series for decades was suddenly replaced by another. Selma acknowledged this with an irritated snort. Then she looked at me and said, "Something has to happen."

"What?"

"Go out with that nice young man sometime, the one from your trade school. What's his name again?"

"Andreas," I said.

Selma asked the optician what *enormous population density* meant, and he translated it for her. It was in a book about New York. The optician bought heat patches for his lower back. The deliveryman pushed his gray-covered cart to the shop door and my father came to visit. He brought me a scimitar, which I gave to Mr. Rödder as a gift. The twin from the upper village, the one who was not the mailman, set crazy Hassel's farmhouse on fire and didn't get caught, and Selma and I stood looking at a tree on the bank of the Apfelbach and wondered if Elsbeth was right about ivy on a tree trunk actually being a person climbing toward redemption and, if so, who it was. The optician said it was a shame we didn't know anyone who was a stamp collector, since we had so many marvelous stamps we'd received with the photography books sent from all over the world and the letters from Japan.

I taught the Häubel children how to tie their shoes on our front steps, Friedhelm married the widow from the House of Contemplation, and on his express wish we all sang, *Oh, you lovely Westerwald*, in front of the registry office—at the wedding the twin from the upper village, the one who was the mailman, asked if I wanted to kiss some more, since he was unattached at the moment—and that winter Palm made a discovery. He was on his way to Selma's with some Bible passages when he saw her gripping my arm tightly, trying in vain to make her way down the snow-covered slope in front of her house without constantly coming close to falling. Palm watched her, thought for a while, and went home. That evening he came back with two vegetable graters. He tied them to the soles of Selma's winter boots with florist's wire.

"Brilliant, Palm," we said.

"Brilliant," Frederik wrote two weeks later, and we almost slapped Palm on the back, but that wasn't allowed.

"Endless expanses," the optician said when Selma asked him, a book of photographs of Australia open on her lap, what *vastness* meant.

Selma pushed her wheelchair over the Uhlheck, Marlies complained about a book recommendation, Palm quoted Bible passages, and the optician tentatively asked if they hadn't already gotten through the entire Bible. "A long time ago," Palm said, "but each passage can be interpreted a thousand different ways," and one night the twin from the upper village, the one who wasn't the mailman, broke into the bookstore.

He hadn't counted on Mr. Rödder still being there, on his knees under the counter trying to hook up a modem. Unnoticed, Mr. Rödder scrambled on all fours to the travel section and held down the twin from the upper village until the police arrived. From then on, Mr. Rödder was much more even-keeled. Even his eyebrows, once in a constant state of agitation, calmed down. Mr. Rödder grumbled less. He no longer sidled between the shelves but strode proudly, conscious of having performed an important act.

"There's always something going on in your village," Frederik wrote, and I wrote back asking if perhaps he didn't have an email address so we could reach each other more quickly, since everything took so long this way. Frederik responded, with a delay, that naturally he wasn't on email and: "By the way, I'm happy gravity is still here. And that we are, too."

My mother, who had started writing poetry, won second place in the local newspaper's poetry competition, and Palm's hunting blind collapsed without him in it. Surprisingly, it was the posts the optician hadn't taken a saw to that had crumbled. The posts he had sawn lasted forever because he and Elsbeth had repaired them so well.

The optician gave the Häubels' third child a stamp collection album, and the mayor died; his heart stopped just as he was trying to attach the wreath to the maypole and he fell from the ladder stone-dead. "Please don't tell me you dreamed of an okapi," the mayor's wife said to Selma, and Selma said nothing.

"What are *enchanting oasis towns*?" Selma asked with a book of photographs of Egypt on her lap, and the optician translated it for her.

Friedhelm sang when he walked through the village and tipped his hat to everyone he met. The optician stuck his head into his perimeter and signaled to the dots that he had seen them. My father came to visit and brought me a glossy poster of a Venetian gondola that was so ugly I wondered if maybe he'd bought it at the gift shop and not in Venice. Mr. Rödder gave an interview to the local newspaper. Over a bowl of Flaming Temptation in the ice-cream parlor he spoke about heroism. And I went out with Andreas from the vocational school so that Selma would finally leave me in peace. Afterward Andreas came up to my apartment and, because I hadn't counted on that and hadn't cleaned up, all the chairs and the sofa were covered with clothes and news-papers. Andreas was about to sit on the still unpacked book-shelf in the corner. "Stop," I said. "Not there, please."

"Where should I sit, then?" Andreas asked, and I had no idea where he should sit.

Alaska needed a hip operation and the veterinarian warned us that he probably wouldn't survive the procedure for the simple reason that, in theory, he shouldn't even be alive. On the evening before the operation I wrote Frederik, "The opera-tion went well. Alaska made it through the procedure extraor-dinarily well and is very lively." On the day of the operation, my father called every half hour, from Alaska, of all places, to ask if there was any news, and only stopped when we told him we needed to keep the line free for the veterinarian.

Alaska didn't die. Alaska began yet another of his countless lives without dying in between, and after I'd put down a piece of the Christmas roast outside Marlies's door and had turned to leave, I heard rattling as she undid the five locks on her door and opened it a crack.

"What's the name of the guy who said people should sit quietly in their rooms?" she asked.

"Blaise Pascal."

"No, the other one."

"Oh right, Dr. Maschke."

The shopkeeper bought a coffee dispenser and wrote COFFEE TO GO on a paper plate and hung it on the front door of the shop, but he soon took it down again because no one wanted a coffee to go. "Where I am supposed to go with a coffee?" the dead mayor's wife asked.

In Selma's television series, Melissa betrayed Matthew with his half brother and Selma would never forgive her; and even though I didn't know where I should put Andreas, he and I became a couple. It just worked out that way. It also happened that right after I'd kissed Andreas for the first time, I wrote to Frederik that I'd met someone who was very nice and whom I'd probably marry, and I was irritated that Frederik, who otherwise reacted to everything I wrote, didn't mention Andreas at all in his next letter. He wrote about the moss on the roof, about work in the fields, about meditation, the guests in the monastery, and only at the very bottom of the last page: "P.S.: Congratulations, by the way."

Everyone thought Andreas was very nice. They also found that we shared the same interests, because Andreas was also a bookseller. Whenever anyone asked how things were with Frederik, I just told them that things hadn't worked out.

"You can't always choose which adventure you're made for," I said.

"That's not how I meant it, Luisa," the optician said.

After one of my father's visits, Mr. Rödder looked at the wall over the travel books for a long time. There was a Buddha mounted on that wall, a Moroccan mask, a necklace with a large Greenlandite pendant, a rug from Lima, a New York license plate, a framed Hard Rock Café Peking T-shirt, the scimitar, a Celtic cross, the saddlebag, a Chilean rainstick, the poster of the Venetian gondola, and a didgeridoo. "We now have more travel decorations than travel books," Mr. Rödder said. He asked if I could imagine taking over the bookstore someday when he was no longer around.

"But you are around," I said, and two weeks later Frederik wrote: "That's a nice offer, but is it what you really want? I think you're actually made to travel the seven seas."

I was on my way to the bookstore when I read that. I ran back to my apartment and wrote Frederik that he was in no position to judge what anyone was made for in life. After all, he had completely withdrawn from real life into a mossy-roofed monastery and from there, talk is cheap. Frederik had started in on my blurriness again in his last letter, so I also wrote that someone who is never around can't judge visibility, either. But as I wrote, I noticed how wrong I was: Frederik and I could see each other very well across the nine thousand kilometers, maybe even better than if we were close up.

"Dear Luisa," Frederik replied, "I'd like to know what real life is in your opinion."

"What does *scenic and craggy* mean?" Selma asked with a photography book about Ireland open on her lap. The optician, who was standing in front of Selma's living room in the dark and could therefore only see himself, translated the words and added, "just like my face."

Selma hung her wash to dry as carefully as if for future generations, Marlies ate peas straight from the can at night when she stood at the window, sure that no one would come to see her, and now and again someone in the village resolved to be more thankful, to take more joy in simple things, or just to be happy to be alive, at least until the next burst pipe or unexpected surcharge.

Because the summer was so hot, the Apfelbach stream dried up. Now that it was dry, the optician spent an entire afternoon jumping over it with the Häubel children, and for my thirtieth birthday, Andreas gave me a gift certificate for a trip to the seaside. He suggested that we take over the bookstore together someday, that we might also move in together, and just as he made that suggestion, lying on my bed, the telephone rang in the hallway. I ran to answer it and although the call came from the other end of the world, there wasn't any static, the connection was crystal-clear.

"It's me," Frederik said. "Happy birthday."

I was hearing his voice for the first time in eight years. I closed my eyes, and on the inside of my eyelids I saw Frederik in black and white in the Uhlheck, standing between other black-and-white monks, his light-colored eyes appearing very dark behind my eyelids. He stood there and said, "My name is Frederik, by the way."

I wasn't prepared for his call, but my blank was. It had been preparing for it for eight long years.

"Thanks," I said, "but this isn't a good time."

Frederik was quiet for a moment. Then he said, "You can't imagine how complicated it is to make a phone call here. At least tell me how you're doing."

"Fine," I said, and then there was silence until Frederik said, "I'm fine, too, thanks. I'm just always hungry."

"That's good," I said, and then Frederik asked how things were with Alexander. "Andreas," I said, and told him I really needed to hang up.

"Don't be so difficult, Luisa, I just wanted to hear your voice."

"Good, very good," my blank said, and I hung up. I lay down next to Andreas and didn't sleep the entire night because Frederik had wanted to hear my voice. Two weeks later he wrote: "Calling is complicated, but not only because of me."

Selma asked the optician, whose face really had become craggy, if it wasn't about time he started thinking about retirement. But there was nothing wrong with the optician, who was almost as old as Selma, that is, almost seventy-seven, aside from a weakness in the muscles of his lower back that rendered them unable to relieve the burden of his disks, and he dismissed the idea energetically. "I will work until the day of my death. That's my preference. You'll see, Selma: I will die with my head in the perimeter." And that was what happened many years later, only Selma was no longer around to see it.

"What does *merciless drought* mean?" Selma asked, holding up a photography book of Namibia. The optician translated the words and added, "as you can see."

The optician was still carrying around the sentence about how something not seen can't disappear, and still no one could explain it. "I'm sorry," Frederik wrote. "Please tell the optician that I don't understand the sentence, either." The shopkeeper asked how things were with Frederik; the optician declared that it really was time to repair the weak spot in Selma's floor properly because it was an impossible state of affairs even though it had been possible for decades, and then he forgot about it again; the widow from the House of Contemplation left Friedhelm because she preferred being a widow after all; the wife of the dead mayor moved in with her daughter in the county seat; and then the Häubels' third child disappeared.

The entire village set out looking for him. We searched in all the houses, the stalls, the barns, and we searched the Uhl-heck. The child was called Martin because he was named after Martin. He was ten years old.

"No," Selma said when we asked about her dreams the previous night. "No, definitely not."

We weren't worried about the usual dangers, but about the most outlandish ones. We were afraid that a door some-where might have opened and the Häubels' child been ripped from life. But three hours later, the boy came home unharmed. He had been hiding in the dead mayor's former cowshed, way in the back next to the discarded milking ma-chine. We'd all passed right by him, and when he heard our collective fear, he hadn't dared come out of his hiding place.

When Andreas gave me a kiss on the forehead one morn-ing before he drove to work, a cursory kiss, like the ones the characters in Selma's series, all of whom by now had been played by multiple actors, gave each other, I told him we had to break up. Andreas put down his backpack and looked at me, not at all surprised, as if he had been expecting it for a long time. "And why?" he asked nevertheless, before listing all the plans he'd made for us. "Why?" he asked again, and because nothing better occurred to me, I said, "Because I'm made to travel the seven seas."

Andreas took from my desk the gift certificate for the trip to the seaside that he'd given me and I still hadn't redeemed.

"You didn't even want to travel to *one* sea," he objected.

Then Andreas left, and I didn't stick my foot in the door as he closed it.

I felt dizzy. I had rarely opposed anything that was happening to me.

While I was considering what to do next, I noticed I was holding a butter knife as I stood in front of the bookshelf that had not been unpacked for eight years. I cut open the packaging. The assembly instructions included twenty-six steps, but I still gave it a try. And while I was assembling the bookshelf, I hought of Frederik's letter in which he'd asked what real life was in my opinion. I thought of Martin and the fogged-up window he had leaned against with his eyes closed in intense concentration, also of the strand of hair on his head that never stayed combed down. I thought of Elsbeth's hydrangea-like swim cap, of Mr. Rödder's breath that smelled of violets, of Selma's old skin that looked like bark. I thought of the table in Alberto's ice-cream parlor at which I'd been rewarded with a small Secret Love the first time I read the sugar packet horoscope aloud by myself. I thought of Alaska and how he lifted his head when he left a room, how he weighed whether it was worth getting up and coming with us, and how he usually decided it was. I thought of the optician, who, all his life, was always ready to help others. I thought of Palm, of Palm's wild eyes when I was young, and of Palm now, how he nodded and said nothing, nodded and said nothing.

I thought of the station clock, under which the optician taught us to tell time and about time zones. I thought about all the time in the world, all the time zones I'd had anything to do with, and of the two watches on my father's wrist. That's real life, I thought, the whole expanse of life, and after the seventh point in the instruction manual, I crumpled it up and kept assembling without it. In the end, I had a bookshelf that stood relatively straight.

On the way to the bookstore, I stopped in the ice-cream parlor. "What'll it be?" Alberto asked.

"I'd like a large Secret Love," I said.

The photography book for Selma's eightieth birthday was one about Iceland, and she didn't ask the optician any questions.

The optician had been glad it was about Iceland because he knew Selma would like it. Iceland was pleasant and the people there believed outlandish things. Elsbeth would have liked it, too.

"You're not asking me about any words," the optician said.

"I'm not reading any," Selma said, and smiled. "I'm much too excited."

Selma had put on lipstick and mascara. Her cheeks were rosy, and she looked incredibly young.

And then, when we heard the first guests outside—the entire village comes to an eightieth birthday party—Selma snapped the book shut.

CHASING AWAY THE DEER

Well?" Mr. Rödder asked after we had squeezed our way through the door into the back room of the shop. "Have you considered it?"

"No, but you're still around," I said.

Mr. Rödder balanced on his tiptoes. "Yes, well," he said, looking at me gravely, "when you saw away at a tree and it falls over, you can't say: 'It will only really be felled once it's lying on the ground.' It's already falling."

"Are you not well?"

"I am valiantly striding toward the age of sixty-five," he murmured. "At that age, you can say you feel the saw."

He was right, but it didn't change the fact that he would go on well past sixty-five. Mr. Rödder would even make it to 101 and would do so valiantly. He would reach such an advanced age the local newspaper would ask him for the secret of his indestructible health, and Mr. Rödder would answer: "I suppose it's the violet pastilles."

"Mr. Rödder," I said, "I need a few days off."

"Visitor from Japan?"

"No, but my grandmother's not very well."

"Oh, of course you can have time off. And please give your grandmother my best, even though we've never met."

A few weeks earlier, Selma had waited for me in her wheelchair in front of the village shop because the ramp had given way under the weight of a detergent delivery. Near her, a bag of rolls sat on the sill of the shop window. Selma didn't know they belonged to the mayor's second wife, who had been so caught up in a discussion with the optician about the advantages and disadvantages of contact lenses that she'd forgotten them. Selma was hungry and her errands were dragging on. She opened the bag, took out a currant bun, tore off a piece, and put the bun quickly back in the bag.

Not long afterward, she started forgetting names. "Remind me the name of Melissa and Matthew's son, the one who got involved in that terrible problem with drugs," she would ask, for example, and if anyone tried to tell her a name, she would call out, "Wait, don't tell me!" because she wanted to remember it on her own. Or because she thought it was enough if someone else could remember the name.

She started forgetting birthdays and doctor's appointments.

"You haven't eaten found bread lately, have you?" I asked her.

"No," Selma said, but then she would have forgotten that, too.

She also lost one of the earrings that Elsbeth had given her for her seventieth birthday, made of two somewhat oversized artificial pearls. When she realized the earring was missing,

Selma started to cry, and didn't stop for half the night. At first I thought she wasn't actually crying over the earring at all, but over the dwindling of her abilities, over Elsbeth and all the other people she had lost in the course of her life. But Selma had no feel for metaphors. She was simply crying over the lost earring.

She started saying peculiar things. "The forest is creeping into me," she said when the optician and I pushed her over the Uhlheck. "You know what? I think the forest is sharing my thoughts."

The optician and I ignored this, as if Selma hadn't spoken, but the forest rustled even louder than usual.

Selma began frequently saying sentences with the words *never* or *always* and said them like someone who had reached the end of her life and could, indeed, form judgments about what had always been and what never had.

"I never really left this house," she said, patting the flank of her home one day when we returned from our walk in the Uhlheck. "I've always liked blackberry jam very much," she said one morning as she spooned some on her toast.

"Isn't it amazing how you live through the anniversary of your death in advance your whole life long?" Selma asked as she copied the dates of birth and death from her old calendar into her new one. "One of the countless twenty-fourths of June or eighths of September or thirds of February that I've lived through will be the date of my death. Isn't that something, when you think about it?"

"Hmm," we replied.

"Do you also ask yourselves occasionally which of your senses goes first when you die?" Selma asked as she tried in vain with her deformed hands to fasten a button that had been hanging only by a thread onto the optician's jacket. "Is it the sense of touch? Or sight? Maybe the first to go is your sense of smell. Or do all senses disappear at the same time?"

"No, we don't ask ourselves that," the optician replied.

When the optician picked me up at the bookstore after work and we drove to the village, Selma suddenly asked from the back seat, "Do you believe your life flashes before your eyes when you die?"

I flinched. I hadn't noticed Selma was in the car.

"I picture it like a slideshow put together by Death," she continued, "but because it can't present your entire life, a selection has to be made. What are the criteria? Which are a life's most important scenes? From Death's point of view, I mean."

"I'm guessing this particular scene won't make the cut," I said. And the optician said, "Please stop with this, Selma."

Selma wanted to talk about death with us, but we wouldn't let her, as if Death were a distant relative we were ignoring because he always behaved badly.

I looked at Selma in the rearview mirror. She smiled. "You're acting like children who believe no one can see them when they cover their eyes," she said.

That night, I slept on Selma's sofa. I woke at three-thirty in the morning and went into her bedroom. Her bed was empty and her comforter on the floor.

I found her in the kitchen. She was sitting at the table in her flowered nightgown. Seven unopened Mon Chéris lay at her feet and she held an eighth in her hands. "I can't unwrap these anymore," she said. "It's like my hands are paralyzed."

I ran to Selma and took her in my arms as awkwardly as you hug someone sitting in a chair. I flung my arms around her thin torso from behind. It looked like I was giving her the Heimlich maneuver.

"Luisa, I believe it will be soon," she said, and I closed my eyes, wishing that ears also had lids you could snap shut. Selma turned to face me, put her hands on my shoulders, and pushed me away a bit so she could see me better.

"Will you affirm the end coming, my dear child?" she asked.

This must be what it feels like when a scimitar is rammed into your stomach, I thought.

Selma stroked my cheeks. I thought of Frederik for a moment.

"You're all crazy," I said, my voice much too loud in Selma's silent, nocturnal kitchen. "You all keep asking me to affirm some nonsense or other."

"Be happy that you're even asked," she replied. "Usually these things are considered valid without any affirmation."

I looked into her eyes and only then recognized that something sinister had played out behind her eyelids.

"You dreamt of an okapi," I whispered.

Selma smiled and put her hand on my forehead as if she were feeling for a fever. "No," she said.

"You're lying to me! Why are you doing that? You don't need to be afraid to say it," I exclaimed, even though I was the one who was afraid.

"I thought for a long time about what I should put in order in my life, and I couldn't come up with anything," she said, patting my knee, "aside from that spot over there, perhaps." She pointed to the red circle outlined on the floor. "But I would have liked to help put your life in order, Luisa."

"My life is in order," I said, and the macramé owl the shopkeeper's wife had given Selma fell at my feet from the wall.

Selma looked at the owl, then back at me. "Do you notice anything?"

"No," I said, and I wasn't lying.

She handed me the Mon Chéri. "Unwrap it," she said.

Just when she'd gone back to bed, about four-thirty in the morning, the doorbell rang. It was the optician. He had a comforter draped over his shoulder and a rolled-up air mattress under his arm. "I have a bad feeling," he said.

The optician lay down next to the sofa. We all slept late, and while we slept, Frederik wrote, "Luisa, please get in touch. I have a bad feeling." But I only read it two weeks later.

The next morning, Selma had a slight fever. Her eyes glittered. I pulled the optician to the door of her room.

"We should call the doctor," I said.

"Out of the question," Selma called from the bedroom. "If you call a doctor, I won't say another word to you."

The optician and I looked at each other.

"Not one word for the rest of my life," Selma shouted, and burst out laughing.

The telephone rang. I hoped it would be my father calling, and it was. "You have to come home," I said. "Selma's not well." It didn't sound right, but I couldn't say: "Selma's doing great, she's just dying."

"I'll catch the next flight," my father said. "I'm in Kinshasa right now."

———

While I was in Selma's apartment on the phone with my father, the phone rang in my apartment. "Please call, Luisa," Frederik said to the answering machine, and the answering machine cut him off. Frederik said: "Making a phone call is very complicated and this damn machine doesn't make it any less compli—" and the answering machine cut him off. "I'm calling because I'm worried," he began, and the answering machine cut him off. A tinny female voice said: "Your connection is maintained, your connection is maintained." With that, Frederik had enough, and the answering machine announced: "End of message, end of message, end of message."

At noon my mother made chicken soup, which Selma had always liked but now didn't want. The shopkeeper brought a plastic bag full of Mon Chéris, each one already unwrapped. But Selma politely declined them, too.

Early that evening I went to the garage, because it was Tuesday and I had to chase away the deer. It was, in fact, standing in the meadow at the edge of the forest, the deer that, after several generations of deer, was no longer the original one. I opened the garage door and slammed it shut. I did it again and again, long after the deer had run away. Suddenly Palm appeared behind me.

"You don't need to worry about the deer," he said.

I slammed the door one last time and looked at Palm, standing there holding a Bible to his chest.

"How is she?" he asked.

"Fine, but I don't think she has much time left. Are you coming?"

Palm followed me to the house but stopped at the doorstep. I turned around. "Come," I said.

But Palm stayed where he was, as if afraid of the weak spots in the floor. He stood there for hours. And no one in the world looked more lost than Palm, standing there in front of the door.

"I'm hot," Selma said. The bedroom window wouldn't stay open. I opened it and propped a photography book against it so it wouldn't swing wide open. It was very windy.

The optician sat on the edge of Selma's bed. He hadn't sat there since he'd told us about blue whales after Martin died.

Nothing in the room had changed since then. The alarm clock in diarrhea-colored imitation leather that ticked too loudly, the quilt and the large flower pattern, the fat lambs in the picture with the carefree shepherd boy, the bronze bedside lamp with a frosted glass shade shaped like a gnome's hat: it was all still there. And again, the optician saw none of it. Again, the room would have been very beautiful in his eyes if he had eyes for anything other than Selma.

"I'd like something to read," she said.

I brought her every possible book and photo album, but not one was right. "What would you like to read?" I asked. "I'll get you whatever you want."

"I don't know," Selma said.

The optician stood up suddenly. "I'll just be a minute."

I followed the optician to the front door to check on Palm, but he was gone. I watched the optician hurry down the slope and wondered if he was going to come back with a bat's heart, but Selma wasn't in pain.

The optician returned carrying two enormous suitcases. I opened the door for him and without a word he carried them past me, down the hall, and through the living room to Selma's bed.

The entire way back to Selma's, his inner voices raged as they hadn't for a very long time, running riot inside the optician. "Are you out of your mind?" the voices screamed as the wind whipped at his hair and banged the suitcases against his shins. They shouted that repression had always worked so well, that fear is a good counselor, that it would all end tragically if the optician finally revealed, at the very last moment, his secret love, never aired for so many decades. "Don't do it," they shouted, panic-stricken. "Don't do it," they shouted again when the optician put the suitcases next to Selma's bed and opened them.

They were full to the brim with paper. The optician smiled at Selma. "It's all here," he said.

Dear Selma, On the occasion of Inge and Dieter's wedding I'd like to finally

Dear Selma, It's amazing how fast Luisa is learning to read. When we were in the ice cream parlor just now and the small Secret Love

Dear Selma, Do you think Marlies is crazy? Like Farmer Hassel is? I mean: that she is mentally ill? I was wondering again today. Speaking of crazy. You'll think I'm crazy when I tell you

Dear Selma, It's been a year today and you are right: we have to find a way to bring back Palm's desire to live. Speaking of desire to live. The source of my desire to live

Dear Selma, The eclipse today was spectacular. Speaking of eclipses. You are the opposite of

Dear Selma, As we discussed earlier today, I also don't believe Luisa really loves Andreas. Speaking of

Selma took one sheet of paper after another out of the suitcase. While she read them, she took hold of the optician's hand without looking up from the papers. The optician sat next to her as if she were studying a photography book, as if he were waiting for Selma to ask him a word she didn't understand.

"What does *unconditionally* mean?" Selma asked.

The optician laughed. "Unconditionally means unconditionally."

"My life is flashing before my eyes," Selma murmured as she read, and we were alarmed. Her time is up, we thought, but Selma said, "No, no, I just mean in these letters. It's flashing before my eyes in these letters."

She read until she could not read any longer. Then she rested her head on her pillow, looked at the optician, and said, "Read them aloud to me."

The optician read to Selma until well after midnight, then he grew hoarse.

"I need a rest, Selma," he said.

She looked at the optician with glittering eyes. She pulled him to her and held her mouth close to his ear. "Thank you for bringing me so many new beginnings at the end," she whispered, "and thank you for not ever telling me. Otherwise we might not have spent as much time together as we did. Imagine."

"I'd rather not imagine that, Selma," the optician replied. His eyes were glittering, too, and he also had a fever, but not one that could be measured.

"I'd also rather not, not at all." At that moment the photography book couldn't hold the window any longer. The window flew open and the wind raged in, pulling at the curtains and rifling through all the piles of paper next to the suitcases. All the new beginnings flew away.

"I need some fresh air," the optician said an hour later while Selma slept. But before he went outside, he stopped in the kitchen.

Frederik's number still hung above Selma's refrigerator. The optician examined it as if the numbers signified more than just a telephone connection. He took the paper with the number down, folded it, and put it in his breast pocket.

On the way home, the optician felt much lighter than he had on the way to Selma's; instead of lugging two suitcases full of papers and a commune of panicked voices, he now carried a single piece of paper, and even the wind that had whipped at him earlier had calmed down.

At home he picked up the telephone and the number and sat down with them on his bed, the bed that was just the right size for one person. He counted forward eight hours. He dialed the nearly interminable string of numbers, then waited an even more interminable period of time until the first monk picked up the receiver. Only six monks later did the optician reach the monk he wanted.

"Hello?" Frederik said.

"Hello, Frederik, this is Dietrich Hahnberg."

There was a short silence on the other end of the line. "Excuse me, but *who* am I speaking to?" Frederik finally asked.

"The optician."

"I see," Frederik exclaimed. "I beg your pardon. This is a surprise. How are you?"

"Could you please come by?" the optician asked, as if Frederik were in the neighboring village and not at the other end of the world.

"Of course," he replied.

I sat on the windowsill in Selma's bedroom. I looked at the carefree shepherd boy with his shawm and wondered when exactly Selma had dreamed of an okapi the night before and how much time remained in the best-case.

Selma woke briefly and looked at me. She lay on her back with her comforter pulled up to her chin. Her eyes were more feverish than before, but also alert.

"So far everything's going smoothly," she said as if talking about preparations for the May Festival.

ON INTIMATE TERMS WITH THE WORLD

The optician went back to Selma's; it was one-thirty in the morning. Just before he reached our house, he noticed, despite the darkness, a movement on the edge of his field of vision. He looked to the left at the meadow through which the Apfelbach flowed. On the far side of the meadow, a figure was standing on the bridge. The optician climbed over the fence and walked toward it.

It was Palm. The optician stepped onto the bridge and stood next to him. Palm's eyes were glassy, his arms dangling. He held his Bible in one hand, a half-empty bottle of liquor in the other.

Palm had been sober for so many years that the optician had forgotten how he looked larger when drunk. When he hit the bottle, Palm seemed bulkier, his shoulders, his hands, his face.

The optician tentatively extended his hand. Palm flinched, dropping the Bible. It fell on the bridge, on the very edge. The optician nudged it to the center with his foot.

The stream, which usually didn't rise above a murmur,

roared in the optician's ears. On that night, the stream was a torrent. Because of the roar, the optician couldn't hear that Palm was weeping, but he could see it. He saw tears streaming down Palm's face, which had turned red, bulky, and ferocious again in a mere instant.

The optician took a deep breath. Then he took a step forward, slipped his arms under Palm's armpits. Palm staggered backward, but the optician pulled Palm to his chest with all his strength, not letting the possibility that Palm might crumble to dust at the slightest touch stop him. There and then, over the thundering Apfelbach, he had to run that risk.

Palm did not crumble, and the optician lifted him up. He let Palm's heavy head sink onto his shoulder. Palm stank of liquor and sweat; his entire body shook with sobs, and the optician's body trembled from the strain. Palm's arms, which had hung along the optician's right and left sides, lifted and embraced him. The bottle slipped from Palm's hand onto the bridge. Palm's sweat-matted hair brushed the optician's neck. His shoulders pressed against the optician's nose and pushed his glasses onto his forehead.

The optician managed to hold Palm up for a full minute but ran out of strength. He set Palm down without letting go, and Palm did not let go, either. With Palm in his arms, the optician first dropped to his knees, then sat down.

They stayed that way for a long time: the optician leaning against the railing with his legs extended, Palm with his torso resting diagonally on the optician's chest. Palm's eyes were closed and he didn't move. The optician sat crookedly, half on Palm's Bible. This wreaked havoc on his disks, but the optician saw no way of changing his position without disturbing Palm.

He stroked Palm's hair. The liquor bottle lay at his feet and he could easily read the label. Only then did the optician notice that the night was surprisingly bright from the light of the moon, the illuminated body whose path Palm had once known so well.

IT WAS YOU

Then things stopped going smoothly. Selma became agitated, turning from one side to the other in bed. I had made leg compresses for her and tried to lay the wet washcloths on her calves, but she kicked them off and the letter openings that still lay on her bed grew limp.

Alaska sat at the foot of Selma's bed. He watched me run back and forth, sit on the edge of her bed, then run back and forth again. He watched me as if he had an important question and regretted not being able to ask it.

The optician returned. I didn't notice how disheveled he looked because I only had eyes for Selma, whose bed we perched on only to jump up again in order to do something that didn't need to be done. Our sense of time disappeared. Maybe it was two in the morning or maybe time had shifted forward or backward, we had no idea.

Selma's eyes were watery. Perhaps the first thing to go was one's eye color. She dozed off, she woke again, her hands clawed at the sides of her bed as if she wanted to hold on to it tight. Then she suddenly gave us an irritated look, as if she didn't know who we were, and said, "I'd like to speak to my son."

I put my hand over my mouth and began to weep. At that moment, I'd have given everything I had to be someone else, to be a receptionist who could connect Selma with her son immediately.

For four hours, until dawn broke, Selma tossed and turned in bed; for four hours she didn't recognize us, and then, at the last moment, she recognized us again; she took my hand and I laid my thumb on her inner wrist, on her pulse like before. Selma's heartbeat raced; the world raced just before it was about to stand still.

Selma put her hand on the back of my neck and pulled my head onto her chest, on her humid nightgown, and stroked my hair.

"You invented the world," I whispered.

"No," Selma said, "that was you," and those were her last words.

HENRY, THE COACH IS BREAKING

Selma stood in the Uhlheck. She was wearing a flowered, ankle-length nightgown and looking at her old feet in the grass. She stood there exactly as she had with an okapi in the dreams that meant some life would soon be over. But there was no okapi in sight, only the trees, the fields, and the wind that always blew here.

And just as Selma asked herself why she had been put here without an okapi, someone emerged from between the trees, someone who moved without a sound and simply stepped out of the undergrowth. He came nearer, and Selma realized who it was. She ran to him as quickly as she could and wasn't at all surprised that it was very quickly indeed, that she could run as fast as a sense of time that hadn't aged.

Then she stopped abruptly, thinking that you can't just fall into someone's arms after more than fifty years, no matter how much you want to, because that person might crumble into dust.

"Here you are," Heinrich said. "It's about time."

Heinrich's hair, which for decades had been light in the

afterimage behind Selma's eyelids, was now black, as in real life, and his eyes were light again. "You're in color," Selma said, and then, after a few moments of silence, "and you're so young."

"Unfortunately, that couldn't be avoided," Heinrich said. Selma looked around. "I'm old," she announced.

"Fortunately," Heinrich said, smiling.

He smiled exactly as he had on the day he turned back to wave at Selma one very last time, on the day he said, Don't worry, we'll be together again soon, I know we will, Selma, I know we will.

"It took longer than expected," Heinrich said.

Selma looked at the Uhlheck. The light was somehow silvery, like it had been during the eclipse.

She stepped closer to Heinrich. "Will you help me?" asked Selma, who had never before asked for help. "Will you help me?"

She spoke as if she were requesting Heinrich's help taking off her coat.

Heinrich opened his arms and Selma fell into them. She embraced Heinrich's still-young body, Heinrich embraced Selma's body that had lived for more than eighty years as tightly as he had when she was young, and Selma could only feel those parts of her body that were touching Heinrich's. For example, she couldn't feel her right shoulder anymore, just as she had lost sensation in it for a time after Martin's death, when she carried me around day in, day out. This time it was different. This time her shoulder wasn't numb. This time her shoulder seemed to have vanished.

"I can't feel my shoulder anymore," Selma said into Heinrich's neck, which smelled exactly as it had in his life, of mint and faintly of filterless Camels.

"That's how it should be," Heinrich said, his mouth against her neck, "that's exactly how it should be, Selma," and his hands stroked her back, her hair, her arms. Selma trembled. It was a trembling she couldn't locate. She didn't know what exactly was trembling, she simply trembled.

And then Heinrich said to her what Selma had said to me when I was five years old and had climbed too high in a tree in the Uhlheck. Selma could see the tree very well from where she stood. I didn't know how to climb down. Selma had raised herself on her tiptoes, stretched her arms up, and held me tight while I still clutched the branch.

"Let go," she'd said, "I'm here."

OKAPIA JOHNSTONI

"Dear Frederik, Selma is dead," I'd wanted to write, right away, on the morning after Selma's death, but I stopped after "Dear Frederik" because no one should write it, no one should set it down, as long as my father still didn't know.

I wasn't the right person to tell my father; my mother should be the one.

"Of course," she said, but when my father called on the afternoon following Selma's death, she wasn't there. She was out organizing Selma's funeral, so I had no choice but to be the right one.

When I heard the phone ring, I pictured my father somewhere far, far away at a public telephone with a terrible connection through which he couldn't understand anything other than "Selma" and "dead."

"It's me," my father said. "Good news, Luisy: I was able to get a flight for today."

"Papa," I said.

"Can you understand me?" he asked. "There's something I absolutely have to tell you."

"There's something I have to tell you, too."

"Luisa, I have seen an actual okapi. A real one. Here in the rain forest. It's an extraordinarily beautiful animal."

I pressed my free hand over my mouth, so my father couldn't hear me weeping. I felt like someone watching a tree fall and thinking, This tree will only really be felled once it's lying on the ground, and there's still time until then.

"Its full name is *Okapia johnstoni*, after the man who discovered it, Harry Johnston," my father explained, "and you know what? He didn't even discover it! In his entire life, he never actually saw an okapi, only parts of it, the skull and the pelt. But he never set eyes on a complete okapi."

"Papa," I said through the fingers of the hand over my mouth and I thought, Papa, you have to be quiet now. You have to let the world in.

"Isn't that something?" my father asked. "In her life, Selma saw more complete okapis than its discoverer. Maybe *she's* actually the one who discovered the okapi." He laughed. "How's she doing? I'll be there tomorrow evening."

I took my hand away from my mouth and said, "She died last night."

Then the only sound was the noise such a sentence makes when it is said very far away from the place where it must be heard.

"No," my father said. I heard his hand with the receiver sink and then rise again. I heard my father's voice repeating softly, "But I'll be there tomorrow evening, tomorrow evening I'll be there."

SINCE YOU'RE ALREADY LYING HERE

Dear Frederik," I wrote, sitting at Selma's kitchen table, "Selma is dead. She liked you very much. The only thing she didn't like about you was your time zone. Perhaps we weren't actually made for each other. That's not so bad. None of an okapi's parts belong together and it's still extraordinarily beautiful . . ." I wrote no more because the optician appeared beside me and said, "It's time."

The optician and I stood in front of Selma's full-length mirror in the entryway, I in a black dress, the optician in his good suit, which had grown ever larger with time. The optician held his *Employee of the Month* badge up to his lapel. "Should I?" he asked, and looked at me in the mirror with tear-filled eyes. "Do you think it would be funny?"

"Yes," I said, and tried to wipe away the mascara that had spread all over my face from so much crying, "very funny."

It rained on Selma's funeral, but only very lightly. The entire village came, and half of the neighboring village as well. My mother made the wreaths. During the brief address given by the pastor from the county seat, my mother and father held hands, because at a burial it's natural for those who loved each other for a long time to hold hands, and for the duration of a funeral the fact that they no longer love each other is irrelevant.

As always, Alaska was overjoyed to see my father. He could not pull himself together at all and jumped up on my father again and again, his tail wagging wildly, and because he was an animal, we couldn't explain that sometimes pure joy is not appropriate.

I stood between Palm and the optician. Palm looked completely scrubbed. His face was red and his blond hair was plastered onto his head, with one strand sticking up. It was hard to step close to Selma's grave. It felt like we were wading in a river against the current. Palm threw a rose into the grave. The optician and I threw handfuls of dirt.

Afterward the village gathered in the community center. I'd baked for three days. There were piles of cake slices on high tables and I was embarrassed that they were so dry. The shopkeeper patted me on the shoulder. "Don't worry about it. Since Selma's dead, it's very fitting that we all have a dull taste in our mouths."

My mother was standing with my father at one of the high tables when Alberto joined them. He put his arm around my mother's shoulders. I looked at my father. Apparently, the fact that two people who loved each other for a long time no longer do is really only irrelevant at the side of an open grave.

I sat down next to the optician on one of the wooden

benches lining the walls. Palm sat on his left, holding a glass. We didn't know if it contained more than just orange juice. I leaned against the optician's shoulder and he rested his cheek on my head. We looked like the two little screech owls that had slept, huddled together in our chimney, every day one summer.

"Now we're all alone," I said.

The optician put his arm around me and pulled me closer. "No one is alone as long as he can still say *we*," he whispered, then kissed the top of my head. "I'm going to get some fresh air, all right?"

I nodded.

"Come, Alaska," he said, and Alaska slowly rose. It took a while for something that large and that ancient to stand all the way up.

The optician walked with Alaska to the end of the village and into the forest. There he lay down.

In his good suit, he stretched out on the damp, old leaves. Alaska lay down next to him. The optician crossed his arms under his head, looked at the sky etched with branches and treetops, and blinked in the drizzle.

Again the optician thought of the sentence he'd been ruminating on alone and with others for so long: *When we look at something, it can disappear from our sight, but if we do not try to see this something, it cannot disappear.* His inner voices had never tried to explain it to him. Why should they? "Since you're already lying here," they now told him, "you might as well die, too. It won't make any difference."

The optician sat bolt upright, so abruptly and orthopedically wrong that he felt a stab of pain in his lower back.

"I've got it," he shouted.

And Alaska stood up, probably because he noticed it was a solemn moment.

"It's about differentiating," the optician said. "To look means to differentiate." He patted Alaska's head. "I could have figured it out earlier, Alaska, given my profession. Listen: if we don't try to differentiate something from everything else around us, then it can't disappear. Because it's not separate. Because it hasn't been detached from everything else, it's still there." Because he was so excited, he asked Alaska, "Do you understand?" and was surprised that Alaska didn't reply, "Of course, I understand perfectly. Please go on."

Selma doesn't disappear if I don't try to see her, the optician thought. And what he wanted most was to run to Selma and explain it to her.

THE OPPOSITE IS TRUE

Can I do anything for you?" my mother asked after we'd left the community center. "Maybe you'd like an ice cream?"

"No, thanks. I'll just go for a walk."

I walked to the edge of the village, to Marlies's house. She hadn't come to the funeral. I was worried something might have happened to her, because nothing could stop her from coming to Selma's funeral—not even she herself. Of that I was certain.

I walked through her garden gate, past her soggy mail, and made a circle around the bee nest. I didn't bother ringing the doorbell, but went straight to the kitchen window at the back of the house. As always, it was ajar. I peeked inside. My heart immediately started racing. I looked away and put a hand over my heart. Calm down, I thought, she can't be serious, and then I looked inside again.

Marlies, in her Norwegian sweater and underpants, sat on a kitchen chair. She was holding Palm's shotgun under her chin.

"Marlies," I said through the opening in the window, "you can't be serious."

She wasn't at all surprised to hear my voice, as if I'd already been standing there for hours.

"Marlies? Are you listening? There's been enough dying. Death hasn't exactly made himself scarce recently. I strongly recommend you don't throw yourself at him."

"Your recommendations are always shit," Marlies said.

She sat directly under the hook on which her aunt, that bad-tempered, intolerable woman, had hanged herself.

"How did you get ahold of Palm's gun?"

"Palm was drunk. He slept so soundly, I could have cleaned out his entire house. Now get lost. It's time to put an end to it all." Marlies looked at me. Her eyes were wilder than Palm's used to be.

Of course, I thought. It is time to put an end to it all when you put all you've got into making sure no one wants to visit. When you haven't chosen any of the things that surround you. When you don't like anything, not any suggestions, no frozen dishes, not a single item in the gift shop, it certainly has to end sometime when everything is all blurry.

I had always thought that time passed Marlies by because her days were all identical and left no trace. But that wasn't true. Time did pass for her, and the worst was: it passed pointlessly.

I leaned my head against the open window. "Please let me in."

"Disappear. Just go away."

I thought of Martin and what he wrote in my poetry album. He had leafed through it to the last page and written in his neat, child's handwriting: "At the very end I've taken root / to keep all others from falling out." When Elsbeth sent us to Marlies's house afterward because someone had to check on sad Marlies, Martin showed her his entry and said, "Just like you, right? You took root at the end."

Marlies didn't understand. But Martin was convinced that Marlies must have moved to the end of the village and was so intolerable because she'd been invented to keep any criminals from attacking us from behind.

I'd asked Marlies to write in my poetry album that day as well. She reluctantly opened the album, flipped past the optician's entry, "Boulders can be crushed and mountains can be scaled, but you cannot be forgotten, you are nonpareil," my father's entry, "The brown bear lives in Siberia, in Africa lives the gnu, the black boar lives in Sicily, in my heart there's only you," she flipped past Elsbeth's entry, "Be happy and full of joy, like a puppy with a brand-new toy," and the shopkeeper's, "Why must you always roam? The good is near at hand. If you learn to catch happiness, you'll never need to leave this land," and my mother's, "Only love knows how to become rich by giving to others." She ignored Selma's entry, "Not every day is Sunday, nor every meal a feast, but you can still be happy and see your life increase," and when she finally found a blank page, she wrote in pencil "Greetings, M."

"Martin believed you would save us all," I said softly.

"That worked out really well," Marlies called, "especially for Martin. And for Selma."

"But Selma was over eighty."

"She left me in peace," Marlies said, her voice breaking slightly. She cleared her throat. "Selma was the only one out of all of you who always left me in peace."

"And she still will."

"Get out of here," Marlies said quietly. "I can already see Death. He's coming for me."

I'd had enough. "Okay, Marlies, you're right. It's time to put an end to it all."

Marlies's curtain rod fell down. The left side had come undone. The curtains hung diagonally at the window.

There's always something falling around here, I thought, there are a lot of things that aren't properly fastened. And suddenly I thought of Selma asking me if I'd noticed anything when the macramé owl in her kitchen fell off the wall after I'd said that my life was in order.

Marlies stared out the window. I thought she was staring because of the crooked curtain rod, but that wasn't true.

"He is coming, Death is coming right for me," she said.

I turned around and saw what she was staring at: a man in a long black robe walking through her garden straight toward us. I took a step back and stumbled against the wall.

"That's not Death," I said, "it's Frederik."

He stopped a few steps from me. "Did I come at a bad time?"

"Frederik," I said.

"It's me," he said, and smiled. "You wear glasses now."

"Frederik," I said again, as if a person becomes more real the more you address him.

"I had a very bad feeling, and when the optician called me, I set out right away," he said, as if he had come from the next village.

"All the way here," I said.

"Yes, it's still less complicated than a phone call. Luisa, I'm very sorry that Selma has died."

I wanted to go to him, but I was afraid to move. I thought that if I moved even just a centimeter from the window, Marlies would pull the trigger.

"I have to stand right here," I said.

"No, you don't," Marlies called.

Frederik came up to me. He looked exactly as he had ten years ago. Only the fine web of wrinkles that showed when he smiled was new. I gestured with my head at the window behind me. Frederik looked.

"Don't look in here," Marlies shouted, "it's none of your business."

"Should I go get someone?" Frederik whispered in shock, but the only person I could think of was Selma.

"She won't do it as long as I stand here, so I'm standing here," I said.

"But we can't stand here forever," Frederik said, and I was happy he said *we*.

I took his hand.

A red-and-white crossing signal had fallen on the tracks at the station when I said to Martin that I didn't believe in Selma's dream. A vision chart had fallen from the wall when the optician said, "But you love him," and I replied, "No, not anymore."

I glanced at Marlies, who looked crossed out behind the half-fallen curtain rod. She hadn't changed position. She sat there with her chin on the muzzle and her hand near the trigger. Marlies would not let me in. She wouldn't open a single one of her five locks and she wouldn't let us talk her into coming out of her house because my recommendations were always shit.

Marlies had to be extracted in a different way, I thought, and thought also that you can't always choose which adventure you're made for. I took a deep breath.

"Frederik," I said, "it was nice of you to come by, but it's not such a good time."

Behind Marlies an air freshener taped to the wall fell to the floor. It fell without a sound.

"What?" Frederik said.

He wanted to let go of my hand, but I held it tight.

"We could talk on the phone once in a while. You always like calling me."

A framed piece of embroidery Marlies had made for her aunt as a child fell to the floor. The glass shattered. Marlies gave it a glance, then put her chin back on the muzzle of the shotgun.

Frederik looked at me the way someone looks when the world no longer makes any sense and decides it's better to stay away from it. Stay here, I thought, don't go now. I thought it with all my strength. Marlies shouted, "Stop jabbering and go away."

"Marlies is my best friend," I said.

Nothing fell.

I repeated it with more emphasis. "Marlies is my best friend," but nothing moved.

"You, Frederik, are a very pushy person," I said, and the cast-iron pan hanging over the stove behind Marlies fell down. Marlies whirled around, and I held Frederik's hand as tight as I could. "I'm absolutely convinced that we don't belong together," I said, and Marlies's kitchen shelves collapsed with all the tins of canned peas. Marlies dropped the shotgun and jumped up. And Frederik, who had been looking back and forth from me to Marlies, now looked only at me. He looked at me and flinched slightly every time something fell, but he no longer looked away. "There's no one I've ever not loved as much as you," I said, and the wall cupboard full of greasy dishes fell with an earsplitting crash. "I'd like a small Secret Love without whipped cream," I said, and the ceiling lamp that had hung next to the hook on which Marlies's aunt had hanged herself fell with a bang and sent glass splinters flying. Marlies, whose door sported too many locks, ran to the window, flung it open, and climbed out over the curtain rod.

For a moment she looked like she might run blindly into the forest, but she remained standing next to us in her Norwegian sweater and her underpants.

"What was that?" she asked, her entire body trembling. "And why has it stopped?"

"Did you listen to me, Frederik?" I asked.

"Yes," he said. Frederik had gone pale, too. "I didn't know you loved me, at least not like that."

Marlies wrapped her arms around herself.

"I knew," she said.

"I need to get some air," Frederik said softly. He turned and without another word set off across the meadow toward the forest.

I watched him walk away. I felt as if I'd lifted something it was anatomically impossible to lift.

"Come, Marlies," I said, "let's get you some pants. And shoes."

"I'm not going in there again," she whispered, "and you aren't, either."

"Fine," I said. I got Marlies's rubber boots that were standing outside on her front doorstep. "Get in," I said. Marlies steadied herself with a hand on my shoulder and slipped her bare feet into the rubber boots.

"Let's go look for the optician, okay?" I asked, and put my arm around her shoulders.

"Hands off," Marlies said, but she came with me.

"Let's find the optician," I said as we walked through the

twilight, down the street, and across the meadow, "and then we'll go to Selma's and eat something. And you'll sleep there tonight. So will I. Frederik, too. I'm sure he'll come back soon. He just needs some peace and quiet. And the optician can sleep at Selma's, too. We'll put all the mattresses in the living room. Selma would like that. I don't know if we have enough pillows. My father sleeps upstairs and my mother at Alberto's. I'll pan-fry some potatoes. My fried potatoes are really good. The sofa cushions will work as pillows. I'm sure Frederik will come back soon. We could ask Palm if he wants to come over. Do you like fried potatoes? Where is Palm, actually? Maybe the shopkeeper wants to come over, too. Are you cold? The shopkeeper could bring a bottle of wine. Although, that's probably not a good idea because of Palm. Where is he, actually?"

Marlies stumbled along beside me. "Could you please stop talking?" she asked.

FREDERIK

Frederik did not come back until it was night. I waited for him in the kitchen.

"Where did you go?" I asked, and for a second I imagined he might have visited Dr. Maschke, as Alaska had once.

"Everywhere," Frederik replied.

He ate three helpings of cold fried potatoes. There was hardly a sound aside from my father's footsteps in the upstairs apartment, where he had withdrawn right after Selma's funeral. No one was allowed upstairs except Alaska. Alaska finally was what Dr. Maschke had invented him for years ago, a furry, externalized pain.

"How is he?" I asked Alaska now and again when he came downstairs so someone would take him for a walk, and Alaska would give me a look suggesting that in this case he was happy to respect his duty of confidentiality.

Frederik washed his plate, then followed me down the hallway to the living room. Just before the door, he took hold of my wrist. I turned to face him.

"You always confuse everything," he said.

I looked at him. Frederik was all worked up. He held my wrist very tightly.

"*Always* is a bit much," I said. "This is only the third time we've ever seen each other."

That didn't change a thing. People you don't see can be particularly good at being involved in a life that is playing out far away and creating disorder, like invisible ghosts pushing precious things over. Besides, Frederik and I had written each other at least once a week for ten years.

He let go of my wrist and opened the living room door. The optician and I had set up a mattress camp. The optician was stretched out on the sofa. Three mattresses lay on the floor next to him. Marlies was asleep on the middle one. She was completely enveloped in Selma's comforter. She looked like a giant flowery caterpillar and she snored.

A few hours earlier, when Marlies lay down, the optician crouched next to her in his blue-and-white-striped pajamas and watched as she wrapped herself in the comforter. "Are you going to do it again, Marlies?" he had asked. "Because if there's the slightest danger that you'll do it again, we're going to show up at your house every five minutes, asking how you're doing." The optician bent down over Marlies, trying to look like a particularly malevolent imp.

"We'd never leave you in peace again," he said. "We would unscrew all your locks and smoke the bees out of your mailbox. And every night"—here the optician had to force himself—"you'd have to sleep at one of our homes." He bent even lower, the tip of his nose almost touching her assaulted hair. "You would, to be precise, have to move in with one of us." Marlies sat bolt upright. The optician just managed to pull his head away in time.

"Never," Marlies said.

"Then it's all settled," the optician announced, and made himself comfortable on the sofa.

I lay down on Marlies's right, Frederik on her left. The optician, on the sofa, sat up and reached for his glasses.

"How nice that you were able to come, dear Frederik," he whispered. "By the way, I found out what the sentence about things disappearing means. Shall I explain it to you?"

"Please," Frederik answered softly, and the optician explained that looking meant differentiating, that something can't disappear if you don't try to differentiate it from everything else.

Frederik nodded but said nothing. The optician looked at him attentively. He couldn't tell if Frederik now understood the sentence or if he himself was still the only one around who understood. For a moment the optician felt very lonely, as if he lived far away on a tiny planet, his only company a grateful sentence, which felt understood only by the optician.

Frederik was abstracted, it struck the optician, too. He was so abstracted, the optician worried that Frederik might become undifferentiated overnight. He waited until Frederik had shaken out his pillow, then he said, "If you'd like, I can examine the voices in your head tomorrow. There's a revolutionary new method from Japan."

Frederik smiled. "They're not so bad," he said.

At some point, the optician fell asleep. Everyone but Frederik and I was sleeping. I could hear on the other side of Marlies how he wasn't sleeping.

I stood up and stepped over Marlies toward him. Frederik's head was right next to Selma's open bedroom door. I closed it, sat down, and leaned against it.

"You're not at all blurry, Luisa," Frederik said softly without looking at me. "You are crystal clear."

"*You* are blurry," I whispered.

Frederik nodded and ran a hand over his bald head. "And drawing a blank as well," he whispered back.

I thought of my first telephone conversation with him, how he helped me get unstuck. "Your name is Frederik. You're actually from Hessen. You're now thirty-five years old. You live in a Buddhist monastery in Japan. A few of the monks there are so old, they probably knew Buddha personally. They taught you how to clean, how to sit, how to sow and reap, how to be silent. You always know what needs to be done. You're actually always doing fine. And most important, you know how to welcome your thoughts. That's a trick that no one here has mastered as well as you. You can say *one thousand years at sea, one thousand years in the mountains* in Japanese. You're almost always hungry. You can't bear to see something stand crookedly. It's very important to you that everything be in its place. You're nine thousand kilometers away. You're seated at a banquet table across from me."

Frederik slipped his arm out from under his head, pulled me to him, and rested his forehead against mine. "I love you, too, Luisa, and have for a very long time now," he said softly. "Maybe not for a thousand years, but close. It's easier to see from the other end of the world. And now I'm afraid my entire life will be upended." He studied me and looked like the most exhausted person in the world. "Three meetings are enough to know it's forever," he whispered, "you can believe me."

The completely swaddled Marlies sat up abruptly. "Could you two stop?" she asked loudly, waking the optician.

"Is it morning already?" he asked, confused, groping for his glasses.

"No," I said, "it's still night."

Marlies fell backward onto her mattress. The optician laboriously made himself comfortable. Frederik turned off the light above him on the coffee table. We looked at each other even though we couldn't see one another.

"I'm going to sleep now," he said. "I don't think I've slept for three days."

He lay down and turned his back to me. Maybe it's a trick you learn in the monastery, I thought, how to fall asleep even though your life is on the point of being upended. I leaned against Selma's bedroom door and waited for my eyes to get used to the dark and for my head to get used to what Frederik had said. I heard Frederik fall asleep. He was wrapped up just like Marlies, but less flowered, and I was happy to sit there the entire night, next to Frederik and the truth of his love that had slipped out. At one point the sleeping optician's hand fell off the sofa onto Frederik's bald head and rested there.

When we woke up and went into Selma's kitchen, it became clear to us that we would never get used to not being greeted there by Selma. The optician said, "I'd like to go into my perimeter."

"I'd like to go for a walk now," I said. "And you two?"

I looked at Marlies and Frederik. Frederik was leaning against the kitchen doorframe in his robe. Marlies was standing in front of the kitchen table as if she had been put there by someone for the dubious reason that he didn't know where else to put her.

Marlies crossed her arms in front of her chest and said, "I don't want anything at all," and the optician rolled his eyes. He'd had the faint hope the night before that Marlies would become a new person overnight, because life starts anew when you don't fire a shot at the last moment after all. He'd thought that you immediately start to appreciate the smaller things, the play of light in the branches of the apple tree, for example. But just as before, Marlies looked like she'd received both an unexpected surcharge and a burst pipe. Marlies had dodged Death but not herself, the optician realized—he had not taken into account earlier that certain changes don't like to be pushed even if threatened at gunpoint.

"There is no nothing anymore, Marlies," he said rather pointedly. "It has more or less canceled itself out."

Marlies glared at the optician and he glared back. Frederik pushed off the doorframe and said, "I'd like to do some cleaning. May I?"

Before, Selma's kitchen had always been sparkling clean. Once her hands became deformed, she couldn't manage the same level of cleanliness and wouldn't let anyone help her. There were spots on the floor and piles of trodden crumbs gathered around the feet of the table legs. Dust bunnies multiplied under the kitchen bench, dark shadows had formed around the handles of the cupboards and the refrigerator, around the knobs on the gas stove, and the glass doors of the credenza were plastered with fingerprints.

"But not right this minute," I said. "Don't you want breakfast first? You're always hungry, after all."

The optician pulled Marlies and me out of the kitchen by our sleeves. "Let him, it will do him good," he said. He took his coat from Selma's closet. *"Every illumination begins and ends with cleaning the floor.* Maybe afterward he can think of connections between things that don't belong together." The optician smiled at me in Selma's mirror. "And you can let them fall apart again as you like."

He patted me on the shoulder and said, "See you later."

Marlies came with me, and that alone proved the optician wrong, because it had never before been possible to take a walk with Marlies. She wore one of Selma's dresses, one of Selma's blouses, and one of Selma's coats. When we turned onto the Uhlheck, I hesitated because it was the first time I had ever walked there without Selma. Marlies looked at me out of the corner of her eye.

"I'll go first," she said, as if it were a matter of chasing away criminals about to attack us head-on.

She stopped in the middle of the Uhlheck, where you can see the village. "It was an earthquake," Marlies said, looking at her house. "An earthquake that only shook my house." She looked at me. "Isn't that something?"

I nodded. Then we walked on to the House of Contemplation and past it. We walked in single file and didn't say a single word to each other, exactly as Marlies wanted.

Meanwhile, Frederik stood in the middle of the kitchen and took several deep breaths. It was finally quiet, so quiet he thought he could hear Selma's traveling alarm clock ticking in the bedroom, the traveling alarm clock that never went on a single trip and perhaps ticked so loud to draw attention to its bungled existence.

Frederik started cleaning the kitchen. He took out all the dishes, all the cutlery, all the pots, pans, and bowls, all the

provisions from Selma's credenza. He got a ladder from
the garage and wiped the lampshade inside and out. In it lay
three dead moths. Frederik picked them up carefully, carried them into the garden in the hollow of his hand, and
buried them there.

He cleaned all the cupboards, top to bottom, inside and
out. He leaned far into the refrigerator and the oven. He took
a pile of paper from the kitchen bench, the optician's book
on Buddhism, old shopping lists and flyers in which Selma
had circled especially good deals. In the pile lay a letter.

*Dear Frederik, Selma is dead. She liked you very much.
The only thing she didn't like about you was your time
zone. Perhaps we weren't actually made for each other.
That's not so bad. None of an okapi's parts belong
together and it's still extraordinarily beautiful . . .*

Frederik folded up the letter and put it in the pocket of
his robe. He put the book and flyers on the kitchen table and
shook out the cushions.

He washed the dishes and the cutlery. He wiped off
containers of flour, sugar, and preserves, polished glasses,
scrubbed pots and pans. He dried everything carefully and
put it all back in the cupboards. He cleaned the windows, the
window frames, and the door from all sides. Then he put
the ladder back in the garage.

When he closed the garage door, he took an involuntary
look at the meadow on the forest's edge to check if the deer
that had to be chased away for its own good happened to be
standing there. Frederik knew exactly what had to be done
or not done in and around Selma's house. He had learned it
in the letters, the more than seven hundred letters.

He went back into the house. His head had been empty the entire time, as devoid of thought as only Frederik knew how to make it. When he opened the door, he was struck by a question, namely if when you enter an old house, the old house also enters you.

In the cubby at the end of the hallway, Frederik found a vacuum cleaner leaning against the drying rack on which Selma had hung laundry exactly as laundry should be hung.

Frederik went back to the kitchen and vacuumed the floor. My mother suddenly appeared in the doorway.

He turned off the vacuum.

"Hello," she said, "where is everybody?"

"There's no one here right now," Frederik said, and gestured at the ceiling: "Except your husband. He's upstairs."

"Once again, I'm too late," my mother said. She leaned against the doorframe with a sigh. "Do you know the feeling? Of being too late?"

"From before, I do," Frederik said. "Where I live now, we're all very punctual."

"I can believe that." My mother looked around the kitchen. "You're also here at exactly the right time."

Her eyes fell on the optician's book lying on the kitchen table. She picked it up. "I write poems now. I'll bring you one sometime," she said, assuming that Frederik would stay long enough that he could be brought things sometime.

She opened the optician's book. Out of habit, the book opened to the passage the optician had often opened to because it held his favorite sentence, underlined multiple times. "*Even a continual mistake can be Zen*," my mother read out loud. "My God, I think I'm a Buddhist, too."

She looked at her watch. "If I leave now, I'll actually get to Alberto's on time."

Frederik smiled. "Then go," he said.

My mother hesitated. "Or should I check on Peter? What do you think?"

Frederik was sure there was no need to worry about my father. "Your husband is mourning and doesn't want to be disturbed in his grief," Frederik wanted to say, but since my mother didn't know that he knew my father very well from my letters, he was afraid she would find such a sentence presumptuous. Frederik only noticed how much he knew about all of us from my letters now that he was trying to hide it.

"I'll be here in case anything happens," he said. "I'll be here cleaning."

"That's good. Both are," my mother said, and she left.

The vacuum cleaner was missing the attachment to reach the farthest corners. Frederik ran a hand brush over the stove, the refrigerator, the sink, the credenza, around the legs of the kitchen table. Then he crawled under the bench and swept the baseboards.

At one spot under the kitchen bench, the wood had pulled away from the wall, and a pearl was stuck in the gap between the wall and the baseboard. It was Selma's lost earring, but despite all the letters, Frederik couldn't know that. The pearl was a bit too large and a bit too artificial. You could see the seam where the two halves had been joined together, as on a globe. At one point there were barely recognizable traces of glue where the earring post had been attached. Frederik rolled the pearl between thumb and forefinger. A small, blind globe in pearl white.

He put the false pearl down next to him and wanted to clean the rest of the baseboard, but the pearl started to move. It rolled purposefully away, across the kitchen, and under the credenza.

Frederik watched it roll. He crawled out from under the kitchen bench, knelt before the credenza, and felt around beneath it with his hand, but he had to stretch out and stick his arm in up to his shoulder until he could reach it. He stood up, looked at the pearl, and then at the linoleum.

"The floor is slanted," he said, because some things are so obvious you have to say them out loud, even if no one is listening. He took a step to the right, as if the floor were so tilted you immediately lost your balance.

And because the floor's slant concerned Frederik so much, he didn't notice that he was standing with one leg right in the middle of the spot outlined in red, which everyone automatically avoided and which the optician always pointed out emphatically, as if the risk were not one of breaking through to the basement, but all the way to Japan, to the void, or to the beginning of the world.

No one had stood there for a very long time. So long that the spot on the floor didn't have any idea what was happening to it.

Selma had stood there when my parents brought me to her for the first time. My mother had put me in Selma's arms, and everyone—the shopkeeper, Elsbeth, Marlies, and the optician—had gathered around Selma and me and bent over me as if I were something in fine print. Everyone was silent until Elsbeth said, "She looks like her grandfather. No question." The optician found that I looked like Selma. The shopkeeper said that I looked like Elsbeth, at which Elsbeth blushed and asked, "Really? Do you really think so?" Marlies, a schoolgirl at the time, said, "She doesn't look like anyone." My father said that he had to agree with Elsbeth.

Beyond a doubt I looked like his father, and Selma looked at my mother, who was standing at the edge of the group and had remained quiet the entire time.

"She looks like her mother," Selma said, and then the doorbell rang and rang. Palm was standing outside the door, breathless and with disheveled hair. "It's a boy," he shouted, and hugged the optician. "His name is Martin. Come see him, all of you."

My father had stood there, in a very young version of himself, and looked out the window, searching for the correct answers. Selma sat behind him on the kitchen bench, asking practice questions for his medical school exam. Suddenly my father turned around and said, "When I finish, I'm going to start a practice here." He smiled at Selma and said, "I'll settle here, near you."

When there's no farm for children to take over, Selma knew, they need to be encouraged to go out into the world. Selma didn't have a farm. She only had herself and a crooked house that might well collapse before anyone could take it over. She knew that going out into the world would be important, particularly for my father. She knew she should encourage him, but instead of encouragement, all she found within herself was relief that her son would stay here, near her. That's why she stood up and went to stand next to my father by the window and stroked his back. "Do that, Peter," she said, "settle here, that will be exactly the right thing," because it was the only thing she could find within herself. Staying put was always exactly right. Staying put.

Selma had stood there, in a very young version of herself, holding her son in her arms, Selma, with no part of her yet in the slightest deformed. She saw Elsbeth climbing up the hill, in a very young version of herself, Elsbeth still slim, climbing unusually slowly, unusually bowed, as if she were walking against a current to which she would have happily abandoned herself in exhaustion. And Selma knew then that Heinrich was dead. She knew it even before Elsbeth stepped into the kitchen and said, "Selma, unfortunately I have to tell you that my brother—" and she could not get any further.

Selma had stood there just a few days earlier. With her son in her arms she had looked at the newspaper photograph that Heinrich had hung on the kitchen wall. "That's an okapi, my little Peter," she said. "Your papa discovered it. In the newspaper, that is. It's the most comical animal in the world." She kissed his head and said, "Tonight I dreamed of one. I dreamed that I was standing in the Uhlheck with an okapi. In my nightgown. Imagine." She pressed her nose into her son's stomach and both of them giggled.

Heinrich had stood in that spot. From it he had watched the shopkeeper go, the last, rather drunk, of Heinrich's birthday guests to leave. It was his first birthday in his own house. Heinrich lit a cigarette and blew the smoke out the window into the night. He looked over the meadow and the slope that bordered the forest, the trees swaying in the wind that always blew.

Behind him Selma was picking up the bottles and glasses from the kitchen table. Without a thought, she put a piece of chocolate in her mouth and drank the rest of Elsbeth's cherry brandy, which was still on the table. "This is delicious," Selma said to Heinrich. She went up to him and wrapped her arms around his chest from behind. "Is there such a thing? Cherry-brandy-flavored chocolate?"

Heinrich tossed his cigarette out the window, turned, and took Selma in his arms. "I don't know," he said, "but if not, you definitely should invent it." He pulled her close. Selma kissed his mouth, his throat, his neck.

"My heart is racing," she said, smiling.

"As it should be," Heinrich replied, lifting her up, one arm under her back, the other under her knees. Selma laughed, and Heinrich wanted to carry her into the bedroom, but they only got as far as the living room.

And Heinrich had lain in that spot, on his stomach, looking in great concentration over the floor that had just been laid. His chin almost touching the planks, he looked from one corner of the room to the other. Then he looked up at his best friend, standing next to him completely covered in dust, who had helped him with every step, with measuring, ordering, laying the planks, everything.

"Hey," Heinrich said, "is it slanted? Take a look. You can judge, as a trained optician."

The optician tried to clean his dust-covered glasses with his dust-covered undershirt, lay down next to Heinrich, and looked across the floor.

"Now that you mention it," he said, "yes. But if you don't know, it's not at all noticeable."

They both gazed over the floor as if it were an unusual

landscape. Then the optician knocked on the spot where they had just lain. "But I do think these boards are too thin."

"Where?" Heinrich asked, as if he didn't know, as if the optician hadn't said again and again: "These boards are too thin."

"Right here, where we were just lying."

Heinrich had walked back and forth across the boards and jumped up and down. "Naw, it's good enough," he said, and to prove it, he kept jumping, so hard that the optician, lying on the floor, bounced up and down. "It'll hold forever. Trust me."

Frederik did not break through. Not into the basement, not to Japan, and certainly not into the void. He stood there, kept his balance, and felt pleasantly heavy, as if one automatically grew heavier when standing on places that had been unjustly labeled for years as dangerously weak.

He looked out the window to see Marlies, the optician, and me. We had collected the optician from his perimeter on our way back through the village and were just climbing the hill. The optician and I had each taken one of Marlies's arms. We were moving slowly because we were trying to teach Marlies how to play Hat, Stick, Umbrella, and Marlies refused to learn. Frederik watched us again and again advance three steps, then stop and take one forward, one back, and one to the side. He heard us say, "Come on, Marlies, join in," and Marlies answer, "Not a chance."

I waved at Frederik and he waved back.

Now lift your feet from the floor, Frederik thought. Step away, open the door, let everyone in.

But because Frederik was so heavy, we were quicker. We came into the kitchen as Frederik was still standing with one foot on the dangerously weak section. The optician stared at him. Frederik raised his eyebrows. "What's wrong?" he asked, then looked down at his feet. "Oh," he said, finally noticing where he was standing. He came up to me and extended his hand holding the false pearl. "I found something," he said.

EPILOGUE

We really need to go," the optician called.

He was leaning against his old Passat, in front of the house, at the foot of the hill, waiting. He sighed and looked up at the sky. It was morning and very clear.

Marlies and Dr. Maschke walked down the street. They stopped next to the optician and looked at him with concern. "What on earth is the matter?" Marlies asked.

"Oh, that," the optician said, and wiped his cheeks with the sleeve of his jacket. Since early morning, tears had been continually streaming down his face even though he was convinced he wasn't crying. "I don't know, they just keep dripping on their own. I'm guessing it's some defect in my tear ducts due to age. Or an allergic reaction."

"Or sadness," Dr. Maschke suggested.

"Has she already left?" Marlies asked.

"No, I'm about to give her a ride," the optician said. He looked at Dr. Maschke. "Luisa is flying to Australia today. In other words, practically to the middle of the Indian Ocean," he said, as if Dr. Maschke didn't already know, as if he hadn't been telling everyone he met for weeks.

"Yes, I'm aware," Dr. Maschke replied, handing the optician a handkerchief.

"She's flying because of the endless expanse," the optician recited what I'd told him, "and because she decided to do it." He said it the same way he had recited the sentence about disappearing, the one no one had been able to explain to him.

The optician blew his nose thoroughly. "We really need to go," he called again in a slightly lower voice.

"I'll be right there," I called down from the front door of the house on the hill. Frederik helped me hoist my enormous backpack onto my shoulders. "Time to go," he said.

He was covered with paint. He'd been repainting the living room while I ran back and forth, packing the last few things.

"I'm definitely coming back," I said, "in exactly four weeks. You can count on me."

"I do," Frederik said.

"And you'll still be here?"

"Yes," he said, "right here. Although I might be in the kitchen. I very likely will, actually."

I kissed him. "And then we'll see," I whispered into his ear.

He smiled. "Yes, then we'll see."

"If anything happens, you have my number," I said, and Frederik wiped white paint off my chin.

"I very much have your number," he said, because I'd taped notepaper with my cell phone number all over the house.

Frederik looked at me. He saw that I was trying not to

ask a question I'd already asked one hundred times for the one hundred and first time.

"Yes, I'll remember Alaska's pills."

"And no one dies," I said.

"No, no one dies."

I let go of Frederik's hand and walked down the hill, turning around again and again to wave at him. It was a morning in summer. I was brightly illuminated.

Frederik watched me go, then closed his eyes. Behind his lids he saw a static afterimage, the frozen movement of a last wave, a frozen smile, and everything that was actually light was dark to his inner eye, and everything that was dark appeared very bright.

ACKNOWLEDGMENTS

Enormous thanks to Gisela Leky, Robert Leky, Jan Strathmann, and Jan Valk. And to Tilman Rammstedt, who accompanied this book from the first idea to the epilogue.

For their helpful advice, I thank Christian Dillo, René Michaelsen, Cornel Müller, Bernhard Quast, Gernot Reich, and the Röseler optical shop in Berlin.

Certain themes from this novel were first aired in the radio play *Der Buddhist und ich* (*The Buddhist and I*), WDR, 2012.

A Note About the Author

Mariana Leky was born in Cologne and currently makes her home in Berlin. After training as a bookseller, she studied cultural journalism at the University of Hildesheim. Though she is one of the very few members of her family who are not psychologists, she still writes a monthly column for the magazine *Psychologie Heute*. Her books have earned numerous prizes, including the Allegra Prize, the Lower Saxony Literary Advancement Award, and the Advancement Prize for Young Artists from the State of North Rhine-Westphalia. Before being published in twenty-one languages, *What You Can See from Here* was named the German Booksellers' Favorite Book of the Year and became a runaway bestseller.

A Note About the Translator

Tess Lewis is a writer and translator from the French and German. Her translations include works by Peter Handke, Walter Benjamin, Klaus Merz, Hans Magnus Enzensberger, Christine Angot, Pascal Bruckner, and Jean-Luc Benoziglio.